O9-ABF-282

The Night Is for Hunting

The Night Is for Hunting

John Marsden

Houghton Mifflin Company
Boston 2001

Acknowledgments

Many thanks to the following, who helped in the writing of this book.

Rachel Angus
Ross Barlow
(Murtoa Secondary College)
Margaret Phillips
Cate Hoffmann
Olivia Hoffmann
Rob Alexander
Gabrielle Farran
Col McCrae
Jeanne Marsden
Julia Hindhaugh
Elie Weisel
Charlotte Lindsay
Nickle McCulloch
Helen Kent
Wayne Gardam
from the Hay Veterinary
Practice in Hay NSW
Tony Porter
from Baynton, Hay
"The One That Got Away"
— Chris Ryan

The title of the book is from "The Law of the Jungle" by Rudyard Kipling.

The poem on page 12 is by Ross Falconer.

First published 1998 in Macmillan by Pan Macmillan Australia Pty Limited
First published 1999 in Pan by Pan Macmillan Australia Pty Limited
St Martins Tower, 31 Market Street, Sydney

www.houghtonmifflinbooks.com

The text of this book is set in 12-point Transitional 521 BT.

Library of Congress Cataloging-in-Publication Data
Marsden, John, 1950–
The night is for hunting/John Marsden.
p. cm. — (Tomorrow series ; bk. 6)
Sequel to: Burning for revenge.
Sequel: The other side of dawn.
Summary: While trying to care for a group of abandoned young children, five Australian teenagers continue their struggle for survival and their resistance against the enemy invading their homeland.
ISBN 0-618-07026-5
[1. Survival—Fiction. 2. War—Fiction. 3. Australia—Fiction.] I. Title.
PZ7.M35145 Ni 2001
[Fic]—dc21 00-044844

Manufactured in the United States of America
QUM 10 9 8 7 6 5 4 3 2 1

An Aussie Glossary

abattoir: a slaughterhouse
Aga: a wood stove
Ag bike: a motorbike used on farms
"all the go": popular
B&S: a dance for young rural people
billabong: a pool of water along a riverbed where the river has stopped flowing
billies: short for billycans
billycan: a container used on fire for cooking
bitumen: asphalt or tar
bloody: a swear word
bloodyminded: stubborn
Blu-Tack: adhesive used to fasten paper to walls
boot: a car trunk
burl: a knotty part of a branch or trunk of a tree
bush: the uncleared Australian countryside
bushbash: to force a path through the bush
cactus: doomed
chemist: a pharmacist
chook: a chicken
Chrissie: Christmas
coolroom: a walk-in refrigerator
cricket stump: a stick used in the game of cricket
crims: criminals
crush: a pan for farm animals
cubby: a hidey-hole constructed by children
cutting: a place where a track is carved out between two high points
Deb: powdered mashed potatoes
didgeridoo: a musical instrument made and used by Aboriginal people
draught: draft, current of air
drop bear: a mythical Australian creature that drops out of trees and attacks people
duco: the surface of a car or truck body
emus: large, flightless birds native to Australia
feedlots: small fields where farm animals are confined and hand-fed
"flat chat": full-speed
floaties: devices for keeping children afloat while they learn to swim

"forty-four": a forty-four-gallon metal container
frogmarched: being forced to walk by someone who's twisting your arm up behind your back
frogmouth: a type of owl
gastro: short for gastroenteritis, a stomach ailment
grog: alcohol
gumnuts: nuts from the gum tree
herbing: going fast
"hiding to nothing": a choice between two bad alternatives
hot water service: heater for water
k's: kilometers
knickers: underwear
"knock him back": reject him
knuckles: a game played by children, using the dried knuckles of farm animals
lollies: lollipops
Maccas: McDonald's products
milkbar: a small corner store, minimart
Milk Trays: chocolates
mincer: machine for grinding up meat
moleys: moleskin trousers, often worn by farmers
mono'd: to ride a bike while making the front wheel come off the ground
mosquito wriggler: mosquito larva
muleser: someone who cuts dirty wool and skin from around the anus of a sheep
mustering: rounding up farm animals
myxo: rabbit poison
nature strip: a strip of grass between the front fence of a house and the road
netball: a sport similar to basketball
op shop: short for opportunity shop, a shop at which second-hand products are sold to raise money for charity
Panadeine: a brand of painkiller
Panadol: a brand of painkiller
petrol: gasoline
poly-pipe: black plastic pipe for heavy-duty watering
pooh-sticks: a competitive game in which sticks are floated down a stream
pressies: presents
PTO: the "power take off" device on a tractor from which attachments can be run

rellies: relatives
roos: kangaroos
shout: to treat
skerrick: a tiny amount
soak: a place where water soaks into the ground from a spring
Social: a social function, dance
spanner: a wrench
"spat the dummy": had a tantrum
swagmen: tramps
tacker: a young person, a kid
"taking the piss": pulling your leg
Textas: colored marking pens
torch: flashlight
tray: the flat back section of a pickup truck on which the load sits
trots: diarrhea
tucker: food
ute: utility vehicle
Vegemite: sandwich spread
Vo-Vos: a brand of biscuits
whinger: a whiner
windscreen: a windshield
wing mirrors: sideview mirrors
yabbie: a crayfish
yarn: to tell stories

For Charlotte Lindsay (Austin),
without whom there'd have been no Ellie

One

It was hot and dusty. The sun sat up there all day without moving. It saw everything and it forgave nothing. Sometimes it seemed like you were alone in the world, you and the sun, and at those times you could understand why people in the old days feared and worshipped it.

I hated the sun. For months on end it had no mercy. It burned everything. Everything that wasn't covered or hidden or fed with water, it burned.

It was mid-December and we were forty millilitres down on the monthly average. The dams looked like muddy pools, and the stock hung around in the drying mud, more interested in staying cool than in eating.

Three of us were working in the yards: Dad, Quentin, and me. Quentin had been late, as usual, and that got Dad snarling.

"Don't know why I bother with him," he said to me as we waited. "If that new woman's any good she'll have half his business in three months."

The heifers milled around noisily. They didn't know what was going on but they didn't like it. We'd penned a hundred and fifty in the yard and run about thirty of them into the holding pen, ready to put them through the race, but of course to do that we separated lots of mothers from calves. So they bellowed and moaned, as they shifted backwards and forwards. Most of the time you were so used to it you didn't even notice, but sometimes it got on your nerves and you felt like bopping the poor things on the forehead with the back of an axe.

Not really. They couldn't help it. They were just being good mothers. Good mothers and loyal kids.

We saw Quentin's little cloud of dust as he came across Cooper's, one of our flatter paddocks. Cooper's is about twenty-five hectares. It's named after a soldier-settler who took up a block near our place after the First World War and lasted seventeen years, longer than most. When the bank got his place Mr Cooper came and worked for my grandfather. He died of liver failure. His block ended up as part of our place eventually: Dad bought it before I was born, and it's now our eastern boundary, only we turned his seven paddocks into three, that we called Burnt Hut, Nellie's and Cooper's.

Quentin arrived, as usual without bothering to apologise. He wanted to lean against the crush and yarn before he started work but Dad wasn't having any of that: Quentin charges by the hour. So it was on with the overalls and straight into it. Quentin's arm, wearing its long glove, disappeared inside the first heifer and a moment later he was nodding and coming back to the pen so we could put the next one into the crush.

My job was pretty easy. The three of us helped fill the smallest yard, then all I had to do was swing down the big steel bar when the heifer was in the crush, and open the gate when she was allowed into the next yard. Occasionally a calf got in there too, which didn't matter if it was in front but did if it was behind, because then Quentin couldn't get at the heifer. That was about the only real problem.

There was plenty of time to think. I spent most of it watching Quentin. It always seemed so unhygienic wearing the same glove all morning. Wouldn't you think he'd pass on infections from one cow to the next? I asked him once and he said it almost never happened. And how come the heifers didn't mind his arm going right up them? With some cattle, the quiet ones, you could fill the race and Quentin would just walk along and do them in there, one after the other.

Homer would say they enjoyed it. But that's just Homer.

I touched the end of the steel pipe that formed the nearest crossbar to me. It was a bit rough, and there was a bolt sticking out near my head. Dad was always saying we needed to take the rough edges off the stockyards. They bruised the cattle, and you couldn't afford that. Marbled flesh was all the go, because of the Japanese market. Everything had to be perfect. It put a strain on farmers. The ones who knocked their animals around didn't survive any more. Even Mr George had given up using a cricket stump to move them through the stockyards. What we really needed was a circular yard, because you get a better stock flow then. Homer's place had a circular yard.

My time of thinking-music was interrupted.

"This one's empty," Quentin said.

Empty. Such an ugly word. You could tell that most farmers — and most vets — were men. A woman would never have come up with a word like that. I let the first two beasts out and slammed the gate shut on the nose of the empty cow. Quentin grabbed his clippers, closed her in from the rear, banged her tail and put the tag on. I climbed over the rails and swung the bar up on the other side, so she could come out into her own little yard, with her new short tail.

"Welcome to Failure City," I said to her. "You're not pregnant. You've failed as a woman."

"Ellie, are you going to get her out or are you going to have a bloody conversation with her?" Dad shouted.

I went red. I hoped he hadn't heard me. I waved my hat in her face and out she went. It was true though, what I'd said. They only got one chance and if they missed, they were finished. You couldn't have them eating all the feed in the paddocks if they weren't breeding. They had little value to anyone once they got that tail-tag. It was off to the abattoirs. Didn't matter if they had nice personalities or a good sense of humour or were good to tell problems to, or were really intelligent. If they got pregnant they had value. If they didn't, they hadn't.

At school, in Year 8, there was this young teacher from the city, I can't remember his name, but one day I overheard him saying something about the girls off the properties being rough as guts. But God, why wouldn't we be? As long as I could remember I'd been watching vets shoving their arms up heifers' bums, feeling their wombs to see if they were empty. I bet that teacher never had to pull grass-seeds out of the eyes of four hundred ewes: all that white mucusy stuff and the slightly off smell which gradually makes you want to throw up. I bet he never had to pull a dead calf out of a heifer in labour; a calf that had died a week earlier and decomposed inside the mother. And I noticed he didn't say anything about the boys being rough. Next to some of the boys, we were Qantas stewardesses.

The next empty heifer might have been reading my mind because she was a bit mad. When she wouldn't move I gave her a tap with some poly-pipe. I didn't like using poly-pipe even, but you have to have something and I don't think poly-pipe bruises. When she still didn't move I bopped her hard. She dug her front hoofs in and lowered her head and stared furiously at me. In the end I had to get an electric prod from Quentin's Toyota, and even then she was stubborn. When I got her into the rejects' yard she stormed up and down for ten minutes, like a yabbie in a billycan.

It wasn't that good a morning actually, not because of the heat but because there were too many empty heifers. Fifteen I think, out of a hundred and fifty. When we'd finished and let the others back in their paddock Dad and Quentin had a chat about it, leaning against our Land Rover.

"Probably this dry weather," Quentin said. "They've lost a bit of condition."

I never liked asking questions that made me look ignorant but I'd learned ages ago that if I listened I could usually pick up the answers. So somewhere along the line I'd learned that heifers won't come into season when they get down in weight. If the feed's poor they don't cycle: they have to be a certain weight before they rejoin. I guess it's Nature's way of stopping them having calves they can't support.

"Hmmm," Dad said. "Maybe I should have given

them more time with the bull. They had six weeks. Probably could have done with a couple more."

"What about another month?" I suggested.

In the end the heifers got a reprieve. Fifteen was too many to write off that easily, so they went back with the bull for another go. If they still didn't get pregnant at least they could have a good time trying.

Today we party, tomorrow we die.

The very next day the rain came, good soaking rain that filled the dams and greened the country, even if it was too late to give us much feed. But I never found out if the heifers got in calf or not, because less than a month after that the soldiers invaded and normal life ended forever. There was no time then for carefully culling poor performers as part of a long-term programme to improve the fertility of the breed. No time for long-term programmes of any kind. From the day the bombers roared overhead, and the tanks and convoys rolled down our highways, there was time for one thing only, and that was survival. All our energy went on that.

Sometimes there didn't even seem much point to it. Why go through hunger, cold, exhaustion, burns, bullet wounds, the death of family and friends, when at the end of the day the invasion had been so successful that we had nothing to look forward to anyway?

I changed my mind about everything every day. OK, I know that's what being a teenager's all about, but it was a thousand per cent worse since the war started. So one day I'd think "Yes, we're not going so badly, there's still hope, we can win." The next day it was more like "Oh God there's no hope, we should give up. If only we'd been caught in the first place it would have been better."

It was unfair: we'd been saddled with this huge responsibility just because we hadn't been caught. Because of this incredible fluke we were expected to put our lives on the line.

On the line? Three of my friends had put their lives over the line. They were dead. I had lost them. They were my friends and they were no longer on this earth and I would never see them again in this life, and it was all because of this rotten scummy war.

It seemed so random. I don't know how Robyn and Corrie and Chris were chosen, if choosing was how it worked.

The stupid thing was that we didn't have to be here. I kept dreaming of our days in New Zealand. It's not like we did nothing there but laze around watching TV, sleeping, eating chocolate, and partying. Well, OK, we did do all of those things for a while, but we did some useful things too, and worked quite hard, visiting schools and raising money for the war, stuff like that. Until the pressure was put on us again. Colonel Finley, the New Zealand officer who seemed so powerful in saying how this war should be run, could be a smooth talker sometimes. I don't blame him for getting us to come back, but I wish it had worked out better. I still burned with anxiety to know what happened to the Kiwi soldiers we lost near the airfield. I was proud of what we'd achieved at the airfield, and how we'd survived by using our own brains and taking some big risks, but it hadn't helped us find Iain and Ursula and the others.

And now here we were in hiding. Again. Half of Stratton was ruined: bomb craters and blacked-out streets and deserted houses. At least my grandmother's suburb wasn't too bad, and her place was OK. It was hardly damaged at all, except for a bit of vandalism. But we were leading a pretty grotty life. We didn't see too many people. Our only neighbours were young kids living much the same way we did, not far from us, and we knew how fierce and dangerous they could be. Sometimes I imagined the streets of the cities and the paddocks of the countryside teeming with feral humans like them, living in burrows and cellars, coming out at night: shadowy half-wild creatures.

Certainly the kids were as scary as the soldiers who patrolled the suburbs on their motorbikes.

All in all, I'd rather be back in Hell. Well, I'd rather be on the farm, helping Quentin and my father move the heifers through the race. Failing that, I'd settle for Hell. I missed that peaceful wildness, that deep sanctuary. But I knew we couldn't just cruise on back there. I had to keep reminding myself of that, and push away the temptation to run out of the house and straight out of Stratton. I knew we didn't dare go back into the bush yet, didn't dare go near Wirrawee. After our little effort at the airfield they'd be looking for us till we were old age pensioners.

And the truth was that while we were in Stratton we could do a bit more to help the war effort. There were still targets in Stratton: soldiers everywhere. I just hoped there weren't any soldiers in Hell.

But there was another reason I didn't want to go back in the bush for the time being. It was because I thought it might be claustrophobic, stuck in the basin of Hell. I had a feeling the five of us might end up in an enormous fight. Until recently in this war we'd got on pretty well, but at the moment things were tense. In Stratton we could get away from each other, and that seemed important. I still wanted them all near me, with me. Needed them with me. But I also needed some space.

The two who especially weren't getting on well were Lee and me. I was so angry at him. Our relationship had hit a problem. And unlike some problems, which are about trivia and in the long run don't matter much, this was extremely horrible and serious. I didn't know where it was heading. I just knew our relationship had hit the gravel and rolled end over end, and was still rolling.

So although I gave myself an occasional little holiday by going back to those lost days before the war, I couldn't do it for long. My memory was fading. I started out deliberately thinking about my parents every day, as a way of keeping in touch with them, with the way life used to be. But it had become harder and harder. There'd been so many days when I was too scared or too tired, and other days when I just forgot. Then, when I couldn't get a clear picture of how they looked I'd panic, and try desperately to remember every single detail of our lives together. That day with Dad and Quentin the vet, preg-testing the heifers: for some reason I could relive that so realistically that when I closed my eyes I felt I was there again. But there were only a few memories I could call up like that. Most of everything else had ebbed away. Getting with Steve at the Year 9 Social, digging out the old well, trying to reach the top apples in the tree, lounging against the Aga while I talked to Mum about the Nelsons' horrible feedlots or the problems with Eleanor and our netball team or whether my short silver dress would do for the party at Robyn's . . . I could remember those moments but I couldn't smell them or taste them or feel them any more.

Other people used tranquillisers or grog or drugs I suppose, to shut out awful grey realities. I didn't have those but I wouldn't have taken them anyway. I clung to my daydreams, and tried to use them. They weren't enough, not by a long way, but they were something. On the really depressing days they were all I had.

Daydreams could be dangerous though. On my school reports teachers wrote "Needs to concentrate harder." It didn't bother me much back then. But in this war concentration became a matter of life and death. You missed hearing a twig break, you were dead. You ignored a truck parked off the side of the road, you were caught in a trap. You blocked out your sense that something wasn't quite right, and the next minute you were lying on the ground with a gun pressed in your neck.

And it wasn't just yourself who got wiped out. You could kill your friends by not concentrating.

Oh, I suppose you could do that in peacetime by driving too carelessly, or using a firearm recklessly, but here the probabilities were much higher. In peacetime there weren't people looking for you to kill you.

So I made myself snap out of my little daydream of the heifers and calves in the stockyards. Daydreams now were like watching TV in the old days — something to do when your jobs were finished.

That was the theory, anyway.

I was standing by the kitchen sink of my grandmother's house in Stratton. I'd half-filled the sink, using a bucket, so I could peel some potatoes. I was thinking about Christmas and wondering when it was. I'd lost track of dates pretty much completely. We'd managed to pass almost a whole year without celebrating any birthdays. Unbelievable. It was mainly because half the time we didn't know what week it was, let alone which day. Sometimes someone would say, "Is this August? Hey, it's my birthday in August." But as we were usually attacking an enemy at the time, or hiding in a blacked-out school building, or changing sentries at three o'clock in the morning, the comments about birthdays tended to float off into the Milky Way, to be read by any passing aliens.

Plus birthday cakes were in short supply.

It was sad though, to think I'd missed a birthday. When I was little it never crossed my mind that this could happen. Birthdays were so important. No, more than important. The whole year revolved around birthdays and Christmas. Months of waiting and dreaming and hoping. The funny thing was that afterwards you didn't spend months reliving the wonderful day. Within twenty-four hours it was gone and you just had to think how long it was till the next big one.

One thing I could never understand about adults was how they didn't seem to enjoy Christmas or birthdays any more. They said sterile things like, "The best present would be if you got better grades in school," or "You don't really want presents when you get to my age."

Not want presents! I couldn't imagine that! For me, that day would never come. Never! But the adults turned it all — Christmas especially — into a nightmare. They spent weeks complaining about stuff like shopping and the rellies and the cards they hadn't written and why you hadn't got a tree yet and why you hadn't put up the decorations. They sounded so tired and cross and cranky, going around saying, "Sometimes I wish Christmas was only every second year," or "It's just a big commercial rip-off."

Didn't they realise that for us kids it wasn't that way at all? Had they forgotten so much already about what it was like to be a kid?

I saw a poem once, in a book, and it was by a kid, and there was a bit that said:

No one can get in
Our world.
It has a wall twenty feet high
and adults
have only ten foot ladders.

Boy, was that ever right.

Yet here I was, peeling spuds and thinking, "Well, Christmas sure doesn't mean much to us any more. There isn't going to be a Christmas this year."

What was that Dr Seuss book, *How the Grinch Stole Christmas*? The soldiers had stolen Christmas from us.

Two

It was Homer who first had the idea of making another approach to the ferals. The ferals was the name we gave to the gang of kids who were running wild in the streets of Stratton. And I mean really wild. They weren't just average naughty little tackers. They were ferocious, dangerous, frightening. They had caught us and mugged us more successfully than the soldiers. They had at least two guns, and a bow and arrow that would be as lethal as a gun, assuming they could use it.

But we'd had vague ideas for a while about doing something for the ferals. It was horrible to see kids so young and so crazy. Homer said once that we wouldn't have given up on them if they were our little brothers or sisters. In a vague abstract kind of way we all agreed with that idea. We just hadn't ever got around to doing anything about it. We had enough worries of our own. And I don't know about the others, but I was pretty damn nervous of these kids. With the frights and the horrors we'd been through already I wasn't anxious to go looking for more trouble.

Once I'd offered them some food. I left it on the footpath near their hide-out, with a sign saying FOOD—HELP YOURSELF. But to my surprise, they hadn't touched it. It was strange, because I was sure they were hungry. When they mugged us in the alley they seemed desperate for food. If they were city kids, like we thought, they probably weren't too good at foraging for food. Before the war they'd probably had a life of supermarkets and milk bars, opening the fridge door and helping themselves to a yoghurt or a tomato or a Mars Bar. Like the Grade 2 kids from the city who'd camped on the Mackenzies' property. One of them asked Mr Mackenzie, "How do you get the wool onto the sheep?"

Anyway, whoever suggested having a go with the kids certainly started something. Fi in particular got quite worked up at the idea of making contact with them again. I suppose enough time had passed for her to forget how scary it was to be at their mercy. My talking about Christmas set her off in a big way. I think she immediately imagined a happy Christmas dinner with everyone sitting around a decorated table and Santa making a surprise visit down the chimney. I didn't get the same picture when I brought it up on my monitor. These kids would eat the reindeer and strangle Santa. But I didn't say anything. I didn't want to spoil her dreams.

Fi's the last of the great romantics.

Kevin wasn't so tactful. "Are you kidding?" he said, when we started talking about it. "You guys told me they were a hair and a freckle away from killing you."

"I agree," Lee said. "We've got enough problems of our own. We're just setting up a lot of grief for ourselves if we think we can save everyone."

We didn't go as far as putting our hands up for a vote, but we were obviously divided. Our discussion, which was in Grandma's lounge room, broke up without a decision.

But I didn't confess to the others that I'd been keeping an eye on the ferals anyway. They were hanging out in a deserted milk bar on Mikkleson Road. I'd taken to going past it at night, just quietly, across in the park, a hundred metres from the shop, so as not to provoke them. I'm not sure why I did it, just some vague feeling that I wanted to make sure they were OK. If I was in the area anyway, it was easy enough: no big deal.

Then I did get closer to them, briefly, but not in a way I'd expected.

It was late in the afternoon. We never seemed to see the motorbike patrols between four and six o'clock, maybe because they were changing shifts. I was doing a little patrol myself, at the other end of West Stratton, near one of those shopping centres that have only a milk bar and a fish-and-chip shop, and a newsagent and a chemist. This one had a computer repair shop and a Red Cross op shop as well, but it was pretty boring, and of course there was nothing valuable left in the shops.

In both Wirrawee and Stratton there were certain houses that seemed to attract attention. Any nice-looking place, or big rich place, was guaranteed to be worked over by looters. My grandmother's was one of the biggest in West Stratton, so it had been plundered, but not as badly as some. We'd learned not to bother with big places much because there was never anything worthwhile left in them, just like the shops. We mainly checked out the smaller houses.

So I don't know why I went into this big house on Castlefield Street. No particular reason. I was wandering. The house was solid dark brick and stretched along the street for a hundred metres. It wasn't pretty but it sure was big. They had a pool in the backyard: Like all pools these days it was filthy and stagnant, the water such a dark green it was almost black. The front door was so solid no-one had even tried to smash it down, and the back door had been attacked but not broken. Around the corner though, was a side door which had been easily forced. It led into a rumpus room, a big area with a polished wooden floor.

As I stepped into that I heard voices. For a moment I thought, "No way, it must be birds outside, or water gurgling somewhere." I'd been caught out by both those sounds before. But then I heard a high-pitched voice say,

"It's my turn," and I knew that it was no bird or broken pipe. It was a child.

The instincts I'd developed during the war gave me a strong message. Strong and unmistakable. "Get out!" was the message, and it yelled at both my ears from the inside. So I couldn't pretend I didn't hear it.

But I went forward. I tiptoed across the room to the far side and crouched next to the door, so if anyone came in they wouldn't see me straightaway. The voices had faded and I thought they might have moved off, but a minute later I heard them again.

"Put her up here," the same voice said, and another child answered, "Wait, I'm changing her dress."

"Hurry up."

Then a new voice, quieter, murmured, "The pin thing's broken. Try this one."

I still hadn't heard an adult. The door was half open and I put my left eye to the crack. There was nothing to see, just a long corridor stretching somewhere, quite dark, with the same polished wood.

I crept around the door and looked down the corridor. At the end was a short flight of steps, only three or four, going up to another half-open door.

The biggest danger was that my boots would squeak. I started along the corridor, putting my feet down carefully and slowly. I was half-way towards the door when it moved suddenly, swinging towards me. I froze. The blood rushed to my face so fast it seemed to burn the skin. The door had moved maybe twenty centimetres.

Then it moved the same distance back again, and I relaxed. The draught was shifting it.

The voices came again, much more clearly. The first child, a girl, said, in a highly aggravated tone, "But she has to be lying down."

I went another five steps, which took me right to the end of the corridor. I could see the beginning of a carpet, a deep red colour with a green crest stamped on it every ten centimetres or so. The girls were heading into a fight now. I thought there were three separate voices and I was sure they were all girls.

"Put her on the bed," one of them said loudly and aggressively.

"No," another one answered. "We did that last time. Put her on the chair. Then the soldiers can come in through this door."

I'd heard enough to know they were playing. The sounds of kids playing are different to any other sounds. You can't mistake them. They get so absorbed in their game, and I think they actually put on more adult voices. That's what these kids were doing.

The argument suddenly flared into a full-on fight. One of the girls, the second one, said, "No, don't touch her, she's mine!" and the third one said, "Yeah, Brianna, don't be so bossy."

Brianna screamed, "Well, you're not doing it right, you're so stupid. Why don't you listen to me for once, you're always sticking up for Casey."

The next minute the door was flung open and Brianna — it had to be her — was standing there. I recognised her from the hold-up in the alley. She'd been one of the noisiest. She was a fiery little thing, all red hair and burning red face. About ten years old and with a haircut that a kid must have given her: some bits too long and some bits too short, and a fringe they might have done with a whipper-snipper. She held a large stupid-looking doll with blonde hair and a dirty bride's dress.

She took one look at me and her mouth opened like she'd seen Jack the Ripper. She made a little gulping noise, clutched the doll, and ran back through the door. "That girl's out there," she yelled at the others as she ran past them, with me right on her heels. But she was too quick. She had the next door open and was through it and gone, like a mosquito wriggler slipping through your fingers in a cattle trough.

I turned around. The other two were heading out the first door, just as fast as Brianna. "Wait," I called. I lunged at the closer girl and grabbed her by the back of her T-shirt. She sobbed and swung around, hitting at me with her spare hand, but missing. I let her go anyway, partly because I didn't have a good grip, partly because I didn't like to hold her, didn't like to make her a prisoner. But when she charged off again she ran straight into the open door, hitting herself hard. Her forehead, her nose, her chin: she really cracked them.

She staggered back holding her face and crying, and I grabbed her a second time. "It's OK," I said, "don't cry. You'll be right." This time she didn't fight, but stood there letting me hug her. She sobbed heavily, like someone who hadn't cried for years, like she was crying from somewhere deep inside. I hugged her for maybe a minute. Then the third girl reappeared at the door, very cautiously. She obviously didn't know what she was going to find. She stared at us for a moment. She was a pretty kid, a dark slight little thing with solemn brown eyes. She looked like an autumn leaf who'd blow away in a breeze.

In an uncertain voice she said, "Come on, Casey."

Casey hesitated, then pulled away from me. I let her go. It actually hurt me to do that, hurt me quite a lot. But I couldn't force her. "If you love something let it go. If it doesn't come back, it wasn't yours in the first place." I didn't love these kids but I felt sorry for them. They were *Lord of the Flies* come to life. One minute they could play with dolls, the next they were a savage street gang, dangerous and violent. Casey looked back at me, kind of sadly. I shrugged and said, "I won't hurt you," and she got a very serious puzzled expression, like "Do I believe her or don't I?" but then the other girl said, "Come on," with a lot of emphasis on the last word, and they ran out together without another glance at me.

I didn't try to follow them, just stood having a look around the room. It seemed like a regular playground. Toys were scattered everywhere. I suppose they had their pick of toys from all around the suburbs. The invasion came so suddenly that there wouldn't have been time for the average kid to pick up his toy collection. But maybe there's such a thing as having too many toys, because the ones in this room seemed to have been given a hard time. I counted six broken porcelain dolls, and a lot of other stuff. A Barbie mobile home, for instance, that looked like someone had sat on it. The remnants of two Hungry Hippos. And a telephone set that had been ripped apart. I guess anything like telephones, which relied on batteries, would have been a bit frustrating when the batteries ran out.

There were lots of toy guns, too. I thought that was kind of interesting. I assumed they'd be so sick of guns that they wouldn't play with them. By now they should all hate guns.

Sitting on a windowsill was one of those cute little bears that are made of plastic or something, and dressed in different outfits. This one was in a suit with a waistcoat and a gold watch chain, and carrying a briefcase. He looked very pleased with himself. I put him in my pocket as a present for Fi. Sometimes we needed our toys too.

I wasn't taking over sentry till midnight, so I decided I wouldn't go straight back to Grandma's. It was a nice evening, the kind where the light fades so slowly that you don't notice it getting darker. It changes gradually, losing its hardness, its brightness. The glare goes. It was at that softer stage now and it gave me the urge to get out of town again. For an excuse I decided I'd look for mushrooms. There'd been a bit of rain, so I figured there should be a few around.

I took a couple of bags from the house on Castlefield Street, and set out along the back streets till I got to the factory area. There were still a few factories that hadn't been bombed, and they often worked nights, so I avoided them, detouring round the back of the bowling club.

I found a lot of mushrooms along the roadside, but it was too dangerous hanging around there, so I went into the paddocks. There were plenty in among the damp grass too, but mostly yellow-stainers, that look like perfect field mushies, but when you scratch them they go yellow and you know they're poisonous. So I didn't do as well as I hoped. Still, I found a couple of nice patches, ate half a dozen on the spot and brought back a bagful to share with the others.

I was approaching the milk bar, still a hundred metres from it, when I smelt something funny. When you're a non-smoker you can smell a cigarette from miles away. You can smell it on someone's clothes the day after they've had a smoke at a party. Or on your own clothes, if someone near you has been smoking. And wafting towards me down the street, was the smell of a burning cigarette.

My first thought was, "Don't tell me these kids are smoking, at their age," which was pretty silly considering they seemed quite capable of murder. When they mugged us I'd wondered if they were on drugs. But I didn't know where they could have got cigarettes. At this stage of the war everything perishable had been looted. Cigarettes and grog were among the first to go.

Still, they could have found a hoard somewhere.

I crept twenty metres closer, and waited. Minutes and minutes and minutes ticked by. The smell of the cigarette had gone but the person who smoked it had to be there. If I wasn't patient before this war I was now. I don't think impatient people survived too long. I didn't see anyone; all I had to go on was that smell. As time went by I started telling myself I might have been mistaken, maybe I'd imagined it, or maybe it was the smell of smoke from our cooking fire, or maybe it was the kids and now they'd gone back into their shop. But I didn't move. It must have been an hour; could have been one and a half. My legs ached — the backs of my thighs especially — my feet got really sore, and I had to keep rolling my shoulders to ease the tension in my neck. I did a little dancing on the spot, but really just wriggling my toes, to stop my calves cramping. I'd almost forgotten why I was there.

Until I saw a shadow flitting across the nature strip. I only got a glimpse, before it disappeared around the corner. I couldn't see for sure, but I'd swear it was a male and I'd swear it was an adult. Then he was gone and I was left with my thoughts and fears and imaginings.

And I did a lot of all of those. In some ways a patrol of soldiers, in uniform and armed, was easier to deal with. You knew where you were with them. You knew what they wanted. But one dark spying figure, skulking around in the undergrowth: I didn't have a clue what that was about. It stirred me up, stirred me deeply. Scared me deeply, to be honest. I couldn't think who he might be or what he might want.

I waited another ten minutes, as my mind got more and more scrambled with the possibilities. When I got back to my grandmother's I rushed to find Homer. Fi and Lee joined in as Kevin listened silently. We were all very disturbed. We felt a bit helpless to know what we could or should do about it. The feral kids didn't want to know us, but on the other hand there was no good reason for an adult to be hanging around them, so maybe we should protect them, whether they liked it or not.

Being the middle of the night, the others didn't really want to do anything. Sure, it was partly because we couldn't think of anything to do. To be honest, though, I think the main reason was that everyone was tired. They were going to bed when I got there, and it's hard to change your mind-set when you're thinking sleep.

I suppose because I'd seen the man — and smelt his cigarette — I was more involved, more convinced of danger, more anxious. I felt a sense of urgency that was on a different level to the others'. Homer just spread his hands helplessly and said, "Honestly Ellie, what can we do? We can try approaching them to warn them, but they're more likely to shoot us. We can chuck a message into their shop or something. But it's the same problem. If they see us coming towards the place they'll go for us. We have to wait for morning."

"I thought you felt sorry for them," I snapped.

"I do, of course I do. But it's not like some TV programme where they show a kid with cancer going to Disneyland and he's a total angel and you're meant to sit there with the Kleenex. OK so these kids are war orphans or whatever you want to call them, and if they were on TV you'd be ordering tissues by the truckload. But it's not quite like that, is it? These cute little orphans will kill us if we're not careful. We just can't go in at night."

A few weeks back Homer was all for helping the kids. Now, when I felt it was time to act, he dug in his heels. And the others more or less agreed with him. They said we should try to get a message to them in the morning. "They're not going to come rushing down the street with tanks just for a bunch of kids," Lee said. "They've probably known for ages that they're there," Fi said. "How do you know it was a soldier spying on them?" Kevin asked. "It could have been someone like us."

I ended up angry and frustrated. I sat there sulking like a little kid for a while. Then, like a little kid, I said, "Well, if no-one else'll come I'll go on my own."

This was breaking all our rules. We had been acting

more independently since coming to Stratton, but not if it meant danger. Only Lee had broken that rule, with terrible results. I knew we had to stick together, but I couldn't help myself. Maybe I was as tired as everyone else. That's my excuse anyway. That's always my excuse. The others just looked at me, totally exasperated. Finally Lee, of all people, said, "I'll go with you."

"It's not that easy," Homer said. "This affects all of us. How exactly do you plan to do it? Bowl up to their front door and ask for a few moments of their valuable time?"

"They're paranoid," Fi said. "They think we're their enemies too. They don't trust anyone."

That was no news to me. But I admit I hadn't thought it through. I had some vague idea that I could go to them with a big stupid grin on my face and they'd throw down their weapons and embrace me and ask me to adopt them as their big sister or their mother. The moment when Casey clung to me in the playroom of the big house in Castlefield Street, that affected me pretty strongly. It triggered deep feelings in me. If I were honest, I think that was another reason I was acting differently now to the others. But I also hoped the kids would give me a better reception than they might Homer or Lee. If the girls from Castlefield Street saw me, I thought they'd be slower to pull their triggers.

On the other hand, as the war went on we'd been forced to improvise, and these days we did it quite well. It had become a way of life. I was starting to rely on it, spending less time planning, as if planning wasn't necessary. That was a big change.

So even though we sat round for twenty minutes trying to figure out a way of handling the situation, at the end of it, all Lee could say was, "Well, we'll just have to play it by ear."

By now the others were more co-operative. My bloody-minded threat, to go on my own, had worked a bit. And no-one had been unkind enough to mention that I was meant to be doing sentry.

All the time we talked I was getting more nervous, thinking that something could be happening already at the milk bar. I was keen to go. Kevin mumbled that he'd do sentry duty for me. I had a few reservations about that, but I needed him too much for me to make any waves. I also wasn't very happy about going off alone with Lee, not after the way he'd sold me out with his black-haired girlfriend. I knew though, that I'd run out of choices. So with Lee by my side I slipped away into the darkness and headed straight to the shop.

We got there six or seven minutes before the soldiers. I shudder to think what would have happened if we'd spent another five minutes arguing around the kitchen table at Grandma's. But we came sneaking towards the milk bar, being shadows among the trees, something else we'd become quite good at. We stood behind a pine tree, silently watching. The shop was completely still. If you hadn't known they were there, you'd never have picked it. But I was sure they were inside, and confident they'd have a security system. The previous experience I'd had with them, near the old stables where they'd been hiding, taught me that. They'd had a cute little booby trap there, a net of pots and pans that made almost as much noise as the airfield blowing up. So I scanned the street and the front of the building.

After about four minutes I pinched Lee's arm and whispered, "See that dark patch along there?"

I was pointing to a part of the footpath about fifty metres from the shop.

"What about it?"

"There's something shiny."

I strained my eyes, squinting, trying to work it out. It was such a dark night, and the area I was looking at was one of the darkest parts of the path, shadowed by an overhanging awning from another deserted shop. I thought Lee wasn't interested because he didn't seem to be looking at the place, but I was wrong, because after a moment he said, "There's another one over there," pointing down the street in the opposite direction.

I moved to get a better view, and it worked. Straightaway I could see what the shine was. Those cunning little rats, they'd put big sheets of galvanised iron in various places along the footpath, mainly around the front of the shop. It meant you couldn't get to the shop without walking on the iron, or, if you wanted to be smart, without lifting it up and moving it. Either way you'd make an awful noise, and they'd be warned you were coming. They'd only need one sentry to cover all the approaches to the shop. And they'd have an escape route too, no risk.

But just as I figured the strategy I heard a faint humming noise, like a pump. We weren't used to mechanical noises these days, so it stood out pretty strongly. I moved back next to Lee. I didn't have to say anything: he obviously heard it too, because he turned his head towards it and listened with full attention.

As it got louder I realised what it was: some kind of heavy truck, a diesel engine, but driven at low speed.

Funny, because it didn't sound heavily loaded. It wasn't one of those grinding straining noises that you get from an engine having to work its big end off. I started getting really uneasy. This shouldn't be happening here, in this suburb, at this time of night. If a truck can sound sneaky, this truck sounded sneaky.

"What do you think?" I said to Lee, urgently.

"I don't like it," he said, looking around a little wildly. "They might be coming here. Or to your grandmother's."

I was horrified at the second half of what he said. It never occurred to me that they might be after us.

But before I could do much with this new idea the truck suddenly sounded louder and closer. I lost any doubt that it was heading this way, and I'd underestimated how close it was. It still sounded sneaky, but it could have been just two blocks down the street.

We peered anxiously through the darkness. Just as I thought I was going to see the truck itself, it stopped. One moment there was the quiet rumble of the engine, the next we were surrounded again by the silence of the night air.

"What are we going to do?" I whispered to Lee. He didn't answer and I realised he had as little idea as me.

"You try to warn the kids," I said. "I'll go and check out the truck."

Again he didn't answer but an instant later he had gone. He could move so quickly, Lee. I caught a glimpse of him three trees away, then the shadows swallowed him.

I tiptoed as fast as I could in the opposite direction. I'd gone nearly the whole block, keeping in the row of trees, when I saw them coming. A line of soldiers on the other side of the street, then a second line on my side. I faded back into the park like I was a shadow myself. As they drew level with me I saw that they all carried rifles. My heart thumped painfully, and bile filled my mouth. I hoped desperately that Lee was successful in his mission. I hoped the kids didn't attack him.

There was no time and no point in my going back towards the milk bar. I couldn't get between the soldiers and the shop. Instead I figured I had to do something that would distract them. As soon as the last soldier was past me I raced to find the truck.

That was easy enough. I got to the end of the park. Next to it was a bombsite: a house, or a shop, that had been reduced to a wreck. Two walls still stood, but nothing else did. The chimney was splayed across the footpath. I stole into the ruins, trying not to turn my ankle on a broken brick. The truck was sitting opposite the wrecked house, by the side of the road, under an elm tree. I could see only one soldier, a man, standing beside it, watching intently down the street. Obviously he wanted to see how his mates were getting on. But I thought as I watched him that there was more to it than that. He seemed to be standing ready to jump back in the cab. He wasn't just watching in a passive way; he was holding the truck door and watching like a man with a mission.

The truck was one of those solid single-axle army ones with a canopy over the back. It was very like the one we'd been put in for the drive to Stratton Prison. It might have been the same one. And I realised suddenly what this man's mission was. He was waiting for a signal from the others. When he got it he would drive down the street and pick up the prisoners — or the bodies.

I tried to think coldly and calmly. In my mind I ran through any number of possibilities and rejected most of them. I was left with only two that seemed workable. One was to disable the truck; the other was somehow to take it over. I preferred the second one. The trouble with the first possibility was that it wouldn't save the kids at the milk bar. The trouble with both of them was that I'd have to deal with the soldier standing across from me.

I didn't have a weapon. But I thought if I was fast enough and brutal enough I should be able to get the advantage. I decided to be ambidextrous. I picked up a piece of broken pipe. Part of a hot water service probably. It was copper, but solid enough. I took that in my left hand and got half a brick in my right. I closed my eyes for a second, as I was moving, and bit my lip. I'd like to have said a prayer but there was no room in my mind for it. I headed around to the back of the truck. On the bitumen it wasn't too difficult to tread lightly. And the guy did seem to be concentrating hard on what might be happening down the road.

I'd figured out what I wanted. There must be a signal, and I needed to know what it was. That meant he had to speak English, but there was a fair chance he would. My idea was that if I jammed the pipe in his back and hit him hard with the brick at the same time he'd be so off-balance, so shocked and dazed, that he'd tell me what I wanted before he had time to think of doing anything else.

He heard me when I was still three steps away. I realised when I saw him start to turn. I covered those three steps in a rush and did what I'd been mentally rehearsing, shoved the pipe so hard into him I'm surprised it didn't come out the other side and brought the brick down firmly — not too hard — on his head. I started saying, "Drop your gun" but before I could even finish the second word he'd fallen to the ground. I was astonished. I was sure I hadn't hit him that hard. I think maybe he might have fainted or something. I honestly slowed the force of the brick as it reached him, because I got scared that maybe I would do him too much damage. Next thing I know he's lying on the ground not moving.

I bent over him, not sure what to do, and even a bit nervous that he might be faking, that at any moment he'd jump up and strangle me. I remembered Kevin talking about a spot on the head where a slight tap could kill someone. I shuddered with disgust and fear. But a moment later I had something else to think about. There was a whistle from down the road, and a torch flashed at me three times.

I didn't need to ask the soldier what the signal was any more. They might as well have set off a fireworks display.

It was time to improvise. I grabbed the cap of the unconscious man from where it had fallen and jammed it on my head, then jumped in the cab of the truck. The keys were in it, thank God. It was a diesel engine but it started quickly. It would have still been warm. There was a horrible grinding noise as I put it in gear, like a chain rattling inside a grain bin. I hoped the soldiers down the road wouldn't hear the bad change, and I hoped it wouldn't wake the man lying on the road. But I drove straight towards the milk bar, putting the lights on high beam as I did so. It was probably breaking all their rules but I had to take the risk; I had to blind them as much as possible so they wouldn't see my face.

With the lights on I could at last see what was happening. It wasn't a pretty sight. There was a pathetic group of kids, five or six of them I thought, the youngest only tiny. They all had their hands on top of their heads. In the middle of the group was Lee, towering above them, because of his height and his age. I mean, he was older than any of them, but as well he's tall for his age. He had his hands on top of his head too.

Surrounding them were four soldiers, and a couple more were away in the shadows.

They didn't even look up as I drove towards them.

At one stage I had the idea that I'd run the soldiers down, but the way they were grouped made that impossible. They were too scattered. So I did the opposite, bringing the truck gently to a halt just in front of them, sweating like hell and hoping desperately that they couldn't see me properly, high up in the cab, or that if they did, the cap would fool them. I didn't know what to do: just prayed for a bit of inspiration.

And at least I got my first wish: they didn't look up at the cabin. They ushered Lee and the kids around the back.

There wasn't much noise or drama. The kids seemed like they'd just woken up, all pale and shocked. Lee looked furious, his lips pressed together and his eyes narrowed. The soldiers hardly needed to speak. They weren't acting berserk; they acted like people going about their normal business. After all, they'd pulled off a nasty job successfully, without any of their buddies getting hurt or killed — as far as they knew — so I suppose their main feeling was relief.

There was a rear-vision mirror which showed the scene in the back. I watched closely. The soldiers helped by shining their torches in as the kids scrambled up. I knew I had to time this perfectly. I'd only get one chance.

Lee was last in, like I expected. The moment he was up on the tray I slammed the gear into reverse and dropped the clutch. I'd wanted to have it in reverse already but dared not, because I thought it would beep, or show reversing lights.

There was a thump and a swearword from Lee as he fell forward, then back. And a few cries from the kids, cries of surprise, fear, shock. I didn't have time to see if they were all right, and it was too dark to see in there now anyway. I was about to yell at them "Get down, get down," because I was expecting bullets, but then I heard Lee yelling it, so I knew he had survived his fall, at least. As we reversed I felt two distinct crunches. I guess I hit two of the soldiers.

I kept reversing, because it'd take too long to stop and find another gear, and also because, now I was past the soldiers, I thought it'd be better to have them shoot at me than at the kids. I tried to think if there were any side streets I could turn down but couldn't remember any. So instead I swung the steering wheel the other way, drove over the kerb, and set off through the trees and into the park, still going backwards.

It was bloody difficult. I'd killed the lights to make us a less visible target, and of course that meant I didn't have tail-lights either. Driving was completely blind. My memory said that once we got through the first line of trees it was clear ground for a while. I just had to hope my memory was accurate.

I got through the trees and went a bit further, then decided it was too dangerous. I swung the wheel hard and put us into a racing turn that went the full 180 degrees. At the end of it we thumped into something: I glanced in the wing mirror and by the brakelights saw a playground swing. I caught a glimpse of it toppling slowly away from the truck, but there was no time to watch it fall. I didn't hear it fall either, because by then I was making too much noise myself. I slammed the gearstick into second and revved it hard. The back wheels spun. We were probably in the sand from the playground. Suddenly the wheels gripped and we took off with a scream of rubber. The tail waggled backwards and forwards like an excited dog.

I don't know if anyone was firing at us at that stage. It was all too dark and wild and noisy to know what was going on. At least now though, I could look through the front windscreen and get a bit of a view. It sure beat trying to use the wing mirrors. We went for a mad swerving drive through the park. As I chucked a crazy left across a big garden bed Lee came slithering into the seat beside me. He did it awkwardly, kind of head first and side on all at the same time, but he was up in a moment and staring through the windscreen as anxiously as me. I had a glimpse of his white knuckles on the dashboard. We crashed over a footpath and straight through a small low fence. We must have been travelling at somewhere between eighty and a hundred k's.

It was a speed of absolute insanity, but sometimes a thought takes over your mind so completely that everything else is pushed into limbo. And the thought that possessed me was the desire to get away from the men with rifles. All thoughts of sane, careful driving, of consideration for the passengers, were erased from my memory. I'd lost them on my computer.

We went straight at the iron railings on the far side of the park. If we could get through them we'd be out on the street a block away from the soldiers. The truck was big and heavy but the railings looked hard and sharp. "Jesus Christ," Lee swore. "Hang on tight," he yelled at the kids in the back. I felt him ducking down as we raced at the pickets. I remembered how well we'd crashed through the fence at the airfield, but this looked to be a higher degree of difficulty. Like, a nine compared to a two.

Just as we were about to hit I saw that at the bottom of the fence was a concrete base. This was going to be the biggest speed bump I'd ever seen. Not to mention the steel spikes on top. I actually hauled back on the wheel as we raced at it, like this was a plane and I was operating the rudder. Then we hit.

It was the most God-awful crash. The shudder came up through the steering column and ripped the wheel out of my hands. I don't know what it did to the suspension but it would have been something chronic. The windscreen dissolved and cascaded all over me, a waterfall of glass. We became airborne. It wasn't like in the movies where you see the car fly across the bridge that's half open, or off the end of the unfinished freeway. In those the car is like a seagull, soaring gracefully. We were airborne for only a second and when we hit the road again it was with a crash that rattled every tooth in my head. I'd scrunched up in the seat, so I didn't hit my head, but there were screams from the back, so I guess they weren't so lucky. I had a mental image of the smallest kid bouncing around like a superball, and felt sick at the thought. The impact was so violent I was scared the floor of the cabin was going to rise and tear open. Everything not fastened down got thrown around: a Stratton street directory and a spanner both hit me before dropping to the floor, and a half-filled bottle of Coke fell from somewhere and lay on the seat pouring its insides out.

We raced across the road out of control, the wheel wobbling wildly from side to side. I had to swing it with all my strength. It wasn't enough and we went over the footpath on the other side of the road and into the front lawn of a house. The best I could do was to straighten up enough to get on the driveway. I didn't have my foot on the accelerator but we'd built up so much momentum that it didn't make a lot of difference. The brakes were cactus, just went flat to the floor. At the end of the driveway was something, some structure: I couldn't quite see what. I prayed it wasn't a brick garage. I was scared to try changing down a gear, because if I missed the change and ended up in neutral — well, we were gone then.

It wasn't a garage. It was a carport, with a little aluminium shed behind it. At the last minute I actually accelerated, thinking it was better for us to try to smash it out of our way. We hit it hard. Aluminium panels went flying, and I saw the roof pop up way above us like a shining silver kite. Then we were through. Through it, and the fence beyond, accelerating still, smash or be smashed, ten tonnes moving at eighty k's. The screams from the back blended with the screams from the ripping metal, till I couldn't tell the human noise from the noises outside. I gripped the wheel like it was a lifebelt and I was in a whirlpool. All I could do was to keep it straight and keep going. I gripped that wheel till I couldn't even feel my hands any more.

Then we were through to the next driveway, back to back with this one, and here there was no garage, thank God, no carport, just an old rusted wheelbarrow that had probably been there since the invasion and which the truck dismembered. I wasn't worried about that: I hardly noticed it, because I had something else to think about.

That something else was getting the truck out of the driveway and around into the street, a turn as tight as a twanging wire. There was pressure back in the brakes, but I knew even as I pushed the pedal that it wouldn't be enough. We had built up too much speed, too much momentum. I also knew I couldn't keep braking this hard and turning at the same time, or we'd be over. I'd roll it and kill the lot of us.

So I had to make a wide arc for the turn. And when I say wide, I mean the front verandah of the house opposite. It was held up by poles and we snapped them like matchsticks. The roof of it started coming down but I didn't see much of that, because we were already through the fence and thumping back over the footpath. Only then could I get the thing under control and straighten up. And suddenly there we were, rocketing down the street in the dark, the fresh night air blowing sweetly on my face.

Three

We pulled up outside Grandma's house. It gave Homer and Fi and Kevin a hell of a shock. I jumped out of the truck and ran across the lawn, but before I was halfway to the front door the three of them emerged from the trees.

"What have you been doing?" Fi asked. "Listen to those sirens!"

I could hear them all right. There were so many that they filled the night air: you couldn't tell what direction they were coming from. It sounded like they were everywhere at once. But the way Fi said "What have you been doing?" almost made me laugh — she sounded so like my father saying, "What have you been doing to those sheep? Why are they making all that noise?"

At the time I'd been riding them around the paddock, until one of them dragged me along the barbed-wire fence. I'd stood there with holes in my moleys and blood running down my leg, trying to look cool while I lied my head off, saying, "Gee I don't know, maybe they heard the dogs barking, or maybe there's a fox around," and all the time the pain was like I had an abscess in every tooth and I was scared I was bleeding to death.

"I'll explain later," I said. "Just grab what you can. We have to get out of here."

"Where to?" Fi asked.

"Where do you think?"

Lee ran past and after a moment's pause Fi followed him into the house. Only then, with them gone, did I notice the chorus of thin wailing voices from the truck. It sounded like a kindergarten that had run out of milk. I was about to go and look but Lee came back with his pack. "What's happening?" I asked him.

"I think there's a few broken limbs," he said. "They're not as used to the way you drive as I am."

My head spun with guilt, and it took me a moment to stop it spinning. Everyone else was in the house getting stuff and I had to join them. I hurried towards the door but as I did I heard the yowling tyres of a car that was horribly close, and I realised we couldn't afford to do anything except go like crazy out of Stratton. I screamed at the house, "Hurry!" and ran back to the truck.

I'm afraid the crying in the back doubled in volume and terror when I put it in gear. I've never claimed to be the world's greatest driver but I was a bit discouraged by their reaction. I didn't think I was that bad.

The others came stumbling out of the house, hauling all kinds of odds and ends. I already had the truck rolling, to encourage them. I know it annoyed the hell out of Homer and Kevin but things were desperate; we'd already wasted too much time.

Maybe they thought it was like that stupid and annoying trick certain adults love to play: they make you open the gate, then they drive through and keep going. Actually not just adults. Homer did it all the time.

They came running after the truck and I slowed down while Lee hauled them in. As soon as Homer's feet were off the ground I shoved the accelerator hard to the floor.

We'd gone two-and-a-half blocks when I saw a flash of headlights away to the left. I wasn't even sure they were headlights, because the high trees and narrow streets cut them off. But a moment later, while I was still asking myself if I'd imagined it, a car came skidding across the road at the next intersection, its back hanging out as the driver tried to get it around. He was aiming to come straight at me.

I only had one chance. There was a little gap behind

the car. I gunned the engine and went for it. The car was fishtailing everywhere. The driver made it worse by swinging the wheel around to get after me. I don't know how he didn't roll it. The car was trying to recover from the first turn and already he was putting it into a second one.

I made the gap. I glanced at the car and saw it go down hard on its nose as the driver got some control again. A blast of smoke came from the tyres. Then we were gone, skidding around the next corner almost as violently as he had. I accelerated hard and we thundered down the street. At the end of the block I turned left, but in the wing mirror saw his lights. He was after us all right, with a vengeance. I was surprised he wasn't closer. He must have had some trouble taking that corner.

I knew if we relied on speed and handling we had no chance. He'd have us by the time we'd gone another block. We had to outsmart him.

I used every trick I knew, and made up some new ones. It was tough work, because the steering and brakes were both in poor shape. I went up a lane, chucked a right, and turned the wrong way down a one way street. He went left, and we lost him for a few moments. I cut across another park. I think he got a glimpse of us at the last second. His lights swung into the park, as we belted under a bridge.

I hit a stretch of dirt, probably roadworks that were abandoned when the war started. The trouble was that we made a lot of dust, and he would pick it up in his headlights. At the end of the dirt I slammed on the brakes, crashed the gearstick into reverse and rammed the truck backwards into a bitumen parking area, outside Bunnings.

He screamed past. His engine made a kind of moaning noise. It was weird.

As soon as he was gone I went the other way. We went back under the bridge and this time I turned left.

We raced along a road that ran parallel to the freeway, but much lower. We were going through another big industrial area. There wasn't much bomb damage, but only a couple of factories seemed to be operating at this time of night.

I heard Homer yell from the back: "He's after us again."

We were just about to drive over a level crossing. I suddenly thought, "Well, why not?" and swung the wheel hard. We bumped along the train tracks. If the suspension was stuffed already from hitting the concrete base of the fence — and it was — then it was really stuffed by the time we'd gone a kilometre along the railway. It got the kids screaming again too. I could hear Homer and the others trying to shut them up, but I wasn't paying much attention.

I paid a lot more attention to the train.

Luckily, like the car, the train was using headlights, or to be more exact, a single headlight. It was like a beam from a torch, but a lot stronger and longer than my Eveready flashlight. I couldn't tell how far away it was, but I'd guess a kilometre and a half, and coming straight at us.

The trouble is that when two objects are travelling towards each other at a hundred k's an hour, a kilometre and a half doesn't amount to much.

I looked for an escape route. It was hard to see far ahead in the dark. My eyes tended to be hypnotised by the light of the train anyway. From the back Homer yelled again: "He's on the train tracks too Ellie!"

I realised he was talking about the car. They were so busy looking out the back that they hadn't seen the bigger problem out the front. Likewise, I'd forgotten about the car.

As far as I could tell, we were heading into a narrower section of the track. We were on a hiding to nothing. If I kept going we might end up in a cutting with steep sides, where a head-on with the train was our only choice. On my right was uphill, leading to God knows what. On my left was downhill, leading to God knows what. I didn't think the truck could handle the uphill. I spun the wheel left and we went for a slide.

It was pretty hairy. For the first fifty metres we were side-on. I knew not to brake; I just had to hang onto the wheel and try to bring the nose around. I was half standing, straining every muscle to make the truck obey me.

At least they'd shut up in the back. I think they were too scared to make a noise.

I'd almost got the nose around when we hit the road. The truck nearly broke in half. I thought I felt it bend. Above us the train rocketed past.

I don't know if it met the car or not. If it had, I think we would have seen and felt the explosion. But by the time they would have met, we were gone, herbing down the road. We were at the outer limits of Stratton and I gunned it. We went for ten kilometres before I started to think that we might just have shaken them off.

There was no slowing down though of course. I went herbing along at over a hundred k's in some parts. At least the road was smoother, and I think a couple of the kids calmed down, but a couple of them were really upset, and I wondered how tough things were back there. Broken limbs sounded like seriously bad news.

The biggest problem wasn't the crying from the back though; it was the steering. It was so badly damaged. I'd point the wheel in a certain direction but we'd go off in another one. The only way we could get around corners was to use the brakes and accelerator, and float in a kind of controlled skid. I got better at it as we went along. It took huge concentration. I couldn't relax for a moment, and what was worse, I knew that if we were going to come out of this alive I'd have to concentrate for hours to come. I had quite a number of lives in my hands.

We didn't need to stop and hold a big conference about where to go. At times of worst stress and worst danger our minds always turned to the one place. That was why I hadn't bothered answering Fi's question.

Hell. The basin of rocks and bush, so wild that no-one except us could get in. Apart from the Hermit no-one else in living memory had been down there.

And now that we'd started out I couldn't wait to get to Hell again. Stratton had its attractions — houses were much better than tents when it rained — but I hated living in the daily fear of Stratton. Or maybe it was just that I hate city life. Whatever, my feelings that Hell might be too claustrophobic, too unsafe, that we could do more important stuff in Stratton — all of that was replaced by an ache to be back there again.

Occasionally I could hear the others trying to calm the kids. The truck was noisy, so I only heard little moments, like hearing the chorus of a song but not the verses. I sure had upset them, but I guess it wasn't just me. It would have been everything they'd been through. I began wondering if maybe they'd be like us when we first met the horrible Major Harvey: we'd collapsed in a heap, and stopped being independent. We'd been grateful to have adults running things again, happy to let them take over. The kids might see us that way. I just hoped we'd do a better job than Major Harvey.

I could only stay on the good road for half-a-dozen k's, and even that was terribly risky. Then it was back to short cuts and detours and improvisation. Creative driving. The steering was even worse on the rough stuff. So I hardened myself against the chaos behind me. If they had to suffer a bit longer then they had to suffer a bit longer. We couldn't compromise our hide-out, no matter what. There was no way in the world I would drive straight to Hell. We had to take heaps of precautions. That wild country may have been the only safe area for hundreds of square kilometres. Without Hell we were lost.

I didn't think about how we were going to get the kids up to Tailor's Stitch. If they were badly injured it might be quite a problem. I couldn't believe they were that bad though. What had Lee said? Broken limbs? That meant arms or legs. Well, they'd survive that. We'd have to worry about it later.

As the crow flies it's not far from Stratton to Hell, but firstly we weren't crows and secondly we sure weren't going the fastest way, even for humans. One old dirt road looked like it hadn't been used since the gold rush. It took us straight down into a steep gully and at the bottom it forded a river that was running hard. I switched on the lights for a minute to look, but couldn't judge the depth. I just had to take the risk and go for it. Halfway across I had second thoughts. The water got deeper and deeper and the road felt rougher and crumblier. If a part of it had washed away we were in big trouble. We hit a couple of huge potholes and lurched around. I felt the rear shift from side to side. Even though the truck had a high clearance, water was coming in through the floor and swishing around my ankles.

I think my armpits were as wet as the chassis of the truck by the time we started up the other side.

I didn't know this country but I knew our general position. The mountains behind our place were away on the left, to the east. When we started to climb a little I thought it was time to head more directly homewards. I swung off the road at the next gateway into a paddock, stopped, hopped out, and opened the gate, cursing a little as I did it. A truckful of people, and I had to open the gate. And shut it.

We bumped slowly across the paddock, disturbing a few Herefords who got up clumsily and turned around to watch. Then another gate and another paddock. And another. And another. At least Homer opened and closed these gates for me.

It was forty-five minutes before we reached the next road. I still didn't recognise it, so we had to start the whole process again, me navigating by instinct as we followed fencelines and old wheeltracks. Any time things looked like getting too civilised — any hint of buildings or small well-cultivated paddocks for example — I'd swing away again. No matter how tired and frustrated I got I could always console myself with the thought that they'd never follow us here. We were making ourselves safer with every gate we opened, every remote paddock we crossed, every creek we forded. And at least in the paddocks I didn't have to worry so much about the truck's steering. It didn't matter if we went off course there.

I was glad to see the sky at last begin its change from black to grey. It gave me a bit more energy, woke me up again. All night I'd been using parking lights or no lights at all, and now I turned off the parkers for the last time. I pressed the accelerator down further and pushed the truck harder. I knew we were getting closer to Hell and the knowledge was sweet. I also knew that we had to get to the bottom of Tailor's Stitch in the next hour, before it got too light, before people started waking up and coming out of houses and travelling the roads. So I used every drop of that new energy, squeezing the bends tighter, forcing the truck up the hills faster, not slowing down for the level crossings. With all the practice I'd had during the night I was getting quite skilled at pushing it through corners, in its controlled drift. There were times when I even enjoyed it.

I was exhausted when we at last got to the track up to Tailor's Stitch. The burst of dawn energy had gone again and my eyelids felt tired and sore, like I'd been partying all night. I switched the engine off and staggered out of the cab, stretching my legs, making them work. I went around to the back, not sure what I'd find. They'd been pretty quiet in there for a while now. I'd heard a bit of retching at one stage, so I wasn't too optimistic about them, or the reception I'd get.

What I saw nearly made me laugh. Homer sat there nursing this little kid. The kid was asleep in his arms, her head hanging back and her mouth open. She didn't look very comfortable. Neither did Homer. He glared at me as if to say: "Make a joke and I'll kill you." So I swallowed what I wanted to say and looked past him. Fi had kids either side of her, hanging on tightly to her shirt. Lee was sitting on the floor next to a boy who seemed to be ill. Even Kevin had a girl asleep with her head on his lap. I was amazed anyone could be asleep. I'd thought the way I drove would have kept everyone awake. More than awake, in a state of shock. Seemed like I was wrong. Sometimes you can be so exhausted, so much at the end of your tether, that nothing keeps you awake. I'd been so exhausted at shearing time one year that I'd gone to sleep on the motorbike, in the middle of mustering. That was a bit embarrassing.

The smell in the back of the truck wasn't too good though. I'd been right about the retching. I guess being truck sick is worse than being car sick. On a bigger scale. Whatever, these guys had been sick. Well, one good thing, I wouldn't need to worry about cleaning it. I had other plans for the truck.

We got everyone out, which wasn't easy. I was so busy helping them, and chucking stuff out of the truck, that I didn't get a clear idea of what the kids were like. I just had an impression of a pale, half-starved pathetic-looking bunch, a lot less scary than they had been back in the alley, when they'd taken us by surprise. They seemed quite organised then. Now they looked about as ferocious as a bunch of starving orphan lambs.

Of course there were fewer of them now. I hadn't had time to find out what happened to the rest. Explanations would have to wait.

I left them to sort themselves out, while I got back in

the cab. I knew exactly what I wanted to do. I put the truck in gear and drove it away, up the track a couple of hundred metres then down to the left, down an overgrown escarpment. A few times before the war I'd been here on a motorbike, when I was just mucking around. No-one else would have known about it, because it was so overgrown that it looked like normal bush. But I knew that under the cover of scrubby grass and little shrubs was a line of solid rock. I knew how to follow it and I knew where it led.

There was just room for the truck. I drove it in almost to the end, not worrying about the trees scraping the sides and scratching the duco, or the rocks threatening to rip open the sump. At five k's an hour, at least the steering wasn't a problem. The escarpment ended in a dark hole: a drop into rocks and treetops. You couldn't see the bottom of it. If elves and goblins lived in the Australian bush, then this was where you'd find them. It was quite a spooky place. Unfortunately the elves and goblins were about to get a rude shock.

I stopped the truck fifty metres from the hole, put it in neutral and took off the handbrake. Then I got behind and started pushing. It didn't take much. It's amazing how you can make a really heavy vehicle move, as long as it's on flat ground and there's nothing to block the wheels.

I got it going all right. It soon took on its own speed and away it went. It reached the edge, paused a moment as though looking at its fate, then dropped slowly into the pit. It crashed through the tops of trees and on, down into the undergrowth. I was surprised at how quietly it disappeared. It didn't make much noise at all. Maybe the sound got trapped by the sides of the hole.

Anyway, down it went. When I peered after it I imagined I could see a dark shape in there, but it was hard to tell.

I went back to the others. The kids wanted to stay there but we were too nervous to agree to that. And right away we had our first crisis with them. They simply refused to go.

Up until that moment I'd found it hard to believe that these could be the kids who mugged us. In my mind, in the little fantasy I'd constructed, I'd stopped thinking of them as vicious crims, more as poor helpless little creatures who needed our love and protection. I'd turned them from *Lord of the Flies* into the cast of *Annie.*

There were only five of them. I'd thought there might have been more. But they weren't all the same ones who robbed us in the alley. I only recognised a couple from there.

While I'd been away pushing the truck over the edge someone had put a splint on one girl's arm, using sticks and the sleeves of Homer's shirt. It looked quite professional, so I hoped it would help her. There was every chance it'd be the only first aid she'd get. The leader of the group seemed to be a boy of ten or eleven. When we asked what happened to the others, he just shrugged and looked away.

"Most of them bolted," Lee confirmed. "They were too quick for the soldiers. I think they were awake already. What we've got here are the sleepers." He said it with a grin at them, like he was trying to make them laugh, but that was a waste of energy. They stared away in their different directions, as though they didn't know what language he was talking.

"Haven't you got any food?" a girl asked me. I realised

she was the same girl who asked that question back in the laneway.

"We've got a fair bit in Hell," I said.

The girl cringed, like she was frightened. "What's Hell?" she asked, in a much more timid voice.

It was the first time any of them had shown interest in anything much, so I guess that was a good sign.

"It's where we hide out. It's a safe place. That's where we want to take you guys. But it's a bit of a hike."

"I don't want to go to Hell," the youngest one said. She started crying again. She sure was good at that. She seemed to have an endless supply of tears. But she was pretty young, about five or six I guessed.

"Is she the only one with anything broken?" I asked Lee, nodding at the girl with the splint.

"I think so," he said. "It's hard to tell."

The girl, as if on cue, said, "I can't walk anywhere. My arm hurts too much." She started crying too. Only then did I realise who she was. Casey, the kid I'd hugged in the house in Castlefield Street. I looked at the other two girls more closely then, and recognised one of them as the third girl from that rumpus room. But Brianna, the bad-tempered red-head, must have been back in Stratton, coping or not coping on her own.

"I'm not going with you lot," the oldest boy said. His voice sounded unusual, slurred, like he'd been on the grog all night. Then the other boy, who was about nine, said like an echo, "Me neither."

I didn't have the patience to deal with this. We'd all had a long night, and the driving had been a tough job. No-one had even thanked me for saving their stupid useless lives. I'd taken huge risks, put my life on the line, for this bunch of snivelling brats. I tried to find some patience and understanding, and failed.

Fi was good though. Fi's the kind of girl who little girls love. Before the war they all followed her around at pool parties and barbeques and Christmas functions. She's one of those people mothers always asked to help out at birthday parties, because she was so good at organising pass-the-parcel and pin-the-tail.

I didn't get approached to do that stuff. I was the kind of girl who got asked to fix the PTO on a tractor, or put a backhoe through rabbit burrows.

So now Fi got to work, even though she looked exhausted. I shouldn't underestimate what it had been like in the back of the truck. Bloody awful. Swinging and bouncing around, getting thrown from side to side, then up and down as well. Seeing kids being sick, and smelling it, and feeling sick yourself, and never knowing what the idiot driver up the front was doing. Never knowing if enemy soldiers might suddenly pull an ambush and kill the lot of you, before you even knew they were there. No, it wouldn't have been a lot of laughs. Casey, the girl with the wrecked arm, had gone beyond pale to grey: she looked like she was sixty years old.

Fi got some water from a creek back down the track, and as they drank it she started encouraging them. "We've got some nice food waiting for us at the end of this walk," she said. Nice food was an exaggeration, but we had a stockpile of New Zealand freeze-dried stuff, which cooked up into a good meal. "And it's hot," Fi went on. "How long since you guys had a delicious hot dinner? And you won't even have to cook it. We'll do all that. You can just sit there and eat."

"Yeah, and Uncle Homer'll make you a special treat," Lee said.

"Yeah, I'll make it with my Swiss Army knife, when I get it back from these little shits," Homer muttered to me.

Give Fi her due, she got them moving. It was a combination of "Let's see who can get to the corner fastest," and "There might even be some chocolate for the people who don't complain," and the old "You don't want to be left here on your own, do you?" routine. The last threat was the only thing that worked with Gavin, the tough little boy who told the others what to do. In fact we all got up and headed along the track at least three hundred metres as he stood watching, as if daring us to leave him. Only when we got halfway around the bend did he give in and start plodding after us, head down, looking like he was at an extremely depressing funeral.

I dropped back and walked with him but he wouldn't answer my questions, wouldn't talk at all. I asked him the names of the other kids, but in the end I could only find out by listening to their conversation, after we caught up with them. The littlest one, who said she was seven, although she looked younger, was Natalie, and the girl always asking about food was Darina.

The boy who seemed like Gavin's shadow was Jack. Like Gavin he walked on his own and didn't say anything.

We had a fight every three minutes. And I'm ashamed to say it was the girls who were the worst. That bloody Gavin, talk about a stubborn little bugger, now he did the complete opposite of what he'd done before. Every time we stopped to have another argument with the girls about why they should keep walking, he ignored the whole thing and went right through the group and continued up the track. And so of course Jack went with him. I'd be watching the girls with one eye and with the other watching Gavin and Jack to make sure they didn't get out of sight. I wasn't expecting any trouble from the enemy, not till we got to the exposed top of Tailor's Stitch, but with these two I thought it was better to be safe than sorry.

I wish I could have felt more sympathetic towards the poor kids. But hunger, fear and exhaustion are quite a combination. They'd make monsters of anyone. And some of these kids had personalities that would turn oranges into lemons.

Somehow we bullied and bribed and threatened and blackmailed them to the top of Tailor's Stitch by lunchtime. Well, it would have been lunchtime if anyone had any lunch. Then we let them stop and have a rest, in the same place we waited that day with the Kiwi soldiers. It felt weird being there again. Last time I'd thought Iain and Ursula were over-cautious, making us hang round till dark before we went over the ridge and into Hell. I still thought that, but this time there was no question in my mind of us waiting long. We had to get food into these little tummies. Both Casey and Natalie looked like they might pass out at any moment.

So we sat there for three-quarters of an hour. The five of us had a quiet conversation while the five of them fell asleep. Three of them fell asleep so fast and slept so heavily that I dreaded the thought of waking them again.

The best thing — the only good thing — was that

Kevin was functioning fairly well. I think he felt important, having these little kids to look after, and I think maybe he was looking forward to the security of Hell. There shouldn't be any danger down there.

"So, what are we going to do?" Homer asked.

"Have we got the radio?"

"Yes," Lee said. "I wasn't going to leave that behind."

"Well, let's call Colonel Finley again. Maybe he'd evacuate these kids. He does owe us a favour."

"Or three," said Kevin, who hadn't done much to deserve any favours.

Everyone seemed to like the idea. I didn't bother to tell them about a slight complication of my own in the plan.

"Have we got enough food for them?" Kevin asked.

No-one could remember very clearly what we'd left in Hell.

"I think so," Fi said. "I know there's some chocolate, anyway."

"Lucky for you," I said. "They'd kill you if we got there and you couldn't deliver on the chocolate."

"There is quite a bit of food," Homer said. "We had plenty of freeze-dried. And some beef jerky. I can't remember what else, but we filled one of those green garbage bags. I remember there were stacks of Deb. If all else fails we can live on mashed potato."

"There's a couple of food dumps further along Tailor's Stitch that we did early in the war, when we were being all efficient," I said. "There'd only be a day's food in them, for this many people, but it all helps."

"I wouldn't mind having a go at making some rabbit traps," Kevin said. "I reckon I could. I've heard old blokes talk about them but I've never actually done it."

"We could raid a farm, too," Lee said. "Bring back more lambs. Get a few chickens even. The security wouldn't be that tight on some of those places."

"What are we going to do about Casey's arm?" Fi asked.

"Do you think it is broken?" I asked.

"I think it is," Lee said. "Just above the wrist. It was so floppy and loose. I think it'd have to be broken."

"It's really hurting her," Fi said.

"Well, there's not much we can do," Homer said. "There's a few first aid bits and pieces down at the campsite, but no morphine or anaesthetic. No X-ray machines."

"It's been better since Fi put the splint on," Lee said. "We can do an even better job when we get down there, and make sure it can't move at all. I mean, the thing is to totally immobilise it, isn't it? Isn't that why you put it in plaster?"

"I guess. I really don't know."

No-one else did either.

"There are pain-killers in my tent," Kevin said. "They'll help."

"Mmmm," Fi said. "As long as she sees we're doing something, that'll make her feel better."

"They've all got heaps of things wrong with them," Homer said. "That younger boy, what's his name, Jack, he's got a bruise right down one leg. And Natalie's got a whole lot of sores that look infected."

I heard Casey crying again, little low whimpering noises, so I went over to see what was happening. She was awake all right, holding onto her arm and biting her lip.

"Is it bad?" I asked.

She nodded, still biting her lip.

"We've been talking about you," I said. "We're pretty sure we've got Panadol and stuff in Hell. If you think you can make it down there we should be able to take the edge off the pain."

She didn't say any more so I sat there with her for a while.

After forty-five minutes Lee and Fi started waking the kids up, but that proved to be a bad idea. They pretty well spat the dummy. The girls actually performed a bit better this time. I think Casey would have come with us, and maybe Darina, but the others weren't interested. Natalie, the youngest one, cried and cried and wouldn't let anyone near her, and Jack took his lead from Gavin. And that was a bad idea. Gavin, in his funny slurring voice, turned on us and said, "We're not going with you lot any more."

I clenched my fists and counted to twenty. I could have counted to a couple of thousand. It wouldn't have made any difference.

None of us could think of anything to say. We gazed at them in horror. "Come on," Gavin said, and to my amazement they started getting up and moving towards him. Apparently they were quite ready to go off into the bush with him, come what may. They didn't look too excited or happy about it, but then they didn't look too excited or happy about anything. I have no idea where they thought they'd go. Back down to the road and wait for a bus I suppose.

They stood in a little group, gazing at us. "You can't walk off like that," I said. "We're miles from anywhere. You're in the middle of the bush. You'll get lost."

"We'll just go back the way we came," Gavin said. "Come on," he said again to the others. "We're going to Stratton."

He started off along Tailor's Stitch, towards the track. We were still down below the ridge, and it was hard for them to walk on the steep slope. But Jack followed him straightaway, then Darina, then, more reluctantly, Natalie and Casey.

"Stop! Wait," Fi called urgently.

"Let them go," I said.

I could see what was going to happen. They would follow the natural lie of the land, but in doing that they would miss the track completely. There was a spur right in front of them which offered a nice easy-looking walk, but it gradually curved away to the south. Eventually it would lead you into thick, impenetrable bush and by then you'd be well and truly lost. That was the bush for you. I loved it, but you had to be constantly on your guard. If it caught you not concentrating it could trick you in no time.

"Oh come on Ellie," Fi said. "We have to get them back."

"Let them go," I said again. "They'll go down that spur and get lost, and then maybe they'll listen to us."

I think Homer agreed with me but no-one actually said anything. We watched in silence as they trudged away. I was right too. They didn't even know what was happening because none of them looked up at any stage. The spur led them gently off in the wrong direction and with their heads down they obediently followed it. It was a bit weird to watch. I had to bite my tongue. I've never seen anyone doing something so totally wrong without saying something. In fact some people think I have too much to say in situations like that.

Soon they were out of sight. The last glimpse I had of them was Casey's sad face looking back at me; the last sound I heard was Natalie crying again. God, could that kid cry. We'd never run out of water while she was around, even if it was salty.

"Hadn't we better go after them?" Fi asked nervously, as soon as they were gone.

"Don't get your knickers in a knot," I said. "They won't get far."

"Don't you believe it," Homer said, then, quoting some bit of trivia he'd picked up somewhere, he added, "They tracked a five year old for forty kilometres, a century or two ago, when she was lost in the bush. And she was dead when they found her."

"I'm going to bring them back," Fi said immediately.

I gave Homer a look and grabbed Fi's arm. "Fi," I said, "I can't believe you haven't learned by now when Homer's taking the piss. Just let them get down the spur a bit. I know it seems cruel, but they've got to learn."

"I don't know why we're so desperate to help them," Kevin said. He had the sulks now, I suppose because the kids hadn't flocked around him, doing whatever he said. For a few hours he'd thought he was King of the Kids. "Let them go, if that's what they want. Stuff them."

We waited fifteen minutes, with Fi getting more stressed all the time. When I got up to follow them she shot off like a dog told to "Fetch 'em up." Sometimes I think Fi still doesn't understand the bush. You shouldn't come to grief as long as you don't fall down a cliff or get bitten by a snake. Sure you can get lost, but keep going downhill and you'll come to something eventually. If you find a fenceline you can follow that. It might take a few days but you won't die of starvation in a few days. And you can always find water. I mean, I'm not talking the Simpson Desert here. Around these mountains there's little pockets of water everywhere, even if some of it's a bit stagnant, or if the cattle have roughed it up a bit.

According to my dad, most of the famous cases of lost children, the ones where they disappeared completely, never to be found again, happened because the kids got to the end of their tether and climbed into hollow trees or fallen logs for shelter. With no food or water they'd go into a bit of a coma, so they wouldn't hear the searchers calling.

Anyway, I didn't think that would happen with these kids. They'd be OK. So I didn't go quite as fast as Fi. At first I thought none of the boys was coming, but just as I got into the tree-line I heard trotting feet behind me and Lee caught up.

"Little buggers," he said. "You'd think they'd be grateful."

I didn't answer. I had to talk to him when we were working together to save the kids' lives. But I didn't have to talk to him now.

He flushed and frowned, like a knitter who'd dropped a stitch. I knew he wouldn't try again. He had too much pride for that. And I had pride too. I still couldn't forgive him for going off with the dark-haired girl.

We concentrated on getting down the spur. It was a nuisance, doing this. We'd have to slog our way back up sooner or later, and it would be quite a slog. I hated throwing away height that I'd worked hard to gain.

The spur was very rocky and soon got thinner. There were three sharp drops, none of them dangerous, but none of them easy. For the third one I had to turn around and go down facing the cliff, so it was as hard as that. I must admit I was surprised that the kids had got this far, and Homer's words were starting to haunt me. But soon enough I heard Natalie's thin irritating crying, and a moment after, Jack's voice raised in anger as he argued with someone.

By then Lee and I had caught up with Fi, so we were together when we came upon the five of them. Although they had been annoying me all day, I have to admit, they were a gritty little bunch. They got a lot further than I would have thought. And even when we appeared they didn't chuck it in. Gavin was saying, "In two minutes we're going," then he realised we were there. They all just stood there — or sat, in the case of Natalie and Casey — looking at us suspiciously. None of them rushed over. They seemed to see us as just another complication in a complicated day. They were so wary. Like a mob of sheep who've been roughly handled and now any time they see a human they're off.

I thought Gavin might have been brainwashing them, making them suspicious of our motives.

I talked to them quietly, like they were a mob of sheep. When you're working stock you assume they don't understand English, so the way you say things is more important than what you say. With these kids I tried to do a bit of murmuring, mainly about food. I was more and more convinced that food was the secret. The way to their hearts was through their stomachs. That mightn't make much scientific sense, but I think it was emotionally true.

When I looked at Jack's wolfish little face I felt a strong desire to put some tucker in front of him. So before I knew what I was saying I found myself making a deal with them. "Look, if you guys promise to stay here tonight I'll go down into Hell and bring you back some food. Something we'll cook up, into a hot meal." At the same time I was thinking, "Oh no! What am I saying!"

"We can't stay here," Natalie whined. "Where are we going to sleep?"

They were very obviously city kids.

"It'll be an adventure," Fi said in her most seductive voice.

"And there are no soldiers out here," Lee added.

"We'll look after you. You'll be safe," Fi said.

I didn't think we would have much trouble with the younger ones, but Gavin stood glowering at me like I was about to put his teddy bear through a mincer.

"Look," said Fi, "we'll make a cubby for you to sleep in." She started busily picking up some big sticks. Lee got into the spirit of it and collected a heap of bark. I was sick of indulging the kids just so we could save their lives, but after a minute I joined in. It seemed easier to make two small cubbies than one big one, so I ran a long stick from the fork of one tree to another, then laid some sticks against it. None of the bloody kids helped one little bit.

It took about fifteen minutes to make the framework, then another fifteen to cover it with bark and dried grass. The kids did get quite interested towards the end, when they saw what the finished houses would look like. The girls drew a little nearer, and Jack actually came and stood close by, peering through the door.

Then Fi and I headed back up the spur, leaving Lee to do the babysitting. I was a bit surprised that Fi wanted to come with me on such a tough assignment, and I think Lee was too, but as soon as we were out of their sight she told me her reasons. I don't think I've ever had a bigger shock in my life.

Four

Fi was furious. Before the war Fi wouldn't have known what anger was. She might have got mildly irritated occasionally, like when the cleaning lady forgot to change the pot-pourri in her bedroom, or a leaf fell on the tennis court, but anger was not part of her life.

Well, we'd all changed in this war. I knew Fi had, and I soon found out some of the ways I had.

It was a funny conversation because we had it while we puffed and panted up the spur. The climb was a grind. It would have been hard at any time, but we were terribly tired and hungry; no energy left. But in between the puffing and panting Fi told me a few facts of life.

"Ellie," she began. "There are some things friends are meant to tell you, right?"

I didn't even answer. I knew I was in trouble. There are some things I didn't want to hear, even from a friend.

Fi gave me a quick look, a troubled look, but she'd obviously made up her mind to say what she wanted, and unless I jumped off the side of the spur, I'd have to hear it.

"Ellie, I know you do lots of great things, and even in the last twenty-four hours . . ." She paused to get over a rock, but unfortunately that gave her enough time to re-think, and once she was over the other side she started again.

"No, I'm not going to tell you how wonderful you are. I always do that and it gets me distracted from what I really want to say.

"Ellie, you've been terrible lately. That's the truth, and if I don't tell you no-one else will. Don't you understand what's happening to you? You've changed so much. This war's making you so hard and horrible, there are times I hardly recognise you. You just seem to be losing all your kindness and understanding and niceness. The way you've been talking to these kids, that's a perfect example. You haven't said one nice thing to them. You're acting like they've come all the way here just to annoy you. I know they're not exactly easy, and I know they took all your stuff back in Stratton, but honestly, you can't blame them. They're only kids. The war's not their fault. They didn't start it. They can't help what happened."

She took another deep breath as she clambered over a big fallen gum tree. Although it was flat on the ground it was still growing. It must have had enough roots to keep pumping the water up to the branches. It looked weird though: a horizontal tree.

"And another thing Ellie."

I knew what was coming and I definitely didn't want to hear this. I had my lips pressed hard together and I was gazing into the distance at the blue ridge on the far end of Tailor's Stitch. I wished I could tell her to stop, but I didn't trust myself to speak. You can't keep out the truth, and that's the truth.

The words fell from her lips.

"You're not being fair to Lee."

I still didn't say anything. I was pulling out a grass seed that had wriggled through my sock and was now drilling its way into my leg. I got it out and straightened up and turned to face the mountain.

"He went off with another girl!"

The words burst out of me. Without Lee and me discussing it, we'd somehow come to an understanding that neither of us would tell the others what had happened. It was our secret.

"So what?"

I was astonished that she didn't seem surprised.

"You mean you already knew?"

She shrugged. "We worked it out."

"Who's we?"

"Homer and me."

I took a big gulp: I didn't know the two of them had been having intimate little discussions behind my back.

"Anyway," she went on, before I could say anything, "Lee didn't have any obligation to you. You hadn't been with him for ages. He shouldn't have gone off with one of the enemy, that's true, and I'm sure it didn't take him long to work that out, but he didn't owe you anything. So why are you punishing him?"

"He let us all down," I said. "He betrayed all of us."

"That's exactly what I mean. He made a mistake. A big mistake. He's been kicking himself ever since. He doesn't need you to put the boot in as well. Ellie, there was a time when you would have been the first to understand how something like that could happen, and you'd have gone out of your way to make him feel better. But now you're so hard that you think no-one's allowed a single mistake, and if they make one, you punish them for . . . well, I don't know how long, because you haven't stopped punishing Lee from the moment it happened. And Kevin, just because he's having trouble coping with all this . . ."

"But Kevin drives everyone crazy. You included."

"He drives you a lot crazier than he drives anyone else."

I was red in the face, scarlet, and it wasn't from the exertion of climbing. But Fi went on relentlessly.

"It's not as though you've never made a mistake. Like, leaving that door open in Tozer's, and not . . ."

"All right, all right, I know every mistake I've made since this war started. You don't have to remind me."

I was scared she was going to mention my screaming at the soldier, in Wirrawee, the terrible mistake that might have cost the New Zealand soldiers their lives. Instead she brought out a name I was trying to forget.

"Well, what you did with Adam in New Zealand was just the same as what Lee did with the girl."

"It wasn't the same," I said hotly.

"If you leave out the stuff about her being the enemy, which affects all of us the same way, then what's left is exactly the same as you going off with Adam."

"But . . ."

I couldn't think of anything to say. I wanted to tell her how I'd had too much to drink and how Adam had more or less forced me into it and how I had no spirit or energy to resist him after all the stuff that had happened to us. But I knew it'd sound too lame.

"Anyway," Fi said again, "in a way it doesn't matter what Lee did. The whole point is, how long are you going to hold it against him? We've only got each other, you know that, and if we go on clinging to grudges, inside a week none of us will be talking to anyone else.

"But even that's not the main thing for me Ellie. The main thing is, I want the old Ellie back. The Ellie who always helped people in trouble, who was there for her friends. If the war's killed that Ellie, then there's no hope for any of us."

I still hadn't looked at her. I climbed the last rocks, my face burning, and walked towards where we'd left Homer and Kevin. All I could think of was a conversation with Fi a millennium ago in Hell, where she'd told me I was going fine, and the only reason I had arguments was my strong personality. Something like that. Seemed like she'd changed her mind a bit since then. Or else I'd changed.

I couldn't speak as Fi explained our deal with the kids. Homer and Kevin weren't too excited to hear that someone had to go down into Hell for food.

"Oh for God's sake," Kevin said disgustedly. "Why do we have to go to all that trouble?"

"It's OK," I said. "I'll do it. No-one else has to come."

I sort of took it for granted that someone would volunteer to go with me, but no-one did. I think that was one of my lowest points in the war. I felt terribly unpopular. None of them even wanted to walk with me, to have anything to do with me. I took myself off towards Wombegonoo, feeling that things had never been worse. I'd gone right to the turn-off when I heard the rattle of gravel behind me, and looked around.

"You could have waited," Fi said.

"I didn't think you were coming."

"I went to the toilet and when I came back you'd gone."

I realised she hadn't been behind me when I thought she was, back at our rest-place.

So I was a bit more cheerful, that Fi didn't mind being with me, but I was still so upset at what she'd said that my stomach felt like a wrestling pit for snakes.

We did a quick slide over the other side, in case anyone in the distance happened to be looking our way, and dived down into the big tree that hid the start of the track. At least it was downhill all the way now. I took the lead, letting my legs do the work while my head and my heart tried to deal with the big mess of feelings stirred up by Fi. I was so unhappy and angry about it, but at the same time I had a horrible idea that she wasn't exactly wrong.

"But," I said angrily to myself, "I've been trying so hard; the way I was nice to everyone back at Stratton. I made a big effort to talk to people more; I even put flowers in the house. She hasn't given me credit for that. And I do heaps of work, more than anyone else. I went and got mushrooms and vegetables and fruit all the time. No-one ever notices that stuff. No-one even thanked me for getting them out of Stratton last night. I saved their lives."

On the other hand . . . well, on the other hand, maybe I was a bit critical of others, and a bit tough on the kids. And because I felt that way, inside, it probably was hard for me to conceal it. Like, it might have seeped out in ways I didn't even notice. The tone of my voice, the way

I'd listen to people differently. But I'd always been critical of others. Maybe Fi hadn't noticed it before the war. We'd been really good friends, but in those days there were so many people around. We never knew each other then the way we did now.

I was avoiding some of the things Fi said though. Was I worse these days? Was I hard? Oh yes. Yes. We all were. How couldn't we be? I'd done stuff I could never have contemplated. I felt often, and very strongly, that my life was ruined. Yet other times I surprised myself by laughing, feeling love, admiring a cobweb, skipping stones across water, enjoying the sight of a new lamb on its wobbly legs.

In depressing times all I had was a flimsy belief that the things we did would give other people a better life, somewhere down the track. In other words, we were doing the dirty work for them.

But the more I thought about it, as I clambered over another slippery rock, the more I was forced to admit that the others, Fi and Homer anyway, had kept something that I hadn't. I'd become grimmer, more humourless. They'd kept some sweetness. The other day Homer had spent half-an-hour putting Kevin's hair in braids. My mind flashed back to the word that floated through it a moment earlier. Humour, humourless. That was one thing I'd definitely lost, my sense of humour. I couldn't remember the last time I cracked a joke. A proper joke, I meant. Not a dry clever joke, but a silly funny one that had everyone giggling helplessly.

As for my treatment of Lee . . . well, that was the one thing I still couldn't face. My whole body burned with such a sense of loss and pain when I thought of what he'd done. Fi brushed it off too easily. I felt so betrayed. I felt so angry. I felt I'd lost him.

We got to our familiar old campsite without me having made a decision about anything. And the struggle of thoughts and feelings in my head was suddenly washed away in the flood of emotion as we walked into that little clearing. This had become the centre of my world, the one stable place, the only safe spot left in the Universe. These days, this was home. It felt good to be back.

I gazed around it fondly, lovingly. I wanted it to be just as we'd left it. I didn't want a single leaf to have dropped from a tree.

And it was pretty much like that. About time something in our lives was predictable. Sure there was a fallen branch here, more strips of bark scattered across the ground, a fresh scatter of possum poo just where Fi and I liked to sunbake. But our little stacks of things were still there: Fi's and mine together, the boys' in separate piles. And over near our fireplace, the bigger pile of billies, frypan, plates and mugs and cutlery, and our food supply. For the first time in our mad rush away from Stratton I realised that we had somehow to provide shelter for these kids. Lucky it was summer. We still had Chris's things, and Corrie's, and some of Robyn's, that she'd left behind when she'd packed up. So there were two sleeping bags and four tents, plus some clothes. Would we ever tell the children that these were clothes worn by people who'd died? It wouldn't bother me to wear Robyn's and Corrie's stuff, but to the kids Robyn and Corrie were strangers, and if I were them I wouldn't be too thrilled about wearing the clothes of a dead stranger.

Anyway, there wasn't time to worry about that yet. Food was our first priority. I was surprised at how much was left. Lucky there was though. With ten mouths to feed we'd be putting a lot more work into keeping up the supply.

We chose a nice selection of freeze-dried, and some biscuits, and the last of the chocolate, then checked out the measly medical supply in Kevin's pile of gear: The strongest stuff we had was Panadeine. It wasn't much for a broken arm, but better than Panadol and definitely better than nothing.

Then, already, it was time to turn around and go back up the steep sides of the basin of Hell. We'd had no rest, but the kids would be getting desperate. So would Lee, looking after them. I was reluctant, unwilling. I had no energy, not a skerrick. There was nothing in my tank. It was like opening a forty-four and finding it empty. Yet somehow I had to get up that cliff. I grimly started putting one foot in front of the other.

Once you start a tough climb you should go right to the top. Never stop halfway. It's all psychological of course. If you stop it's so hard to get going again. You just promise yourself a rest when you reach the top.

That's the way I've always done it. Especially during the last year.

Now though, my spirit failed me, and at the first of the big boulders I had to stop. I leaned against the rock, my head down, sobbing for breath. Fi sat on the other side of the track, head between her legs. I guess we were both pretty dead-beat.

Neither of us said anything for a while. Then it was "Are you OK?" from Fi, and a nod from me.

After a bit longer I said, “Let’s go.”

“Wait a bit,” Fi said. I wasn’t sure if she was saying it for my sake or for hers. But I waited. Then she said, “You haven’t said anything . . .”

I knew what she meant. I hadn’t answered all the stuff she’d thrown at me.

It wasn’t that I didn’t want to. I couldn’t. Every time I thought of answering her, acid burned through my stomach and short-circuited my brain, so when I opened my mouth nothing came out, except smoke maybe. I wanted to say something but I didn’t trust myself.

So we got up and kept going, each of us pretty unhappy with the other, I guess.

God it was a grind. I’d cooled down with the stop and now every metre was an awful struggle. The aches went right up the back of my legs. I could feel the muscles pulling and tightening. Pain stabbed through my bad knee. I was half tempted to knock off a few of Casey’s Panadeine. My steps got shorter and my feet stayed closer to the ground, so I tripped over every root and stone. I had to stop four more times before we got to the top.

It wasn’t just the exhaustion of the drive out of Stratton; it was also the effect of being slack in Stratton for quite a long time.

At least after we got to Tailor’s Stitch it was relatively easy. The spur was downhill of course. The hardest part was waking up Homer and Kevin. They had the decency to carry the food for us. We staggered and slid over the steep bits. And there were the kids again, all of them as asleep as Kevin and Homer, with Lee, the only one awake, sitting against a wattle tree gazing glumly at his child-care centre.

Five

At first I was quite impressed with the baby-sitting Lee had done. He seemed to be a good supervisor. Maybe it was all that experience with his little brothers and sisters. But we soon found out that he hadn't done so well.

Things went OK for a while. If there was a danger sign, it was the way Casey and Darina hung around me as we ate. A few times they seemed about to say something but they'd hesitate and look at each other and at Gavin and then shut up. I didn't think much of it, although I remember wrinkling my nose at how Gavin controlled them. It was like he was keeping an eye on them.

Casey's arm seemed a bit better. The splint was doing its job and the Panadeine probably helped. Her face lost a little of its greyness.

At least everyone cheered up with the food. We lit a fire and fed it with dead dry wood so the smoke was virtually clear. It took only twenty minutes to cook the meal. That freeze-dried stuff sure was good. It tasted like regular food. I couldn't imagine how long it was since these kids had a hot meal. They wolfed it. They wanted more, but there wasn't any, and anyway, I was sure a big meal would make them sick after their semi-starvation.

What happened then was all the more amazing when you think what that meal must have meant to them. It goes to show that these brats had huge willpower. Of course they never would have survived in Stratton otherwise.

We decided to wait until late afternoon before moving up to Tailor's Stitch. The idea was that we'd go into Hell after dark, when we could get over the ridge without being seen. Now that they'd had some food we thought we could afford that luxury, of waiting. Anyway, the more rest the kids got, the better. It didn't cross my mind that they had any energy left after the wild and frightening escape from Stratton.

So I went off on my own and sat on a rock looking out at the treetops below. They looked like a nice soft cushion. I wondered if I could jump and land in them: if they'd hold me gently and softly, rocking me in the quiet breeze. I thought about the things Fi said, and wondered if I'd ever get back a sense of humour. Or is it like trust, virginity and Easter eggs: gone once, gone forever?

I wondered what the others were doing.

In fact they weren't doing anything much. Same as me. Lee and Fi went to sleep. Homer and Kevin found a tree with a swarm of bees nesting in it, and chucked rocks at it. From a safe distance. Before the war Homer and I had a bad habit of shooting up wasps' nests, but since the war started I didn't feel any desire to damage or destroy anything outside enemy stuff. I don't know why the poor bees had to be harassed.

Anyway, what it boiled down to was that everyone ignored the kids. I suppose we all thought someone else was looking after them. Or we thought they didn't need looking after. I assumed most of them would be asleep again.

At around five o'clock I wandered back to the clearing. The only one there was Lee, who had just woken up, and was sitting on a rock looking very bleary, like most people do when they've just woken up. A moment later I saw Fi coming through the trees from the southern side. There was no sign of Homer or Kevin or the kids.

"Where is everyone?" I asked.

"I don't know," Lee said. "Gone for a field trip maybe. Studying flora and fauna."

He was more right than he realised.

I still didn't think anything of it until twenty minutes later when Homer and Kevin turned up. I looked at them, feeling quite surprised, and said, "Where are the kids?"

"I don't know," Homer said. "I thought they were here."

We all got alarmed at once.

"When did you last see them?" I asked Lee.

"When I went to sleep. They were here then. They were at the other end of the clearing, sitting on that green patch. They were just talking I think. I didn't really take any notice."

Fi ran over to have a look around, like a detective searching for clues. Homer stepped into the centre of the clearing and gave a few cooees. I didn't like that because it was too much noise. We couldn't assume the bush was safe any more; couldn't assume unfriendly ears weren't listening.

After a few tries he gave up and came back to us.

"Where the hell are they?" he asked irritably.

"They must have gone for a walk," Fi said.

"Gone for a walk!" I said. "How could they be so stupid?"

"Do you think they're lost?" Fi asked.

"I haven't got the foggiest. It just seems so weird. Surely they wouldn't go off on their own again?"

"Perhaps they've been abducted by aliens," Kevin said.

I hardly noticed Kevin, I was so annoyed, and preoccupied, trying to think.

"Well, what are we going to do?" Lee asked.

"We'll have to look for them," I said.

There was a silence as we thought about what that would mean.

"We could wait a bit," Fi said. "See if they turn up."

"We don't even know how long they've been missing," I said.

"What's the time?" Homer asked.

"Half-past five," Kevin said.

"I don't think we can afford to wait," I said. "We've got to find them before dark, or we're really in trouble."

"Little idiots," said Kevin angrily. "When we do find them, I'll have their guts for garters."

No-one else said anything, so I assumed they agreed with me. I was about to suggest we split up and go in different directions, but then wondered if we ought to think a bit first. "Time spent in reconnaissance is seldom wasted."

"Where do you think they might have gone?" I asked them all, but Homer especially.

It was Homer who answered.

"I think they must have gone deliberately again," he said.

"Why would they run away from us?" I asked in frustration. "And where would they go this time?" I pounded the trunk of the nearest tree with my fist. Suddenly I was shouting. "Bloody little idiots! Where are you? Come back!"

I made more noise than Homer's "Cooees." No-one said anything. They just looked at me. They seemed to be studying me, like they were scientists examining an interesting new specimen. I struggled, and got control of myself again. I said to Homer, "After what happened this afternoon I wouldn't think they'd try it again for ten years. They don't know anything about this area."

He didn't answer, just shrugged. Fi, who'd come back empty-handed, said, "I don't understand them going into the bush unless there's someone with them."

I couldn't help thinking Fi was talking more about herself. These kids were gutsy enough to do anything, but they were also really ignorant when it came to the bush. Being gutsy and stupid at the same time is a big worry. Not a good combination.

Anyway, we hadn't come to any conclusions, and time was slipping by. "Well, I know they didn't go that way," I said, pointing to where I'd been.

"They didn't come up the spur," Kevin said.

"And they didn't go up there," Fi said. "I was sunbaking at those rocks."

This was exactly what I wanted to hear, because if I had to pick the most likely route for the kids, it was down a little animal track to the south. I picked it because it was downhill, because there was a defined track, and because it seemed to lead towards a clearer area, with fewer trees. For them, in their tired and confused state, it would have looked more attractive than going uphill or into heavier bush.

I headed off that way with the others following. The light was still good so I did my Aboriginal tracker impersonation, looking everywhere for the slightest sign. The track was very thin, disappearing in places, but mostly well-worn, sometimes even cutting a gutter between little banks of grass.

We got fifteen minutes along it with no sign of the kids, and I was getting worried. If this was the wrong way then we'd wasted a lot of time already. Then the dry hard surface changed. The track crossed a bit of muddy ground, where a spring was leaking slightly. There were hoof marks and trotter marks and paw prints. And a couple of definite heel dents, from small human shoes.

Now we could go for it. I put my head down and stepped up the pace. As long as we were following this track we could be pretty sure we were going the right way. And I was thinking that Homer must be right, they were deliberately running away. How else to explain the fact that they were heading in the opposite direction to Tailor's Stitch?

We were in a patch of thick bush now. Fed by the underground spring probably. The trees stood high and straight, white trunks draped with bark, as though they were undressing from the top down. The bark was incredibly noisy to walk on. I lost the track in thick undergrowth a few times, where it went under low vegetation. Then Homer went around me and on up a rise. I knew what he was doing, hoping to find the track further along and save us time. I kept looking around where I was, as insurance, in case Homer failed, but I was really pleased when after a few minutes he called, "Got it."

We were virtually ignoring the others by now. Lee and

Fi were as much help in the bush as a Barbie doll, and Kevin was bumbling around talking too much instead of using his eyes and ears. I ran up the slope to join Homer and we followed the path again, heads down, like dogs on the scent of a rabbit.

We travelled at a fast walk, sometimes a jog. We went for, I'd guess, half an hour, without any clues. Imperceptibly we passed from the thicker bush into flatter country, still timbered, but much more open. I wasn't surprised to see a small mob of Angus grazing at one end of a large clearing. There was plenty of good feed around here, and another spring, to give them reliable water. Half the clearing was quite muddy and cut up by the hoofs of the stock. It was a big area; a real swamp. These cattle probably belonged to Colin McCann, who still had one of the old leases that let him run cattle on crown land. They were wild now though; like most stock that'd been left alone since the invasion. The nearest ones lifted their heads and watched us uneasily for a moment. Then they mooed their concern to the others and they all trotted off quickly through the trees. We were at least two hundred metres away, so they were being very wary. I pitied the poor person who one day would have to round them up. It'd be a challenge.

The trouble was that the track petered out in this country. It was kind of predictable — the roos and wombats and wallabies who used it didn't need a track any more. They would have spread out and fed on the juicy green grass. I looked at Homer desperately.

"What do we do now?"

"Wait for the others to catch up. We need a breather."

We'd been going quite a while and Homer was red-faced and hot. The others were out of sight but a moment later they appeared through the long grass, Lee leading the way. As we waited I tried to think of where I would have gone if I were the kids. Homer, looking at me, must have guessed my thoughts. He said, "They wouldn't have gone through all that mud."

"True." I brightened up at once, thinking we should turn right and go in the opposite direction. But Lee, arriving in time to hear Homer's comment, said, "Wait a second. If they have done a runner then at some stage they'll try a few cute moves to throw us off the scent. Don't always assume they'll do the obvious."

He was right of course. I was a bit stuck then. I'd never heard of anyone tracking people who didn't want to be found. The police must have had to do it sometimes, but it wasn't a feature of daily life in Wirrawee.

"So what do you think?" I asked Homer again.

He answered slowly. "It's no good racing away on a false trail. We should either split up or else look round for another clue."

With darkness getting closer all the time I didn't like the idea of splitting up any more. It might have been the logical thing to do, but we had to think of ourselves too. So I said, "Let's have a good hunt around this area. See if we can find a sign of them."

Fi and I went off to the southern end of the clearing. Lee and Kevin went in the opposite direction, into the swamp. If tracks were there they should be easy to see. Homer started searching the slope to the east.

As we looked, Fi and I talked.

"What do you think they're doing?" she asked me.

"I haven't the foggiest. I guess they just want to be their own bosses. But honestly, it's infuriating. We can't let them run around here on their own. Especially poor Casey."

Fi switched tack suddenly and said, "I'm sorry about what I said when we were going down into Hell."

"Let's save it for later. I don't want to think about it right now."

That was for sure. It was too heavy altogether. We kept searching, but in silence. I was concentrating my energies on looking for some slight sign of human traffic.

We were out of sight of the others, and getting back into heavier timber, when I found what I was looking for. A perfect small footprint, in a cowpat, and beyond that, bits of manure in a line to the south-east, where it had dropped off the sole of the shoe. So we not only had proof that they had come this way, we even had a line to where they were going.

I left Fi to round up the others, and I went on, as fast as I could.

There was no path, but I could see where I thought they'd be heading. An old black stump stood like a lighthouse in the distance. It was on the crest of the ridge, away from other vegetation, and beyond it was clear sky. I thought it would attract the kids. So I went towards the stump, and the others caught me as I came up to it.

The stump was a deceiver though. Clear sky was a long way away. Instead we were looking at a series of gullies, full of bracken and fallen timber. They seemed to go on forever, like waves at a beach. Beside me Kevin swore.

"Are we meant to follow them through that?"

"Might be time for a team meeting," Homer said. "I don't think we're going to catch them tonight. Do we want to keep going after dark?"

"No," Lee and Kevin said simultaneously. "I'm getting hungry," Kevin added.

Homer looked at me. "What do you reckon?"

I realised his question had really been addressed to me in the first place. It was pretty much irrelevant what the others thought, or wanted to do.

"They'll probably stop when it gets dark," I said. "Which is all the more reason we should keep going. The problem is to make sure we're on the right track."

The others didn't say anything now.

I looked up and down the first gully. There was such a tangle of vegetation that I couldn't see any easy way through it. Yet these kids, tired and unsure, would look for an easy path. I had to second guess them. Halfway across the first gully was a fallen tree, lying parallel to the gully. Maybe that would attract them, as a place where they could pause and get their breath. While the others watched I ploughed my way down into the gully and across to the tree. The bracken was so high in places that I felt I was swimming in a sea of it. The kids would have disappeared completely. They could have been hiding in it, ten metres away. They'd only have to crouch low and wait for us to go away again. Of course now I accepted that they were deliberately running from us. I didn't know why they would, but there was no other way to explain their behaviour.

I got to the log and stood up on it. Almost at my feet was a fresh white scar, where something had knocked off a large splinter, about the size of a comb. It wasn't much to go on but it was something. I scanned the rest of the trunk carefully. Further to my left was a scuffed-up patch that also looked fresh. It could have been made by a foot. I walked down to the end of the tree and checked all around there. Nothing. Still not confident enough to call the others, yet conscious of all the time we were losing, I went to the other end, almost losing my balance in my hurry. I peered down there. And almost smiled, at the same time as I felt a little sick. On the ground under the big base of the trunk was definite proof that humans had been here very recently. A little brown pile that was already bringing in the flies. Yuck. We had our own rules about going to the toilet in the bush: the main one was that everything had to be covered, and preferably buried. In some places that was easy but in others, where the ground was hard or rocky, it was a real nuisance. This kid, whoever it was, hadn't even tried.

"They've been here," I called to the others.

"How can you tell?" Fi called back as they started through the bracken.

"You wouldn't want to know."

They fought their way over to join me.

"Fancy them going to all this trouble," Fi said, panting a little.

"The question is, where did they go from here?" Homer said.

"I think they've probably kept pushing across these gullies," I said. "Once they started they wouldn't want to go back. But the more tired they get, the more they'll drift downhill. They won't even know they're doing it. I'll bet anyone a Mars Bar they drop height fast from here."

No-one argued with that. What it meant in practical terms was that we might be able to make up some time by cutting straight to the bottom of the first gully and traversing on the easier ground.

We bush-bashed our way down pretty quickly and made good speed for about fifteen minutes. But we were losing the light too fast now. Again it crossed my mind that the kids could be hiding from us. The old hollow tree trick again, or the log on the ground. We might have passed them a long way back.

Homer called another halt. It was now so dim that I could see only the trunks of the trees: several times I almost had an eye put out by sharp twigs invisible in the dark.

"What now?" Homer asked me again.

I had an answer ready this time. I'd been thinking about it for the last twenty minutes. "You and Lee go back to Tailor's Stitch and get a couple of packs. Once we've got them we should have enough gear for an overnight camp. Kevin can stay here and start a small fire. Fi and I'll go on a bit and try to pick up more signs. We could even call out their names maybe? If they're tired enough and scared enough and hungry enough they might answer. Casey'll be hurting heaps. Natalie'll be crying."

"I don't think we should call out their names," Fi said. "Our best chance is if they don't know we're following them. Don't forget they've been hiding from the enemy in Stratton for nearly a year. They'll be pretty good at this stuff."

"This is all Gavin's fault," I said angrily. "I'll bet it was his idea."

No-one commented and for once no-one objected to

my plan. It was a fair hike to the other packs but Homer and Lee went off without grumbling. In the dark, over rough ground, they'd be quite a while, especially as the moon hadn't come out yet.

I said to Fi, "Well, are you up for it?"

"I guess. I don't think we'll find anything, but we might as well give it our best shot. Have a go."

"You little Aussie battler you," I said.

I don't think Fi heard me. We picked up some kindling for Kevin, but left within a couple of minutes. I had no clear plan in mind, just a hope that we'd find another trace of them, and a feeling that we shouldn't give up. A night can be a long time in the bush.

We moved slowly and carefully along the run-off from the gullies. There weren't many trees through this section, so my eyes were safer from branches. But the ground was getting rougher and the general direction was downhill. Increasingly what we were walking in resembled a creek bed. "We have to go all the way back up this hill," Fi grumbled. I didn't answer. There was nothing to say, and besides, I was too busy scrutinising the ground, trying to find a clue in the dark.

It was nearly midnight when we got back to the boys. We'd kept searching as far as we could, but as time went past with no sign of the kids, nothing to encourage us, we gradually lost heart. The last half hour was pretty meaningless. We just stumbled along, hoping I suppose that a ray of light would beam down from Heaven and there they'd be.

I was losing my confidence that there was no real danger in the bush. It seemed incredible that in these modern times people could still get badly, seriously, lost. But the kids, undernourished and bruised and a bit off their heads, were the last ones to be wandering around on their own in an environment they didn't know. You had to be seriously worried about them.

The boys were still awake, huddled over Kevin's little fire, waiting patiently for us. I appreciated that they'd stayed up. We were all so dog-tired. We didn't have much of a conversation, because there was nothing worth saying; just curled up under a rough bark shelter Homer had made to keep off the dew.

At dawn we were away again, all five of us this time. We thought there was every chance the kids wouldn't get moving this early. It was a freezing morning and I hugged myself as we hurried along. Being hungry didn't help: we'd learned in this war that if you wanted to leave a campsite early, the only sure way was to skip breakfast. Even the quickest of breakfasts seemed to hold us up at least half an hour.

Skipping breakfast this particular morning wasn't such a problem because we didn't have much food anyway, just the remnants of the stuff Fi and I had brought from Hell: a packet of prunes, and half a packet of survival biscuits that could break your teeth but were meant to be full of nutrition. Fi said prunes were good for the bowels. Maybe that's why no-one had eaten them yesterday.

We tried to walk fast and look for signs of the kids at the same time. We knew clues would be difficult, because Fi and I had followed the same route last night, so any human tracks might be ours. But that didn't stop me scrutinising soft earth, leaf litter, water soaks. I found some squashed kangaroo poo, that might have been trodden on by a human foot, and which was higher up in the scrub than where Fi and I had walked. More importantly, nearby was a piece of bark that had been dragged along for a hundred metres. It was a long way from its home on the trunk of a stringybark tree. You could see the little trail it made in the dust. Maybe, just maybe, some unhappy kid had picked it up and dragged it along behind her for a while.

They were the only clues. The good news, though, was that there were no obvious detours they could have made. The gully, or creek bed, followed a pretty definite path, and to leave it would take a tough climb up the sides. I was sure they wouldn't have enough energy left for that. Still, we'd underestimated them on everything else. I hoped I wasn't underestimating them on this.

By eleven o'clock I was ravenous. We had a break, sitting on the edge of the gully, talking quickly and urgently about our options. We were now seriously worried. At first we'd been half anxious, half furious with them for being so stupid and annoying. But the time for being angry was long past. In their weakened state they were at real risk. With hundreds of square kilometres for them to wander in and no-one but us to search, they were in a lot of danger. "The only good thing about it," I said, "is that when we do find them they should at least be grateful. They mightn't kick up such a fuss about coming with us this time."

"If we find them," was all Fi said.

"Do you have the slightest clue where we are?" Lee asked me.

"I've got a rough idea," I said, a little annoyed that he didn't give me more credit. I'd been carefully noting landmarks the whole time. "If we kept going this way for long enough we'd come out close to Wirrawee. Our property's back there, over the hills and far away."

"And ours is over there," Homer said, pointing. I reckoned he was out by about twenty degrees.

Fi amazed me then by saying, "I think it's more that way," pointing almost exactly to where I thought. For once in my life I had enough smarts to shut up. Instead of saying, "Yes, you're right Fi, Homer doesn't know what he's talking about," I said precisely nothing. Homer looked like he'd been hit by a koala dropping from a great height. I don't think Fi had ever disagreed with him before, especially on bush stuff.

Luckily Kevin suddenly said, "What are we going to do about food?" and that changed the subject.

We made a lot of decisions in a short time. The main one was that we'd continue for an hour, following the gully to see if it opened up, offering different routes. At the end of that time, if it was still going on indefinitely, two of us would return for food. And that meant trekking all the way into Hell, a horrible idea that appealed to no-one.

Ten minutes later however, completely unexpectedly, we did come to the end of the gully. But it didn't open up. The first I realised the trouble we were in was when I saw Homer, ahead of me, drop to his hands and knees and crawl forward.

I came up behind him. Then I realised. He was peering over the edge of a cliff. A trickle of water from the gully, the best it could do in this dry summer, even with the recent rain, was gurgling over the side. Fi and I stared anxiously at each other. If the kids had come upon this, suddenly, in the middle of the night, as they staggered along tired and lost and upset . . . I wondered if I looked as pale and scared as Fi.

"There's no sign of anything on the edge here," Lee said to me, meaning, no scratches or torn moss or disturbed rocks. I was grateful that in spite of what had happened between us he was still trying to be friendly, to do the right thing. But I wasn't reassured about the fate of the kids. I felt cold and clammy when I remembered the cliff into the Holloway Valley: how I'd lost my grip with no warning and slid down, losing my fingertips on the way. And that cliff had been a garden wall compared to this monster. This was sudden and sheer and very very high.

"Come away," Fi said to Homer. "It doesn't look safe."

True, the edge did seem crumbly. As if to prove it, a little shower of soil and rocks disappeared over the side when Homer stepped back.

"Could you see anything?" Lee asked Homer.

"No, nothing."

"So what do we do now?" Fi asked.

"Spread out along the sides," I suggested. "It's going to be a hell of a job to get down there. We shouldn't even try until we're certain they're not up here."

It was the best news I'd had for a long time when Kevin called us to a spot about four hundred metres from the waterfall and showed us where lots of scrapes and muddied grass marked the spot where the kids had climbed over the edge. They'd picked quite a good place. There was a cleft in the cliff, as though God had hacked into it with a giant axe. From where we stood it looked like the cleft ran right to the bottom.

"How long do you think since they went over?" I asked Homer.

"Some time this morning," he said. "I don't think this grass would look so freshly crushed if it was last night."

"Must have been horrible for Casey," I said.

The time had come to split our forces. Homer and I somehow got elected to go down the cliff. The other three convinced us they could find their way back to Tailor's Stitch OK. Despite Lee's question earlier I thought they shouldn't have any real trouble. Our path had been pretty clearly defined all the way down, and I told them a few landmarks to watch for.

It left us with only two people searching, which was hopeless considering how serious things had become. But what else could we do? We needed a lot of new supplies from Hell. We'd be no use to anyone if we lost any more energy or strength. We were low enough already. All morning I'd forced myself along the gully, driven by fear and determination. I hadn't allowed myself to feel the tiredness and despair which were damming up inside. The wall holding those feelings back was Glad Wrap–thin, bulging in all the weak places, threatening to break the barrier and flood through my insides. When it did, it would be like the Great Flood of 1991, when the Herron River burst its banks and half the country between our place and Wirrawee was under water.

I had to stop that tidal wave of exhaustion washing away my defences.

So I gritted my teeth and pressed my lips together and I think I got a terrible scowl on my face, because Fi asked, "Do you want to go back to Tailor's Stitch instead

of me, Ellie?" But I didn't want that, I was just trying to round up any last little bits of determination I could find skittering around inside.

I went first down the funnel, not because I especially wanted to, but because I happened to be closer than Homer when the time came to get started. I went pretty damn gingerly too. I'd lost some confidence on cliffs after my fall in the Holloway Valley.

I used both arms and both legs, like a crab. Above, Homer's heavy bulk overshadowed me in a way that made me even more nervous and I had to ask him, "Don't get so close. Give me some room."

Even so he didn't stay back much; well, he did for a bit, but within a few minutes he was almost on top of me again.

The only good thing was that I could see traces of the kids in plenty of places. Stones dislodged, finger-lines in the dust, scrape marks from shoes.

Halfway down, just as things were getting trickier, Homer dislodged a heap of small rocks and dirt. He gave a warning yell but not fast enough: I couldn't get my hands up in time, so I had a sudden shower of debris.

I yelled back at him. I was really furious. "I told you to stay further back."

"Sorry. Are you OK?"

"Yes." Then, after a minute, and thinking of the conversation with Fi, "Sorry I yelled at you."

I started again, testing each foothold. The cleft was narrowing fast, and glancing down, which I tried not to do too often, I saw that it seemed to run out completely a bit further on. A few more loose rocks from Homer's feet rattled past either side of me but before I could say

anything I dislodged a few myself. At this rate we'd start an avalanche. I had to reluctantly admire the guts of the kids to take on such a dangerous climb. God knows what was waiting at the end of it. I hoped and prayed, as devoutly as I knew how, that we wouldn't find anything horrible down the bottom.

But then I concentrated on my own position again. Just as I feared, the funnel was coming to an end. I'd been fairly successful with my four-limbed tactics, pushing into the sides of the cleft to give enough grip. That wasn't going to work any more.

I paused, looking at my feet, to see where I could put them, when Homer called down, "How's it going?"

"Not very well. The funnel's running out."

"Yeah, I was afraid of that."

I wouldn't have been surprised to see the kids in a little huddle somewhere around this point, helplessly waiting for us to come along and rescue them. The fact that they were nowhere to be seen increased my respect for them further. I'm not sure when I first started to respect them but somewhere along the line I'd begun to appreciate the strength they showed, the guts that brought them this far, the guts that had apparently got them off this cliff. I glanced down again, hoping they hadn't got off the cliff in the worst possible way. But still there was no trace of them.

Meanwhile I came to a complete halt. The funnel ended on a little platform. By putting one foot on top of the other I was able to stand there, safe but not comfortable. I glanced up at Homer. He was perched ten metres above me, not looking at me but looking all around for a path I could take.

Our eyes met. He said, "If you can get about five metres over to your right there's another chimney you can go down."

I swallowed. That was easy for him to say. I felt a funny kind of fluttering under my ribcage, just above my stomach. I licked my dry lips. The strength suddenly left my limbs; both arms and both legs. They felt like useless, stupid, floppy things stuffed with rags and sewn on by a few weak stitches. I didn't look to where Homer was suggesting, until he said, "Hey Ellie, relax. It's not that hard."

"From there maybe."

"Are you still thinking of your last cliff climb?"

"I guess I am a bit."

"Well, believe me, this is radically different. Your feet can do all the work, along that ledge. Just concentrate on keeping them solidly planted."

Then I took a look and thought, "Oh yes, OK, maybe I can do that."

The ledge was between me and the start of the next funnel, but I could only see it by peering around the pillar of rock beside me. All I had to do was step around the pillar and shuffle along.

"Don't look down," Homer said.

I wriggled around the column of rock, looking steadily upwards and feeling with my feet for each step. I took it slowly, tiny step by tiny step, until I thought I must surely be nearly there. I looked across to my right and realised to my intense disappointment I was only halfway. But glancing up again my eye was caught by a remarkable sight. It's funny how a foreign object shows out so strongly when you're in the bush. A bit of plastic, a cigarette butt, a piece of paper: you can see them hundreds of metres away. But only when they're fresh. Once they've been there a week or two they fade into their surroundings.

Just above my eye-level was a tiny fresh fragment of Casey's bandage. I recognised it straightaway. It looked so bright. In a few days it would become weather-worn and dull. For now it stuck out like a dark green little flag.

I didn't tell Homer till I was safe at the start of the next cleft, but then I called out excitedly, "They've been this way. I just found a bit of Casey's bandage."

The discovery gave me the energy and willpower to keep wriggling my way down the new chimney. Towards the bottom it became quite easy, and less than ten minutes later I found myself dropping, with a sense of relief, onto the safe firm ground at the base of the cliffs.

I stood clear and waited for Homer. When he jumped the last two metres to the ground we looked at each other and grinned.

"Thanks," I said.

"You sure love those high places," was all he said.

"We'd better get on with it."

We cast around like bloodhounds. Not that I've ever seen bloodhounds, but I imagine they keep their noses to the ground and sniff enthusiastically. That's what we did. Homer went to the right and I went to the left. This was all flat, dry, lightly timbered country, so it was vital we found a clue, or we'd have no idea where to go. They could have walked off in any direction. I crisscrossed the ground over a large area, eyes down, scanning constantly, looking for the slightest sign.

I found nothing. I felt increasingly sicker, knowing we were wasting ten, twenty, thirty minutes. The kids would be losing strength and condition, losing heart too no doubt. Already they'd been gone nearly twenty-four hours. Well, they'd survive that. They'd probably even survive forty-eight, although I wouldn't like to think of the condition they'd be in. Beyond forty-eight hours, I didn't like their chances of surviving. All I had to go on was my experience with weak lambs and motherless calves. An orphaned lamb would be dead in a day or so. These kids were stronger than newborn lambs, but every time I tried to make myself feel more optimistic by thinking of Gavin's tough determined little face, I'd also think of Natalie's scared eyes and Casey's grey complexion and Jack's tiny thin legs.

Six

When forty-eight hours had come and gone, and we'd spent our third night in the bush, sleeping in nervous fits and starts, waiting for first light so we could get going again, I knew we were facing our last chance. We had to find them today. We simply had to. The whole of the previous day, Homer and I, and the other three when they caught up with us, had scoured the bush. We called the kids' names now. We had no trouble making that decision. We felt sure they would answer if they could hear us. If they were conscious to hear us. If they were alive.

Each time I called, I just hoped an enemy soldier didn't answer.

The trouble was that this kind of bush was so featureless. I love the bush as much as anyone but there was nothing to love about this bland scrubby stuff. It seemed to go on forever, the light green leaves of the gum trees, the light brown soil, the light blue summer sky. The colours were dull, the brightness leached out by the relentless sun. There wasn't even much wildlife to speak of. The most obvious were the ravens, like big black rags floating down onto trees. And often the only sound to be heard was the cawing of the ravens, hoarse and ugly, the voices of death.

Searching was a lonely business. Landmarks were so hard to find that we had trouble fixing meeting points where we could come together every hour to report our lack of results. Later in the day, as we got more desperate, it was every two hours. We got so confused about landmarks that I'm sure we went over the same ground a number of times without knowing. By the time Lee and Fi and Kevin caught up with us there wasn't much left of the first full day of the search, but we spent all that next day scouring miles of bush, for a total result of zilch.

We didn't talk much about it. There wasn't much to say. We knew this was a job we had to see through to its finish. For once there were no choices.

During those hours I thought many times of the stories I'd heard from my father and grandmother, about kids lost in the bush and the huge distances they travelled, the endurance they showed. But most of those kids were from the country in the first place. Dad sang a song sometimes, about a kid who'd gone missing for ages in the New England Ranges in New South Wales. "'Where's my daddy, where's my daddy,' cried the little boy lost." I tried to remember how long Stephen, the boy in the song, had been lost, but I couldn't, even though I must have heard it a hundred times. "Another night, another morning, another day, another dawning." I remembered that bit but I wasn't sure if it meant one night or two had passed. And then there were those three kids from Daylesford in Victoria, who'd disappeared completely in the 1880s or '90s. No-one had seen a trace of them again.

On the whole I preferred the song. At least the Armidale boy had been found. "She prayed to God in Heaven for the little boy lost."

Her prayers had been answered. Would mine be?

The day had passed in slow motion. Round about lunchtime I'd given myself a sharp talking-to, because I realised I'd reached a stage where I didn't really expect to find the kids, so I wasn't looking keenly enough. I was gazing at the ground without seeing anything. So I had to tell myself to keep my mind on the job.

Things were made worse by the fact that I suspected the kids had no access to water. The trickle over the clifftop ran away for a couple of kilometres before disappearing into a soak which had no run-off. We checked the soak carefully, but there were no tracks in the soft ground around it, so we had to assume they'd left that gully. And in all the huge area we'd searched since then, none of us found a single trace of water. In this hot summer weather nothing would kill them faster than thirst and dehydration.

In the morning we skipped breakfast again. There was a sense of such urgency now, such desperation, that we just grabbed a handful of food each and disappeared in our different directions. We'd agreed the night before to concentrate on a big area of stringybarks that had been cleared by loggers maybe six years ago and was now full of difficult new growth and mounds of rotting trunks.

It was only an hour and a half later, the rising sun still enormous and yellow in the sky, that I thought I heard a cooee in the distance. It seemed to be to my right. I turned that way. A moment later I heard another one, much closer. I ran at a jog towards the second one and soon saw Fi coming through the trees.

"Who was it?" I asked.

"Kevin I think. He was on my right."

We hurried in what we hoped was the direction. Our rule was that you could only cooee if you'd found something, or if you were passing on a signal from someone else. Otherwise it'd cause too much confusion. I was on the left flank; there was no-one to my left, so I hadn't had to pass on Fi's call. We walked a little but jogged most of the time. In about five minutes I could hear voices, so I swerved to the left, with Fi following. There were Lee and Kevin, and a moment later I saw Homer hurrying up from the opposite direction.

By then I'd reached Kevin and could see what caused him to call out. It was a boy's shirt. A green check shirt with a torn collar. None of us needed to say anything but Fi said it anyway: "That's Jack's shirt."

"He must be feeling the heat," Lee said.

"Thank goodness we've found it," Fi said. "At least we're on their trail again."

I didn't say anything, just looked at Homer. He looked back at me. His gaze was steady but his mouth turned down as I watched, and his jaw jutted out more strongly than ever. We both knew what it meant when people start shedding their clothes. It means they're near the end, they're losing it, their body temperature's way too high. "Go back to our campsite and get all the water you can," Homer said to Lee. "Fill the containers, and put them in a pack. Then come after us. If we leave this track I'll put a marker out for you."

Without another word, and without waiting to see if Lee was doing what he asked, Homer strode off. The good thing was that the kids could only have gone in one direction. The track Homer mentioned was an old logging road, overgrown with waist-high saplings, but still clear enough. It led away from us in a straight line, and that's the line Homer took.

We trotted along behind, like kids out for a nature walk. When Homer was like this it was a struggle to keep up. He was no runner but he had a long stride and he was determined now, determined to the point of desperation. Like the others I shut my mouth and followed.

Ten minutes later we found another bit of clothing, a yellow shirt that Natalie had worn. Then nothing for nearly half an hour. Suddenly though, Homer stopped. "Look at this," he said to me. I peered from around his back, because he wouldn't let me step on whatever he'd seen. I could see straightaway what he meant though. The ground told a story as clear as a Hollywood movie. There was a big patch of crushed grass, squashed and broken, then a kind of trail for ten metres, the grass still bent over all that way.

"What is it?" Fi asked, trying to peer over my shoulder.

"Someone's sat down here," I said. "Or fallen down.

Then someone else has dragged them along for a bit, and made them keep going."

No-one said anything and we resumed our frantic chase. "Bloody little idiots," I thought. "If only they would stop." They'd save energy. They must know we'd be looking for them.

Occasionally now one of us called out, but there was no response. Most of the time we saved our own energy. I can't speak for the others but I know I had little enough left. These days of dawn-till-night-time searching, more than sixty hours, on the bare minimum of food, wracked by terrible fear about the fate of the kids . . . it drained everything, gave nothing back. And however bad it was for us, at our age, it must have been ten times worse for the kids.

I was getting breathless, tired and sore, and starting to fall behind Homer. I glanced over my shoulder and realised Fi had dropped a long way behind me and Kevin was almost out of sight. It made me all the more determined to keep up with Homer's broad back.

From then on there was no lack of clues to what was happening. You didn't have to be an Aboriginal tracker any more. In the next couple of kilometres we passed a string of shoes and socks, and several more places where the kids had either collapsed or stopped for a rest. Twice we came to forks in the old logging track, but a few minutes were all we needed to work out which way they'd gone. We made big arrows for Lee, then kept going.

My own weariness was bad enough, but underlying it was a sense of despair, that we were going to fail. And to make matters worse, to fail by just a couple of hours, or even minutes perhaps. It was hard to tell exactly when they'd passed this way, but it had certainly been this morning. It was now around noon, entering the hottest part of the day, and if they'd had no water since coming down the cliff none of them would still be alive by sunset.

I marvelled at their endurance. I expected at every turn to find them lying under a tree, hiding from the heat of the day, sheltering in the shade. But no. They just kept going. I remember thinking that there was still hope for us in this war, if other people showed the guts of these five. It seemed a long way from the alley in Stratton where they'd mugged us on that desperate morning. Seemed like years ago now.

Then my thoughts were interrupted by a cry from Fi, behind me. I swung round, feeling a sick surge of horror in my throat. Something in the way she'd called out . . .

She was hurrying into the scrub on the side of the track. I ran back, forgetting my own exhaustion. I saw at once what had caught her eye, and wondered that neither Homer nor I had seen it as we passed. A little body lying inert under a small gum tree. A little girl, wearing only a grubby pair of knickers, her body deathly pale.

Natalie.

Fi was kneeling beside her, holding her hand and trying to talk her back into life. I ran to them and grabbed the other, tiny arm, feeling for a pulse. I'd done a bit of first aid on an Outward Bound course, ages ago. We all had, except Fi, who'd been on a horse-riding camp. But it was only a very little bit, and it was a long time ago. When I couldn't find a pulse, I didn't know if it was my ignorance of first aid or whether there was no pulse to be found. I only knew that the skinny wrist, the size of a half-inch hosepipe, felt cold and clammy.

At that moment Lee, who sometimes has no sense of timing but sometimes gets it exactly right, arrived with the water. He grabbed Jack's shirt, which Fi had been holding ever since we'd found it on the track, poured some water on it and started bathing Natalie's face.

When I saw the tenderness Lee showed then, the way he held her and the desperate gentle way he touched the water to her lips, I felt the old emotions about Lee come back to me, stronger and more intense than ever.

And when Natalie suddenly wriggled in his arms and shook her head and then opened her eyes and mouth simultaneously I felt such a surge of love that I could have fainted. Guess it was just the tiredness and hunger and relief, but for a moment Lee seemed like a miracle worker, someone who could revive the dead.

I had to get a grip on myself then, remind myself that Natalie was only one-fifth of the job at hand, and what's more, this wasn't the place to be thinking about my feelings for Lee.

It seemed best to leave Natalie to Fi, so I said to Lee and Kevin, "Come on, let's get after the others. Bring some water. Bring heaps of water."

I grabbed a water bottle and ran after Homer.

The finding of Natalie gave me another burst of energy. Unfortunately it didn't last long. I was too exhausted for adrenalin to do much for me.

Homer was well out of sight. I chased him for, I'd guess, three kilometres, before I finally saw him pounding along at his steady, effective jog. I had to slow to a walk then. I had nothing left at all and even walking was a huge effort. My legs ached from my hips down to the soles of my feet. Every muscle, every tendon was in pain.

I knew from previous experience that I'd take days to recover. Maybe a couple of hours in a hot bath filled with bubbles might have done it, but I had a funny feeling that I wasn't going to get that.

Anyway, I reminded myself angrily, I had to stop thinking about my problems at a time like this. What did my sore legs matter when these kids were facing death; for all I knew were dead already?

I put in a few little stretches where I tried to walk faster and eventually caught up with Homer.

"We found Natalie," I panted. "Off the side of the track."

"How is she?" he grunted, glancing sideways at me but not slowing down.

"She was coming to life when I left."

We didn't talk again, but spent all our time scanning the bush as we hurried along, anxious not to miss another little body huddled under a tree, someone else who'd staggered off the track and collapsed.

In fact we could not have missed the next one. She was right in the middle of the track. A pathetic pile of rags, hiding a body so small that I thought it really was just a pile of rags. More discarded clothes maybe. But this was a child who hadn't discarded any clothing, except for shoes and socks. I ran to her. I was a little surprised to realise when I turned her over that I was looking at Darina. I'd thought she was stronger than Casey, and I'd half made up my mind that it would be Casey we'd find next. But no, the closed eyes and the slack lips were those of Darina's dark face; the eyebrows her thin lines of black hair; the little rounded nose unmistakably hers.

She lay completely slack and loose in my arms, so light she could have floated away, and I sensed with a sickening pain in my stomach that that was exactly what she had done. Floated away. She felt different to Natalie somehow. I was sure she wasn't breathing. Trying desperately to remember my first aid I put my mouth to hers. I felt her dry cold lips. Then I realised I could cover her nose and mouth with my mouth, so I did that. It was the strangest weirdest feeling, blowing into this empty body. Her chest swelled a little with my breath, but it didn't seem real somehow. I searched for the pulse in her neck, but there was nothing. I knew I had to go to CPR, and there was some special rule about how to give it to kids, something about the way you place your hands, I think just using one hand, so I put the heel of my left hand on her chest.

I pushed down with the bouncy motion we'd been taught. Two or three centimetres was the rule, I thought. I remembered they said not to be afraid of pushing pretty hard. Her pigeon chest felt tiny, and I thought I would break her ribs. The instructor had said something about that too, but I couldn't remember what. Did she say not to break them, or that it didn't matter if you did? I gritted my teeth and kept pressing and bouncing. A sudden thought: I was meant to have her head tilted back. To clear the airway. I stopped the massage and did it, but even as I did I felt another wave of despair. Her body was so limp. It wasn't exactly cold, but it wasn't warm either: just felt like something had left it. And I knew what that something was.

I breathed into her again. I breathed desperately, trying to transfer my oxygen, my life, into her. Then I resumed the CPR. I heard running footsteps and felt rather than saw Lee standing next to me. At some point Homer must have left, but I hadn't noticed.

"Do you want some help?" Lee asked.

"Am I doing it right?"

"I think you should have your hands up a bit higher."

I moved them to where he suggested. He watched for a minute then said, "You're doing fine, but I'd better get the water to the others." I nodded. I knew that was the right thing to do. I heard his footsteps running on again and felt terribly alone and deserted. I hadn't even asked him how Natalie was. Kevin ran past without stopping: he just yelled, "Are you OK?" and when I didn't answer he kept running. There was no sign of Fi.

Darina had felt cold from the start but she seemed colder and colder as the minutes passed. I started to feel angry, more than angry: enraged. I know my anger affected the way I was doing the CPR — I was pressing harder, doing it more jerkily — but I don't think that made any real difference.

I didn't give up until suddenly the coldness of her lips made me feel ill. Like, nauseous. One minute I was still going all right; the next I wanted to throw up. I felt guilty about stopping but in another part of my mind I knew it was no use, I'd known from the start it was no use. I didn't have the slightest clue how long I'd been trying, but I was fairly sure it was a long time, maybe as long as half an hour. I sat back on my haunches, wiping my mouth. It's a terrible thing to say, but I felt like I'd been drinking milk that was off. I didn't cry. Maybe I'd had enough time during the CPR to get used to the idea that she was dead.

After a time I stood up and looked along the track in both directions. There was no sign of anyone. I felt something then, by God I felt something: another of those unbearable floods of loneliness that rushed through me, that had been rushing through me since this war began. It happened in the Hermit's hut down in Hell, it happened in the school in Wirrawee, it happened in the middle of the bush at night when my horse was shot dead from under me. Each time it happened I thought it was the worst ever. I didn't know any more if this was the worst; I only knew it felt absolutely devastating to be alone on the rough old overgrown bush track with the cold body of a child whom I hardly knew. Somewhere Darina probably had parents, maybe a brother or sister, friends, a home, a school, a street she once played in. Now, thanks to a horrible war, she had lost her life among these grey-green trees, in an anonymous patch of bush that looked like any other patch. If you went back along the track, around the corner, you'd see a stretch of scrub that looked exactly the same as this. If you went on ahead, around the next corner, I was willing to bet it'd look the same again. I suppose it didn't matter but right then it seemed tragic and hopeless that Darina had died in such a boring featureless patch of bush, that this was the last view her eyes had seen before they closed forever, instead of somewhere beautiful or unique or memorable.

I cursed all rotten foul and ugly wars.

I didn't want to go after the others. They could be anywhere. I most wanted to go back to Fi, to see how she was getting on with Natalie. Well, I told myself that was the reason. Of course the real reason was I needed the comfort of being with Fi again, the only person I wanted at times like this, despite the telling off she'd given me on the way down to Hell. That seemed like weeks ago. It was actually only a few days ago.

I should say, Fi was the only person nearby who I wanted to be with. It was no good dreaming of my parents or grandmother. Might as well wish for the man in the moon.

In the movies when someone died away from ambulances and doctors, their faces always got covered with a handkerchief. That's what I remembered them doing. I looked at Darina and felt no wish to do that. Her face was calm and pretty. Her mouth was a bit slack. The tension had gone out of her lips. I gazed down at her, trying to get used to the idea that she was dead. Death was the weirdest thing in the world. How could she be living, thinking, dreaming, laughing one minute, and the next minute nothing? A complete stop. I wanted to believe in stuff like reincarnation, but being on a farm makes it hard, because there's so much death. I couldn't quite believe that all those locusts and European wasps and mosquito wrigglers in the tank got reincarnated, and if they didn't, then why should people? What made us so special?

Without thinking about the emotional side of it, how I was leaving Darina there — even more alone than I felt — I started off along the path after the others. I was so lost in my thoughts I didn't do it consciously. I'd gone around three or four bends before I realised I'd left Darina and was on my way forward, instead of going back to Fi. I guess it was the urgency of the search. There were still three missing children and only the three boys looking for them. I had to try to shake off the memory of Darina for the time being and catch up with the other searchers, do all I could for anyone who was still alive.

Wearily, feeling as tired as death myself, I started jogging again.

Luckily for me I didn't have to go far. Even with the motivation of the lost kids I couldn't do much better than a tired stumble. My steps were so short I felt I had elastic tied between both ankles, and it only stretched fifteen centimetres. It wasn't just the physical tiredness either; it was the terrible emotional weariness. Death, death, death, that seemed to be the story of my life these days. Story of all wars I guess. Talk about walking through the valley of death. For a while I forgot the successes we'd achieved, the applause of the people in New Zealand, the bond that Fi and Homer and Kevin and Lee and I shared. The senseless death of one little girl had taken all that away.

A kilometre further on my search came to a sudden end. It was a shock to come upon such a crowd after being on our own for nearly seventy hours. Six people in a tiny clearing, a clearing the size of our front porch at home, seemed quite a crowd. I went through an awful minute trying to work out if any of the three kids were alive. Then I saw Gavin sitting up and struggling to drink from Lee's water bottle. I looked frantically for the other two. Terror sat on my shoulder ready to grab me around the throat at any moment. Casey was lying on her back. Homer wiping her face with a wet handkerchief. I saw Jack curled in a little ball, Kevin holding him. Just as I got to them the water Kevin was forcing between Jack's lips reached something, and the little boy coughed and spluttered and retched some of the water back up. He started groaning like he had stomach-ache. Then I saw Casey's eyes blinking, and suddenly she was breathing with fast shallow breaths.

I sat down next to Homer and Casey. "How's Darina?" Homer asked, glancing up at me. I think he knew as soon as he saw my face, but I said it anyway. I wanted to know how the words would sound, the strange words coming out of my mouth. I tried to say, "She died, she's dead," but my voice wouldn't form those words. I found myself saying, "We lost her," but even that wasn't accurate enough because I felt like I was the one who had lost her; her death somehow belonged especially to me.

There was no time to explore that idea right there and then though. There was too much to do. I patted Casey and held her hand for a minute, then checked the boys again. It seemed like they were doing OK. I said to all of them, "I'm going back to find Fi and Natalie." No-one answered or even looked at me, but that was fair enough. They had enough to think about.

I hurried back along the track. I passed Darina's tired body but hardly had the courage to look at it now. I felt scared of it somehow. I guess it's just the effect death has on you. There are so many superstitions about it. Halloween and headless horsemen and haunted houses and swagmen drowned in billabongs. They can't help but get to you, in one way or another. So I hurried past Darina, feeling guilty as I did, and pushed on down the interminable track, through the endless monotonous bush, looking for Fi and Natalie at every new turn. I was starting to realise how long Fi had been back here, alone with Natalie. What if Natalie had died too? I didn't like to think of poor Fi alone with a dead child. It had been bad enough for me, but I always thought I was stronger than Fi.

Natalie, tough little bugger, looked in better shape than any of them. She was sitting up and talking to Fi, in her baby voice, sounding more like a three year old than a seven year old. I couldn't blame her though. Maybe that's what happens when you go close to death: you go backwards in age. When you reach zero you die. Whatever, we'd got to Natalie just in time.

We'd definitely got to the other kids just in time. I'm no doctor but I think if we'd been another half an hour we'd have lost the lot of them. That's how close it was. I never want to be that close again.

Seven

I had to learn even more patience in the next few days. There had been times before the war when I was patient. If a pump at home needed priming I'd stand there trickling the water in for twenty minutes. And getting rid of possums in the roof: that was a different kind of patience. It could take a week in our big house to work out how they were getting in, and another week to block their hole successfully. They were crafty and persistent and bloody-minded.

Since the war started my patience had come and gone, in fits and starts. But with these kids in such a bad state we had to grit our teeth and have the patience of saints. Just getting them up the mountain and into Hell was a major operation. It took three and a half, nearly four days, and of course during that time we had to supply them with food and water. I made three trips up and down the hill to the top of Tailor's Stitch and three trips down into Hell and up again. My legs just refused to carry me sometimes, I was so tired, but even when they felt like useless lumps of dead meat I had to keep going, and I did.

We all gradually took on different roles, without ever planning it that way. It just happened, as a result of our different personalities. I became the packhorse. Kevin was the cook. Fi was mother. Lee was the security guy, because after all, we were still in a war. No way could we relax our defences.

One of us certainly took on a new role. A role that no-one knowing him before the war could have predicted. A role that didn't seem related to his personality. Homer became father. In fact when he was in a good mood we called him Big Daddy to his face. It was the most amazing transformation. You just never saw him away from the kids. From dawn till dusk he was feeding them, clucking over their cuts and sores and bruises, trying to get them moving around, trying to get them to play a game or laugh at a joke or show a bit of interest in life.

It was hard work, and I'm glad he was the one doing it, not me. I might have shown plenty of patience at times, but I knew I hadn't got enough to cope with that kind of stuff.

I thought the kids' biggest problem would be coming to terms with the death of Darina, but it was really the opposite. They were almost unaffected by that. They must have seen so much death in this war that they didn't register much reaction at all. We buried her under a river red gum, a very beautiful, very big tree that I thought would protect the thin little body we placed there. Fi and I were a mess. We bawled. But the kids didn't cry. They stood around looking awkward and depressed as we said a few prayers, but they didn't join in. Didn't even say "Amen." Even if they'd never been to church in their lives, they must have known that you end a prayer with "Amen." It made me angry, a bit, that they could be so unfeeling about their friend, although I understood why. But I couldn't help thinking that they would be the same about any of us, if we were killed, and that didn't impress me one bit.

Natalie was the one who would have irritated me the most, if I were Homer. Anyway she irritated me. She wanted attention all day long. The moment she wasn't getting it she started whingeing. That thin little voice wailing across whatever clearing we were camped in at the time got on my nerves faster than anything. Worse than fingernails down a galvanised iron roof. If I ever had kids, I vowed, whingeing would be the one totally illegal activity. Any kid who whinged would be sold off to Mr Rodd to be trained as a sheep muleser.

I guess I should admire Natalie's imagination, because she was so good at finding new things to whinge about. "I've lost my gumnuts," she would cry. "There's too much Vegemite on the biscuits." "Jack hit me." "My shoe's hurting." "I've got ants on my legs."

Ants on her legs! It didn't seem to occur to her that maybe she could brush them off.

At least the shoes were fair enough to complain

about. They were a serious problem for all the kids except Gavin. They just weren't made for the kind of punishment they'd been put through during the trek to nowhere. All of them were split or worn away or falling apart. Only Gavin had what my grandmother would call "sensible" shoes.

Gavin was the exception to everything. We never could work out why the kids marched off in the first place, but it seemed to be something to do with a fight between Gavin and Lee. I didn't ask too much about it, because Lee never got around to mentioning it, so I figured he didn't want us to know. I thought the whole thing might be best buried and forgotten. Lee was so independent, and Gavin was fiercely independent too, a tough little guy who had been doing things his own way for a year now, since the war started, and he wasn't going to let a bunch of strangers come along and give him orders. It wasn't a big surprise when Casey told me Gavin had chucked a rock at Lee, back in the clearing when Lee was looking after them. Apparently Lee had told the kids to stop making so much noise.

The other kids trusted Gavin and took their lead from him. If he'd told them to follow him into a whitewater rapid with only their floaties they would have done it, no questions asked.

Even while Natalie was clinging to Homer and Casey was asking him to teach her how to pluck a pebble out of her ear (the only trick Homer knew) and Jack was tying Homer's bootlaces together and thinking he was a hell of a smart operator, Gavin kept away. He was good with a knife and spent most of each day whittling: carving animals and cars and people. I'd go over and pick one up and admire it and he'd put down his knife and gaze into the distance and not say anything, just wait for me to go.

We'd been landed with a funny little group of refugees. Gavin was short for his age, but solid as a four-wheel-drive vehicle. His right eye was always slightly closed, like he was about to wink. He was one of those guys who didn't really have a neck, which made him look all the tougher.

Natalie was a dark-skinned kid, with a pretty dollface. She could have been Maltese or Lebanese. There was a blush of pink in her cheeks, even when she was pale and exhausted. Like all the kids she had lots of evidence of the rough life they'd led, and the lack of adults to look after them. With Natalie, the main thing was ulcers down both her legs. They were pretty horrible, half-a-dozen big open sores, all red and weepy. No wonder her eyes were always red and weepy too.

The first time I'd seen Casey was in the big house where they'd been playing, and for that moment as I'd grabbed her I felt really close to her. She had an intelligent face, a kind of sensitive look, with deep hazel eyes. of all the kids she was the one we were most worried about. Her broken arm seemed to take so much life out of her. We had to work hard to get her to eat. I thought there was a real danger that we might lose her like we lost Darina. She didn't seem to have much will to live.

She had brown hair, but it was hacked around by someone who'd played hairdresser. I couldn't wait to get her down into Hell, so I could fix it up. I had a pair of scissors, but I didn't bring them back on any of my trips; I thought I'd wait till we were down there before I set up my salon.

Jack reminded me of Steve, my ex-boyfriend, when he was a little tacker in Wirrawee Primary. Brown hair, kind of lanky build, typical rural kid I would have said, except that Jack had lived in Stratton all his life. Jack must have been to the same hairdresser as Casey. If his haircut had been done with a proper pair of clippers it would have been a number two. The way it looked it could have been done with a chainsaw. The effect was pretty wild. It wasn't just his haircut though: he had a kind of cheeky face, little nose turned up and a scatter of freckles on each side. One of those boys you imagine out playing cricket, telling everyone else where to stand and sledging the opposition, wanting to bat first, and complaining loudly when the umpire gave him out.

So that was our bunch of passengers; the four kids who'd changed our lives with all the power of a cyclone.

We'd been with them a day and a half after the rescue before we found out Gavin's secret. I can hardly believe we were so unobservant. I can hardly believe I was so unobservant. But on that second afternoon I was sitting against a tree, totally exhausted, having just staggered in from my second trip to Hell in two days. I was digesting lunch, which didn't take long because there wasn't much of it. Nine people went through food so fast, and we'd put ourselves on fairly strict rations. Gavin was sitting against another tree, on the opposite side of the clearing. Behind Gavin, coming out of thick scrub, probably after going to the toilet, was Jack. I'd just caught my first glimpse of him when suddenly he jumped sideways and screamed, "Snake! Snake!"

I leapt up but as I did I noticed something weird: that for a moment Gavin didn't move. Not only didn't move, didn't react at all. He went on calmly whittling with his knife. It wasn't that he was super-brave — although he was a tough little critter — because as soon as I jumped up he looked scared and jumped up too. But there'd been a delay of a full second. Then I was racing across the clearing to Jack, as Fi and Homer, the only other members of our group at the campsite, converged on him. Gavin came around the side of his tree and stared excitedly at the snake, which did the smart thing and slithered away as fast as a fish. It was a copperhead, about a metre and a half long, so it had the potential to be nasty. Jack now decided he was a big hero. Both boys got right into it, screaming and jumping around.

But once the snake made its escape it was Gavin I was interested in. He was doing a pretty good impersonation of the snake to Jack, using his right arm to show how the snake flicked away from us.

I said to Jack, "Gavin's deaf, isn't he?"

"Yeah," Jack said, taking his eyes off Gavin's snake impersonation and staring at me in surprise. "Didn't you know?"

Homer and Fi and I just looked at each other.

"Are you kidding?" Homer asked me.

Gavin seemed to realise now that he was the subject of our interest. He glanced at me. Although Jack had assumed we'd worked it out, I'm pretty sure Gavin knew we hadn't. When I said "You're deaf?" he just shrugged and said, in his unusual, thick voice, "So?"

I was stunned. And suddenly filled with admiration for him. What a gutsy little character he was. To lead this group of kids, this funny mixture of personalities and ages, to make them do what he wanted, when all the time he couldn't hear them — boy, did that show force of personality.

I think that's when I first started paying Gavin the respect due to him. I suppose I could be hard and say he caused Darina's death. But how could you blame him? It was just inexperience, and his natural suspicion of everyone, that he'd learned in Stratton during the last year. There was no doubting his strength of mind. And I've always admired strength.

Anyway, we were all a bit stunned when we realised. "These bloody kids," Homer said in a sort of mock exasperation. He said to Gavin, "How deaf are you?"

Gavin shrugged. "I can hear some stuff," he said.

Jack said, "In Stratton, he could hear things like a big truck going past. He'd look up and say, 'What's that?' And if you yell really really loudly, he can hear you. But I don't think he'd hear anything out here in the bush. There's nothing loud enough."

When we told Kevin he didn't believe us at first. I don't know why he wouldn't; I mean it's not the sort of thing you'd normally get around to making up. But of course being Kevin he had to do something dumb: in this case testing Gavin to see if it was true. So for example the next morning he came up behind Gavin and yelled, "Boo!" which as it happened was so loud that Gavin did hear. He turned around and looked. So then Kevin went through this stage of thinking Gavin was faking it, and he spent the next few days trying to "catch" him again. It was really quite pathetic, and one of those times when I didn't like Kevin much.

At least Gavin seemed to relax a bit when he knew we knew. But a bit was only a bit: it meant that he muttered

"Thanks" a couple of times when I did something special for him, and he actually forgot himself so far as to spread me a biscuit at lunchtime one day. When he realised he looked so shocked that I didn't count on it happening again for a while. I was right about that too.

If he had been in a fight with Lee I think he must have forgotten; in fact if anything he developed a secret admiration for Lee, because I noticed him watching Lee closely on the rare occasions that Lee dropped in. Lee was the complete fighting unit these days, coming into camp only to grab some food and a few hours' sleep. Instead of our normal system of sentries Lee was now it. I don't know how far he roamed to protect us. The danger came from the west: that's where the road was, that's where the farms and houses were, so we were a bit uneasy about the threat from that direction.

The kids were so weak we couldn't do anything with them. They spent most of each day resting.

On the fourth day we had to get them over Tailor's Stitch and down into Hell itself. We'd nursed them up the spur, and it was a big strain too, as they wanted to stop every few metres. Poor little buggers: they had no strength, no stamina, no energy. We talked to them, joked with them, gave them a piggyback occasionally. There was no water up here but we told them about the beautiful clear cold stream waiting for them over the hill. I think we ended up making it sound like some kind of fabled magical river with healing powers. Casey probably thought she could dip her arm in it and it'd be instantly fixed.

Fi's way of motivating them was to make up a story about the water fairies. "Do you know," she said as we sat in a grassy spot halfway to the top, "in the river in Hell there are little rock pools where fairies live? They sit there at dawn combing their beautiful hair and arranging their gossamer wings." Jack sighed, rolled his eyes at Gavin, then lifted a leg and farted loudly. Despite this Fi was keen to go on. She said, "And the prettiest fairy, whose name is Princess Rainbow —." At that point Homer retched loudly over the back of a tree trunk. Fi glared at him, but personally I was grateful to Homer. I don't know how old Fi thought the kids were. For a moment Natalie looked like she might have been impressed by the story, but she picked up pretty quickly that it was uncool, so she turned her back on Fi and started chewing on a piece of grass.

I had a sudden thought that maybe Fi actually believed in her river fairies. I didn't want to pursue that idea: I pushed it out of my mind fast, before it did any damage.

As we made our slow slow way up the spur Lee hung well back, making sure we weren't followed. Then, when we were close to the top, he overtook us to go on up and check the ridge. He sure had become lean and fit. As he passed Gavin, the little guy, to my surprise, yanked at his T-shirt and asked, "Can I come with you?"

I made one of those faces at Homer that says "Can you believe it?" I was pleased when Lee nodded though. It was the first time Gavin had shown any open interest in us or the things we were doing, and I'd have hated for Lee to knock him back.

So off they went and that was a minor relief for me, because it meant one of the kids was more or less at the top, on Tailor's Stitch. Only three to worry about now, although for this kind of stuff they were the three most difficult. We toiled on upwards, me just about ready to jump off the nearest cliff, but using precious energy to cajole and humour and encourage.

With an hour of light left, I finally saw the familiar ridgeline ahead. It had been the slowest trip I'd ever done. I could have knelt on the rock and kissed it, like the Pope when he turns up at an airport. But again we decided to wait, like Iain and Ursula and the Kiwi guerillas, before going over the top. I hadn't always thought it was necessary, then or at other times since, but at dusk, with a largish group, it seemed sensible.

The kids flopped against the rocks and made their usual grumbling noises about how tired and hungry and sore they were. I passed out the last of the water and tried to ignore the grumbling. I could almost wish Gavin was there. At least he wasn't a whinger.

It took the whole hour of daylight for them to get their breath back, even though we'd been progressing at the rate of a snail with a wooden leg. I was hoping to get into Hell without another stop, despite the track being so narrow and slippery and overgrown. It was downhill all the way.

Then Lee reappeared suddenly with Gavin, and bullied us into getting up and moving fast to the top of the track. He was very impatient, and it got everyone's backs up. I didn't know what the big hurry was, but it misfired, because the kids virtually went on strike. In the end, to shut them up, I carried Casey, Homer carried Jack, Kevin carried Natalie and only Gavin walked in on his own. Natalie was asleep by the time we got to the campsite, which says a lot for the gentle way Kevin carried her.

It was a horrible night though. The track was always difficult, and in the dark, when we were tired ourselves, it was too much. As if that wasn't enough it started raining in the last half hour, and it got as greasy as a frypan.

Luckily none of the kids wanted anything to eat. We shoved them into two tents. We had four tents altogether these days, all of them doubles. We'd had three empty places for quite a while. The little kids fitted into their two tents easily and then we drew bits of grass to decide who'd squash in with them. Lee drew the short straw.

I crashed, and I assumed the others did too.

When Lee woke me I figured he must have been even more uncomfortable than I'd expected. Through the opening to the tent, behind his lean shoulders, I could see it was barely dawn. There was just a dark grey in the sky to contrast with the black of the night. It was still raining, a depressing drizzle that looked as though it might go on forever.

"What is it?" I asked sleepily. I was gradually working up to feeling annoyed, but I didn't have enough energy for that yet. The first morning in ages I had a chance to sleep in, and Lee had to wreck it.

"Can you come for a walk?" he said. Then he disappeared. For a moment I lay there wondering if I'd dreamt it, but I could hear him moving around outside. Cursing silently, so I wouldn't wake Fi, I pulled on my boots and crawled out of the tent. When I did I realised he meant what he'd said quite literally. He had a pack on his back and was obviously set for a hike.

I couldn't believe it. I didn't have the energy for this.

But I knew Lee well enough not to waste time asking questions. It took only a minute to get ready. I'd slept in my clothes, as we usually did these days. I grabbed a sweater and trudged off to our toilet site for a leak, doing up my boots as I squatted there.

When I got back Lee did something that chilled me to the bone. He handed me a rifle.

We had a strange little arsenal in Hell. A collection of guns from all over the place, starting with the .22 and the .303 we'd brought from our own homes after our discovery of the invasion, and others we'd picked up along the way. We didn't bother with them much, because they were so heavy to drag around, and we had so little ammunition. Plus, it was a good idea not to have rifles if we were caught. We still clung to the faint hope we could get away with a cover story of being innocent kids who lived in the bush and hardly knew there was a war on.

I took the rifle Lee handed me though. I was getting scared. Lee looked so damn serious. "Hadn't we better tell the others where we're going?" I asked.

"I left a note for Homer," he said.

We didn't talk again until we were coming back up onto Tailor's Stitch. The path from Hell led towards Wombegonoo, a bare rounded peak with good long views in every direction. But before Wombegonoo the track ended in a gum tree with multiple trunks. The tree was concealed from anyone standing above it. From the trunks you walked up a sheet of bare rock, which was good because it meant you left no footprints.

I lay against one of the trunks, wanting to groan with utter weariness. Only pride prevented me from giving up and telling Lee I wasn't interested. It was too hard, too hard. Especially on an empty stomach. I think Lee needed a rest too, because he was leaning against another trunk, looking quite grey. But all too soon he straightened up and looked at me as if to say "Are you ready?"

I nodded. Pride again. We went over the top of Tailor's Stitch taking maximum precautions, rifles ready, keeping low and scanning the ridge in both directions. I still didn't have a clue what we were doing, and that annoyed me more and more, but I was in the mood now to be annoyed by anything.

On the other side we followed the usual policy when we were going along the ridge in daylight, keeping well below the skyline. Again Lee made it clear that we had to be extra-careful, moving with extreme caution. We went about three-quarters of a kilometre I'd guess. Then Lee turned to me and put his fingers to his lips to tell me to be especially quiet. We began tiptoeing downhill, moving with excruciating slowness and looking around at every step. At one point we waited at least ten minutes while Lee stared through the scrub. I stared equally hard in the opposite direction, not sure what I was looking for, but feeling bloody nervous. It was well and truly light by now and still raining, but the type of rain had changed. Instead of a steady drizzle it blew in gusts, sometimes stopping for a few minutes, then starting from a slightly different direction. It was a miserable morning for summer. Warm enough, but miserable. I kept reminding myself that we needed the rain, but it didn't help my attitude.

We went on, but soon stopped again. Peeping over Lee's shoulder I saw a large clearing. Something about the way he crouched and peered into it for so long made it obvious that this was our destination. We waited half an hour. That was pretty typical for us. We usually tried to err on the side of caution. "Time spent in reconnaissance."

At last though, Lee was satisfied. He led me into the clearing, right to the middle. We stood, staring down at our target. I felt like Robinson Crusoe, looking at Man Friday's footstep in the sand. Because at our feet, in a place no-one should have visited for twelve months, in an area inhabited by no-one but us, were the nice fresh remains of a campfire.

I knelt and ran my hand through the ashes. It was like a grey-white porridge. Even in this damp and squally weather a little cloud of white powder blew away when I stirred it up. My hand was whitened by ashes that stuck to my skin. I pulled up my sleeve and burrowed in further. There was still a faint trace of warmth in the heart of the fire. I was satisfied. Not much rain had fallen on this.

"It's still warm in the very centre," I said to Lee.

He nodded. "So what do you think, the last twenty-four hours?"

"No, you can't say that. If they left it to burn itself out, it could have been three or four days ago."

The rule for a fire was that you had to stick your hand in its middle. If you couldn't, the fire wasn't out. So the first thing I knew was that experienced farmers or bushwalkers hadn't lit this fire. They'd never walk away without putting it out properly, especially in summer.

I asked Lee, "Do you know who's been here?"

"Not a clue. I didn't see them. But I found the fireplace last night, just as you were about to go down into Hell. I had Gavin with me and I didn't want to spook him, so I didn't make a fuss. I don't think he even noticed it."

"Was it still smoking?"

"Maybe. Hard to tell. It could have been smoke, or it could have been wind blowing the ashes."

"Let's look around."

We made like detectives, combing the grass, looking for evidence, at the same time listening anxiously for any sign of the people returning. The first thing we found was their actual campsite. They'd had four tents, bigger than ours. You could tell, because the grass was still flattened slightly. And to prove it, I found the holes where they'd hammered in their tent pegs, and even a rock they'd used as a hammer. It had little chips out of it, little white scars.

That was all we found. I was surprised, because I thought they'd have left some food remains, like empty packets and stuff. I wondered if they'd buried them, the way we did, and I started looking for signs of a hole filled in. I couldn't find anything. They mightn't know how to put out a fire but at least they seemed to respect the bush enough to clean up their mess.

Then Lee appeared out of a patch of bush and beckoned. I went down there and he showed me a path leading to a spring, the water supply for this campsite. It was a pretty path, winding around through dainty little green plants like teardrops on the ground, with moss spread among them. Tiny white flowers peeped out from under the leaves.

I thought, "If God created them he must have fantastically skilful fingers." I'm too clumsy to make something that beautiful and delicate.

Five minutes into the trees we came to the spring: a gurgling flow of beautifully clear water seeping from a thick mat of undergrowth. There were a couple of small pools but most of the water ran over rocks, with that irresistible bubbly sound like soft laughter, that must be about my favourite noise in the whole world.

I wandered along its banks, looking for anything that might give a clue to the identity of the phantom campers. They were either friends or enemies — everyone fell into one category or the other these days — and they were nearly certain to be enemies, but it would help a lot if we knew something about them.

By the second pool, a large shallow one surrounded by rocks, I knelt to have a closer look. There was something filmy about the water here, as though a cloud had slipped out of the sky into the pool. Not a full-on cloud: more like a trace of mist. I put my mouth to the water and drank like a dog. In the first gulp I tasted what made the water cloudy. It was a slight soapy flavour. They'd used this pool for washing. The water was so pure, so fresh, that you could see and taste the traces of soap, even though it might have been several days since the campers had been here. I sat up, wiping the soapiness from my mouth. As I did I noticed a trace of colour among the moss, a colour that did not fit in. I felt in there and pulled it out. It was a fragment of paper, still stiff and new. I smelt it. The soapy smell again. This was the wrapping paper from their cake of soap. I looked at it. The writing on it was not English. It was not our alphabet. I had seen the paper before. In the barracks of the Wirrawee airfield, when I was checking it out, that terrible exciting day that we tore the place apart. In the store cupboard of the barracks I'd seen dozens of cakes of this official army-issue soap, all with the same labels. I knew now who our mystery campers were.

Eight

The truth was that we couldn't do much about the enemy visitors. For one thing, we still didn't know a lot about them. They could have been a patrol searching for us. They could have been a patrol having a general look around the mountains, making a routine inspection. They could have been a group of off-duty soldiers taking a stroll to admire the beautiful scenery. All three theories were equally possible. But if there was one thing that made me lean towards the first theory it was my fear of the results of our airfield attack. That attack took us out of the nuisance category and put us into the category of major dangers, who must be caught and eliminated. At all costs. That's the way they'd be thinking. "If they're there, find them. No matter what it takes, kill them."

If they also connected us with the hit on Cobbler's Bay and the breakout from Stratton Prison we were lucky they hadn't nuked half the country in their determination to get us.

Our only real hope, in the long term, was that they'd think we'd gone away. A long way away. Like, to Alaska.

Preferably Northern Alaska.

I didn't want to have to put sentries on Tailor's Stitch

every day and night. The cost to us would have been too great. Hell was where we came to rest and recover. If we needed one of the five on duty all the time there'd be no real rest for anyone.

Our biggest advantage was the geography of Hell itself. It was such a wild place, a casserole of trees and rocks. From above, standing on Tailor's Stitch, you could see only the tops of the trees, and a glimpse of huge boulders. I had lived all my life on the other side of Tailor's Stitch — the position of our farm made us the closest humans to Hell — and I had never heard of anyone finding their way into it. Except for the vague rumours of the Hermit, a hundred or so years before. Certainly no-one I knew had found the route. We'd fluked it.

So the chance of soldiers, men and women unused to the bush, making the same lucky discovery were pretty thin. Nevertheless we weren't going to take the risk lightly. When Lee and I got back to the others we had an emergency meeting. We agreed to double and triple check our security. We covered the first two or three hundred metres of the track from Wombegonoo with bark and dead leaves, to make it look like an old animal path. We put a lot more camouflage over our tents and cooking area, so that planes or helicopters would be even less likely to see our campsite. When we had a cooking fire one of the kids got the job of standing over it with a piece of stiff bark, fanning the smoke away. I knew smoke could be visible for a couple of kilometres, but flames can only be seen from a few hundred metres.

As time passed and we did all the obvious things, and as we (and the kids) started getting bored, we got more creative. Or sillier, depending on how you look at it. Lee wanted to do booby traps, and of course Gavin and Jack thought that was a very cool idea. After all, they were specialists. I must admit though, I was impressed by how clever the ferals were. All those months in Stratton, surviving in a totally hostile environment, had taught them a thing or two. Gavin started digging a huge hole in a dark shadowy part of the track, that he planned to cover with branches and fill with sharp sticks. He was a blood-thirsty little boy. Jack was a bit more practical. Instead of trying to dig one huge hole he dug four little ditches, each one just wide enough for an adult foot. His idea was that someone running along the track, chasing us, would put a foot in the ditch and break an ankle. Cute. He also got Lee to help him string some tight wires on steep downhill sections of the track, at neck height. He and Gavin made lots of grotesque jokes about soldiers breaking their necks, or even getting their heads ripped off by these wires, if they hit them at high enough speed.

The problem for us was to remember where they'd put these things, because when it was dark, or you were tired, you'd stomp along the track forgetting all their little surprises. I seriously did nearly break my ankle in one of Jack's ditches. When I'd finished swearing at him and his stupid booby trap I felt impressed that it worked so well. Jack was secretly delighted I think, although he was smart enough not to show it while I was going off at him.

Needless to say, Gavin never got around to finishing his huge hole.

Fi and I didn't get too involved in the booby trap operation. We had our minds on something else.

I'd been thinking for a while that I wanted to do

something good, something happy and positive for the kids. Maybe for us too. I remembered again the time I stood in my grandmother's kitchen peeling potatoes, trying to work out when it was Christmas. I'd been quite bitter and depressed that the invasion had stolen our birthdays and Christmas. But now it occurred to me that we were kind of conspiring in the process. No-one could steal Christmas without our permission. We were stealing it from ourselves.

When I realised that I went looking for Fi.

And that's how we started to prepare for the strangest Christmas ever. It wasn't just strange because it was a little late. It was more that it was a Christmas of our own invention, because we didn't have too many of the traditional props. No midnight Mass, no angel sitting at the top of the tree, no holly or ivy, no turkey and stuffing, no plum pudding with old-fashioned coins hidden in it, no stockings to hang on the end of the beds. No beds. If Santa was going to visit Hell he'd have to find something else to shove the pressies in.

It was strange in at least one other way too. There we were getting ready for the peaceful time of Chrissie, when a kilometre or so up the track Lee and two of the little boys were happily making booby traps designed to maim or kill.

For all that though, the kids were genuinely excited when we told them it was time for Christmas. They had no idea what month it was — in fact they hardly knew what year it was — so they took it for granted that we were talking 25 December. It didn't matter. Oh, it might have mattered to a priest or someone religious like that, but Father Cronin wasn't around, so we just decided to go for it.

We realised early on that we'd need to raid a house or a farm. Mainly because our food supplies were disappearing fast, with nine mouths to feed. I couldn't believe how fast they were going. Fi and I — I don't know why it was still always the girls who did these jobs — sat down and did the big stocktake the day after we brought the kids into Hell. And then we worked out a rough menu. We thought we'd be right for ten days if we were careful. We were quite proud of ourselves for being so organised. But after six days, almost every container I picked up was empty, or near enough to it. I said to Homer, "Have you guys been pigging out again?"

"Me? No way. Look how thin I am."

"Well someone must be. We're going through the food like there's no tomorrow."

"Don't look at me. I'm innocent, as usual."

"Might be the kids."

"I haven't noticed them eating that much. No more than you'd expect from a bunch of half-starved little piglets."

"What about Kevin and Lee then?"

"Doubt it. Why don't you ask them?"

He had me there. "I don't talk to Lee much these days. Or Kevin for that matter."

"Yeah, I'd noticed."

There was a bit of a silence. I could guess what Homer would think of my poor communications with Kevin and Lee, but I sort of wanted to hear him say it. I don't know why. The only person who gave me advice these days was Fi, and sometimes that wasn't enough. I needed to hear what a guy thought, and the guy I respected most in the world, outside my father, was Homer. I wanted to know if he agreed with what Fi said to me on our way down into Hell that time.

After a while Homer said, "I thought you two might have sorted things out on Tailor's Stitch when you were looking at that campfire."

"I guess we should have. We were too busy trying to work out who'd been hanging around up there. Looking for clues. Anyway," I laughed, "it was too cold and wet."

Homer ignored my laugh. He was reading a book that we'd had down in Hell for ages, *Red Shift*. I think Chris originally brought it in. Homer only read a book when he was desperate, but we'd banned any activities that might make noise. Most of the stuff Homer liked doing involved noise. So some days now, when he wasn't operating his child-care centre, he was reduced to reading to pass the time.

Now he sat playing with the corners of the pages, riffling through them like he was shuffling cards.

"You're not a happy camper at the moment, are you Ellie?"

"Well, I don't see any of us actually laughing for joy with every passing day."

"You know what I mean."

I tried to think, not of what to say, but of how to say it in a way that wouldn't frighten Homer off. I had to translate it into his words. What I mean is, you can't say stuff to Homer like "I'm in love with Lee but I don't think I can trust him any more." The way you talk to Homer is a lot different to the way you talk to Fi.

Eventually I said, "I still can't believe the way Lee went off with that chick in Stratton."

"Well, he's a guy. That's the way we are. Learn to live with it."

I didn't bother to jump at that bait. And Homer didn't expect me to. He was just going through the motions. Old habits die hard, and he wasn't going to give up stirring girls when the chance came along. But his mind was already ahead of itself. Without waiting for me to reply he said, "The thing is, how many mistakes do you let a bloke make?"

"Only one, if it's big enough."

That stopped him for a while. He actually started making little rips in the side of one of the pages, which shocked me. I never like to damage books. I got in trouble for scribbling on my grandmother's encyclopaedia when I was three, and I guess I learned my lesson.

But after a few minutes he came back at me again. Very stubborn guy, Homer, kind of dogged.

"So do you hold this against him for the next fifty years?"

I tried to explain.

"If it was just a bad call, Lee losing his brains and his balls for a couple of weeks, I can get over that. But what if it shows that he's got some huge character flaw, like so serious that he can never be trusted? That's what sticks in my throat. I'm scared there's a side to him that I didn't know about before."

"Do you think there is?"

"No."

I felt a great sense of relief when I said that. It was something I'd never been able to confront, never been sure about.

"You could at least talk to him about it," Homer grumbled.

He sounded so like his father, trying to persuade my dad to go see the local member, and make him do something about the bad roads or the wool stockpile or petrol prices. I almost laughed again.

But I was grateful to Homer. I found myself getting quite sentimental about him. Once again he'd proved himself a true friend. I just couldn't get a handle on how to solve my problem with Lee.

In the meantime I sat down with Fi to plan Christmas Day in more detail. It wasn't easy, because of the mess our food supplies had got into. Our first decision was that we had to raid a farm for new stocks of food. We could leave the details until a group meeting, but I figured we needed to get going within forty-eight hours. If the raid failed we could forget about Christmas.

How I longed for a trip to the supermarket. I tortured myself with memories of aisle after aisle crowded with canned peaches and All Bran and Snack chocolate and Jatz biscuits, and the refrigerated section, with the ham and salami and King Island Brie, and then there was the freezer: Sara Lee Chocolate Bavarian and Paul's Ice-cream and chicken nuggets. When I was tired of those sections I'd start on the deli and the meat and fish and the bread and the fruit and veg. The supermarkets of my mind gave me more pleasure than the real ones ever had before the war.

But I had to push daydreams away. It was time to put our tired imaginations to work.

"Let's do the brainstorm," I said to Fi.

"Butcher's paper," she said automatically. "Textas."

"That's my joke. Come on, get serious. Let's start with the essentials. Santa Claus?"

"Absolutely. For Natalie's sake," Fi said firmly, then added, "And for mine."

"But what's he going to bring? I mean, it's not going to be mountain bikes and roller blades and a box of Milk Trays."

"No. I suppose when we raid a farm for food we could try to get something . . ."

"Oh sure. We're really going to pass up an armful of pasta for a Barbie camper van to give Natalie."

Fi laughed for about five minutes. It gave me quite a shock. That kind of laughter was rare these days. I was glad I could still make her laugh, considering how angry she'd been at me. She said, "I can just see Homer with bullets whistling around his ears, stopping to pick up one of Barbie's sandals."

"Well, if Santa's going to bring pressies we'll have to get busy. What can we get for Gavin?"

"Nothing would please Gavin."

It took two and a half hours but we finally nutted out a list. Not just presents, but everything: decorations and food and drink and games. We had to give up on a few things, like wrapping paper and plum pudding, but I thought we'd done OK. I was exhausted though, and we hadn't even done any of the work. I began to realise why parents weren't always quite as excited about Christmas as we were.

The other problem we had while we talked was keeping it secret from the kids. Casey in particular was a sharp little operator. She knew we were talking about Christmas and she always wanted to know everything that was going on. We kept sending her off on fake errands but she tried to sneak up on us, dodging in and out of trees, so she could eavesdrop. That year in Stratton had taught the ferals tricks that would stay with them a long time. Luckily our year in the bush had taught us a few tricks too, so I think we stopped Casey hearing too much.

I made her sit on a tree stump while I checked her arm again. It was hard to know what to do about it. As far as I could tell it was healing fairly well but I didn't like to mess with it too much. I was a lot more nervous dealing with injured people than injured farm animals. I took the strapping off again. I'd been doing that daily, and washing it in the creek with my own laundry. The arm looked pale and a bit thinner than the other one, but you'd expect that. It wasn't totally straight, but I didn't know if that meant anything. The lump had definitely gone down.

"How is it?" I asked her.

"I don't know. I guess it's getting better. It doesn't hurt as much."

"Well, as long as you don't knock it again."

The day before, she hit it when she was chasing Natalie through the trees, and the screams of pain brought us all running. It wasn't just scary because I thought she might have damaged her arm; it was scary because the noise she'd made was so dangerous. If there was an enemy patrol lurking on Tailor's Stitch, they would have heard her for sure.

It did seem like she had a way to go before the arm was OK.

By the next day the food supplies were looking very

bare. The boys had been avoiding the whole subject, because we were so dog-tired, and the thought of trudging up to Tailor's Stitch again, and down the other side, into yet another horribly dangerous situation, wasn't attracting any of us. But I told myself that there's no point postponing pain. If you've got to suffer, you might as well get it over and done with. I wasn't totally convinced about this, but I blocked off any dubious thoughts and waited till the five of us were together, after tea.

We were washing our plates by the creek. The kids were up at the fireplace. We didn't have enough plates to go around, so for messy meals, which you couldn't eat with your fingers, we had two shifts, the kids first, then us. But as I scrubbed hard at a bit of burned noodle I said very firmly, "We've got to go out tonight to get food. It's no good putting it off any longer. We're going through it like possums in peach trees."

I bullied them into agreeing. The only trouble with that was that I seemed to be the one automatic member of the group chosen to go. After a bit more talk we agreed we'd need two others. Homer and Fi were the lucky candidates. No-one said out loud why it had to be them, but I knew why. It was because we couldn't leave Fi and Kevin back in Hell on their own. If something went wrong, which was horribly possible with enemy soldiers prowling around on Tailor's Stitch, we couldn't be sure Fi and Kevin would cope. Fi was strong enough in her own way, but like the rest of us she had her limits, and dealing with a situation like that, with only Kevin to help, would be outside her limits.

Somehow we found ourselves standing on top of Tailor's Stitch without me noticing that I'd got there. It happened quite quickly once we made the decision. And it was a lot easier having empty packs and no rifles. I floated up the steep sides of Hell wishing life could always be this easy. The pack on my back was so light; only the load in my mind was heavy, and I was getting used to that. So much unfinished business was in there. The kids of course. Casey's broken arm, Natalie's incessant crying, Jack's long silences. And Gavin's deafness. That was a new one for me. I didn't know anyone who was deaf, except Mr Jay, and he was about a hundred and ten.

Then there was my fight with Lee, the things Fi and Homer had said to me, the presence of strangers on Tailor's Stitch, the shortage of food . . . the list seemed like it would never end.

But somehow, standing in the clear night air, under a sky that glowed like a shower of sparks, none of that stuff mattered. It slipped off me. It was like shedding your clothes before you step in the shower. I felt I was down to essentials again. In fact I felt very close to God at that moment. I guess if you're ever going to feel close to God it'll be while you're looking at the heavens. I wondered sometimes how it must have looked in the old days, before pollution started drifting into the sky. Even up here, in this pure air, there was a heap of invisible pollution. We were looking at the stars through a dirty, murky screen. A thousand years ago the stars at night must have burned almost as fiercely as the sun by day. No wonder all those old civilisations were so into stars when they told their stories and thought about their gods. It'd have been hard to ignore a sky that glowed with a billion fires.

There wasn't really time for thinking about that

though. We spent ten minutes standing in silence, like we were at Anzac Day or something, watching and listening. It was partly the effect of the burning sky but to be more practical, it was a safety measure too. If there were people on Tailor's Stitch we wanted to know about them before they knew about us. But it was quiet enough. And the right kind of quiet. Not the dead silence where the air is beating with tension. And, on the other hand, not the anxious noises you get in the bush when something's wrong: the clatter of frogmouth wings, the scrabble of possum paws up a tree trunk, the wild flight of a sleeping bird suddenly disturbed. None of that.

So it seemed OK, and when Homer glanced at me and raised his eyebrows I nodded "Yes."

We moved softly and silently. Homer first, Fi second, me third. We didn't so much walk, more prowl. Soft feet. Mr Addams, the PE teacher at Wirrawee High, talked about soft hands when he was teaching us cricket. "The best players have soft hands when they're batting." I didn't know quite what he meant but I remembered the expression, because it sounded funny. But walking along Tailor's Stitch I concentrated on having soft feet.

We'd gone about two kilometres — in fact we were about to turn off the ridge to go down towards my place — when I first heard a noise that didn't belong. I didn't even know what it was. But there's no mistaking a noise in the bush that doesn't belong. I think it was probably a scrape of a boot on rock. Whatever, I knew straightaway that we had a problem. Fi was a fraction too far ahead to call her but I don't know if I would have risked it anyway. Instead I picked up a pebble and chucked it at her. Typical Fi, she didn't notice. Just kept gliding quietly over the rocks. It was a terrible moment. I thought if I made any noise I might cop a bullet in the back, but of course I couldn't let her and Homer keep walking if there was danger. So I ran forward. The trouble was that the buckles on my empty pack rattled and jingled as I accelerated. I hadn't bothered to do them all up. I cursed myself for not thinking of it earlier. But even that noise didn't catch Fi's attention. It wasn't until I tapped her on the shoulder that she turned around. She got a huge shock too, when I did tap her; she jumped as though a drop bear had gone down the back of her shirt. I wished she'd been paying more attention, but that's the trouble when you're travelling in the middle of a group: you think you can relax.

At least Homer was quick to react. He heard the noise Fi made when she jumped around, and he jumped around too, then came back to us very quickly. And quietly for a big guy. Neither of them said anything; just looked at me. When I nodded behind me they melted into a band of trees so fast that I was quite impressed. It struck me, almost for the first time, that we had learned a few things, that we'd actually become rather good at this. We'd become genuine bush fighters, even Fi.

Before the war she wouldn't have done anything more dangerous than stay at a party till midnight.

But there wasn't time for congratulations. I melted into the trees as fast as the others, and stood behind a medium-size trunk gazing out at the track. I felt the heat of Homer's body, then the heat of his breath as he whispered in my ear.

"What was it?"

"I heard something."

"What?"

"Don't know. A boot maybe."

Homer edged away. I stood and waited. A cool breeze played up my legs and onto the back of my neck. A few minutes earlier I'd been thinking the breeze was sweet and pleasant. Now it seemed cold and unfriendly. But I didn't think about that for any longer than I thought about how we'd become such great bush fighters. Instead I strained my ears so hard I could almost feel them growing longer and longer, out of each side of my head. I was like the guy in the Shakespeare play, the bloke who turned into a donkey. But try as I might I couldn't hear a thing.

After fifteen minutes Homer loomed up beside me again in the shadows. He looked at me with a big question mark written all over his face. I knew what the question was. "Are you sure you heard something?" He didn't have to say the words.

Of course by then I wasn't sure. At first I'd been confident that someone was behind us. The longer I stood anxiously behind my tree the more I started to doubt myself. The problem was there are just so many noises in the bush at night. It always seems like there's more noise at night than in the daytime. I don't think there really is; it's because at nighttime you hear them so strongly. They stand out. I knew I'd heard something. I just didn't know what it was.

We were under pressure of time too. If we were to get to a farmhouse a fair way away — and it had to be a good way off so no-one would connect us with Hell — we had to get a move on. By dawn we needed to be back in the mountains, back in the safest place we knew.

So after another five minutes I shrugged at Homer and Fi and moved out onto the edge of the track. We stood listening for a couple more minutes then took up the same positions as before, me in the rear. And off we went.

The road, rutted and rough as it was, did a few funny things on its way down to the paddocks. Dad and I had put in detours where there were washaways, and in a couple of other places where wheel ruts were so deep that even a four-wheel drive would get lost in them. One of these detours was a faint track over soft grass, on a flat piece of land. Homer chose that track rather than taking us through the deep ruts. We were on the grass when I heard another noise that I knew simply didn't belong.

I stopped hard. This time Fi was paying close attention, and she stopped too, within two or three steps. And Homer, watching through eyes at the back of his head, stopped straightaway. We all moved quietly off the path, to the left. I tiptoed up to where Fi was waiting for me, arriving at the same time as Homer.

"Well?" he breathed.

"Same again."

"What is it exactly?" Fi whispered.

"First time was a boot I think. On a rock maybe. This time was a stick breaking."

"Where?"

"Back on the main part. Where we went off on the detour."

No-one said anything for a few minutes, as we waited and listened anxiously.

Finally Homer murmured to me, "We've got to take the initiative."

"I was just thinking that."

The last thing I wanted was to stand around waiting to be caught. Without any more discussion Homer and I moved off in different directions. I went to the right, Homer to the left. Fi, sort of knowing this wasn't her scene, stayed put.

I went so carefully. I lifted one foot, let it hover like a helicopter while I looked for a good place, then planted it firmly but gently. Then the next one. At the same time I peered through the darkness, looking for the slightest sign of a patrol. In a way — incredibly stupid though this is — I half-hoped some soldiers would be there. I'd be left looking like a complete idiot if they weren't. And I'd have held up our trip for a dangerously long time.

Of course I didn't really want them to be there. I just hated to think of the act Homer would put on if he found a wombat caused the noises.

When I was within twenty metres of the place I'd heard the stick breaking I stopped again and stood, sniffing the wind like a dingo. And knew at last that I wasn't mistaken. Someone was there. I smelt him, I felt the vibrations of the air as he moved slightly, I sensed him. That was as much as I needed to know really. I got ready to withdraw. Now that I was sure, everything became easier. We would have to abort the food trip, take to the bush, circle back to Tailor's Stitch, and at the same time try to check out who was shadowing us in the darkness.

I took three steps backwards but as I did I saw a glimmer of movement. It seemed like the person on the track had gone to the left, a little further downhill. I felt a flare of fear in my stomach. I was fairly sure he was moving as a reaction to my movement. I hadn't been as careful and quiet as I thought. Suddenly this whole situation, dangerous enough before, was out of control. And a moment later I realised something worse: in moving to my left the soldier was likely to run into Homer.

We had no weapons on us, but I was desperate enough to look for one. I crouched down and ran my fingers across the ground. There were plenty of stones, but at the furthest reach of my hand I felt my fingers close on a rock the size of an orange. I would have liked one even bigger, but this would have to do. I grabbed it and started creeping forward. I had to be quicker than before, so I paid a bit of a price as far as silence went.

Suddenly everything happened at once. It was like a game of chess became a game of football. A patch of black in the darkness ahead moved quickly, even further to the left. At the same time I saw Homer's bulk loom up on the track. He was coming up the hill towards the guy. Homer yelled out, a kind of grunt of surprise, when he realised they were about to run into each other. I yelled, to distract the man, and chucked the rock as hard as I could, straight at the dark shape. A rock versus a rifle didn't seem like a good deal, but it was all I had. I missed, but only by the width of my little finger. And I was already following up, charging straight at the guy, bellowing like a thirsty heifer. Anything to distract him and give Homer a chance.

As it happened Homer and I sandwiched him. Or we would have done. We arrived either side of him, simultaneously. He's lucky we didn't sandwich him. We would have broken every bone in his body. He deserved it too. Bloody Gavin. A steak tartare sandwich, that's what he deserved to be. And the worst thing was, he thought it was funny. He laughed when we grabbed him. A nervous laugh, sure, but a laugh, no doubt about it. He was a tough cookie, but sometimes I wondered how much the war had stuffed up his common sense and judgement. That particular night I wondered in a big way.

"What are you doing, you moron?" Homer said, shaking him like he was a clogged up tomato sauce bottle. Homer was even angrier than me. I was angry, but probably more relieved than anything. It could have been someone much worse than Gavin.

I don't know how much Gavin could lip-read in the dark, but you wouldn't have to be Einstein to work out what questions we were asking. He grinned at Homer and said, "I followed you."

We didn't have to be Einsteins to have worked that out already. "Why?" I asked, but Gavin was looking at Homer and didn't see me, so Homer repeated it.

Gavin shrugged. "I'm not a baby. Whatever you do, I can do. I wanted to come." I realised he was actually very nervous. Close up you could see his body trembling. And behind the grins he did look anxious.

Homer looked helplessly at me. "What do you reckon? What do we do with him?"

I'd already made my decision. "We have to take him along. Otherwise he'll just follow us again. The only choice is for us all to go back to Hell."

"No way," Homer said, to that last suggestion. He rubbed his chin with his hand. "Have we still got time to do it tonight?"

"Well, I guess. Depends how far we go. I was thinking of the Whittakers' place. We've got time to get there, but we wouldn't get back to Hell by dawn."

"I guess that's not such a big problem. We can hang out around here somewhere."

So the decision was made. We set out again, going as fast as we dared. Gavin, give him his due, kept up without a complaint. He was second last, between Fi and me, so I got a good view of him, and he seemed able to go the pace. We went past the outlying buildings of our property — just the old machinery shed and the barn — but we were too far away to see the house. Perhaps that was for the best. I could get by most days without the grief that had paralysed me so many times since the war began, but I never knew when it would strike next, and seeing the house in the middle of the night, with strangers living in it . . . it was better not to go too close.

By road the Whittakers' place would be fifteen k's from ours, but that didn't mean much. We cut straight across the paddocks. Homer and I both knew the way, and once we got out there, away from other buildings, we relaxed, mentally at least. In this open country, at two in the morning, we knew there'd be no-one else within cooee. For kilometre after kilometre our only company was four-legged or two-winged — or two-legged in the case of the kangaroos. The light was better too, with no more trees in the way of the stars and moon. We walked so fast — we had to, thanks to the time we'd lost — that we could hardly get enough breath to talk. I don't know about the others but I was red in the face and puffing.

We kept the pace up pretty well. Of course we slowed down after a while, but we didn't stop. Twice Homer tried to persuade Gavin to sign off: to hole up somewhere and wait for us. Both times he turned us down flat. Maybe he thought we wouldn't come back for him. Homer didn't press it. There wasn't time for that either.

The Whittakers' place was a big sprawling house surrounded by a famous garden. We were sure it would be occupied: it was such a beautiful house that it would have been one of the first to be taken over.

I thought the garden would give us plenty of cover. It had all these big bushes and garden beds and stuff. I wasn't sure exactly how we'd break in. Back in Hell we'd talked about it quite casually, as if that would be the easiest part of the job, but now that we were closer it suddenly looked a bit more difficult.

At 3:05 we came over a ridge and saw the Whittakers' house, the galvanised iron roof shining in the moonlight. It sure was big. It was a single-storey place, but it covered about a hectare. Well, that's what it looked like. At least there were trees going almost to the house, so that suited us.

We dropped flat on the ridge and wriggled forward to have a look. Gavin was right beside me and for a few minutes all I could hear was his panting. Seemed like the effort to keep up cost him more than I'd realised. One thing I'd noticed about him though, he was very good at keeping quiet when necessary. It must have been hard for him, because he couldn't hear whether he was making a noise or not, but somewhere along the line, maybe in Stratton, maybe before the war, he'd learned. Lucky he did. It would have been a matter of life and death for him and his mates, and now it was a matter of life and death for us.

Homer's big body came around behind me and he dropped down on my left.

"What do you reckon?"

This was the same question I'd been asked a thousand times since the war started. "What do we do now?"

Not for the first time, I didn't have an answer. I said rather doubtfully, "It's not going to be easy. But we have to work out where the kitchen is."

"Don't you know?"

"Nuh. Why should I?"

"I thought you knew the place."

"Why'd you think that? I've never been here before in my life. I've just heard my parents talk about it."

He sighed, as if to say, "Well, you're a great bloody help," and moved away again. I could hear the rumble of his voice as he complained about me to Fi.

I wriggled over to them. "Come on," I said, "let's check out the other side. That's where the kitchen should be. I've just heard my parents talk about it."

We set off on a wide circle around the house. It was soon obvious enough which room was the kitchen. The Whittakers had extended their house quite a long way out the back, on the right-hand side, using the same colour bricks, so you couldn't easily tell it was an extension. But in the moonlight you could see that the reflection on the new bricks was shinier. Plus there were bigger windows. Through the three middle windows I could see kitchen-type stuff, especially the gleam of a stainless steel sink.

I stole a little closer, first on my stomach, then bent low and running. The house was silent, so I took my life in my hands and went all the way to the windowsill. After all, how much danger should we expect at 3:30 in the morning? I stood on a pot-plant and peered over the sill. It was the kitchen all right. I saw two large refrigerators, like solid white ghosts, and I drooled a little at the thought of what they might contain. A hand grabbed my shoulder and I jumped, with a shocked squeal. "Shhh," Homer said. "What can you see?"

"It's the kitchen. I can see the fridges. And a big fruit bowl."

Homer tried lifting the window, but either it was locked, or too stiff to move without a lot of noise. I went to the right and tried that one, with the same result. Time was going fast, and we had to get in this house. I took off my jumper, held it firmly against the window, and punched hard and cleanly with my fist, a bit like I'd done at Tozer's. The glass broke easily this time but it fell inside the room with a tinkling sound that seemed to go on forever.

"Jesus Christ," Homer gasped.

We both moved away fast, until we got to where Fi and Gavin were watching, from behind a silver birch. There'd been no movement inside the house but we figured we'd better wait a few minutes before we went back to the window.

For me there was something chilling about that wait. I kept imagining I heard footsteps behind me. Perhaps it was the memory of Homer's hand grabbing my shoulder. Or the memory of Gavin stalking us on the way from Tailor's Stitch. I looked around so many times that I made the others nervous too, until Fi said, "Ellie, are you expecting visitors?"

After ten minutes Homer and I went back in. By now it

was so late that I accepted we had zero chance of getting to Hell before daybreak. I'd been clinging to the hope that we might still manage it. I knew now that we'd have to find somewhere safe during the day. That irritated and frustrated me. I was sick of hiding, sick of the boredom of those long hours spent in holes or dark rooms. The thought of doing it yet again distracted me. In fact I was concentrating more on that than on the job ahead.

We got to the window and I waited while Homer pulled out the jagged bits of broken glass left in the frame. Everything seemed quiet, so I called Fi in, with a quick wave. To my annoyance Gavin came too. I didn't realise until I heard a little muffled cough. I looked around and there he was, a few metres ahead of Fi, like an enthusiastic dog who hates to have you in front of him. I couldn't believe it and I waved furiously at him to go back. What a waste of energy. Gavin pretended not to see me and Fi rolled her eyes and whispered, "He's impossible."

Obviously having a fight with Gavin right here, outside the kitchen window, was not a good idea. We were stuck with him. It wasn't part of our plans, but on the other hand if he could carry out some food — well, every bit helped.

The bottom of the window was at the height of my chin and the pot-plant was too small. Homer had to give me a leg-up. I perched on the windowsill for a moment like a trained monkey and checked out the dark room. There was no noise except the shudder of a fridge. A couple of red lights gleamed at me. They could have been the eyes of a deadly reptile. They were probably batteries charging overnight — on a torch or telephone maybe. I ignored them and dropped as lightly as I could to the floor. Fi followed, really lightly, then Gavin, lighter again, and finally Homer, as heavy as a hippopotamus. Something in the fridge rattled when he hit the floor.

I went to the door on my left, and squeezed it open. The long corrider was dark and silent. I stood there for three or four minutes, while behind me the others waited. But the house slumbered on. I closed the door again.

So there we were, the four of us, in the kitchen, with no time to lose. We had three backpacks to fill, but I thought if I could find a bag for Gavin then at least he could pay his way. I went to a tall cupboard at the end of the room, and checked that out. It was the broom cupboard, like I'd thought, but there were no bags in it. I started opening the big deep drawers down at ankle level and in the second one found a heap of supermarket plastic bags, stacks of old junk mail, and a couple of string bags. The Whittakers were pretty glamorous people but this was their less glamorous side. I gave Gavin the string bags and half-a-dozen plastic ones, then joined Homer and Fi, who were rifling through the pantry.

It was a good score. Sure a lot of the stuff wasn't any real use to us. Spices, pickles, herbs, sauces: they were luxuries, and we couldn't afford to waste space in our packs or be weighed down by them. But there were some nice nuts: cashews and almonds and macadamias. And there was a big bag of rice, full — a twenty-five kilo bag — and another one half full. And quite a lot of cans. Some tuna and some pineapple and some baked beans. Homer eyed the twenty-five kilo bag of rice as though he'd like to hoick it over his shoulder and make off with it, but even for Homer that might have been a bit much. However we did manage to get the half-full bag into his backpack, with some shoving and remoulding. The trip was worth it for that alone, I thought, as Homer did up the buckles. Fi was enthusiastically stocking up with cans. "Wait a second," I whispered. "You won't be able to carry them all." I repacked some in mine then gave a few to Gavin. I added lots of bags of stuff: polenta, borlotti beans, cannalini beans, kidney beans, split peas. Then a dozen packets of rice snacks, some packets of spaghetti, and a few other bits and pieces.

We were there only six or eight minutes. As we headed back to the window I started grabbing fresh fruit and shoving it at Homer and Gavin. I was pleased to see Fi get some vegetables from a stack of red plastic shelves near the microwave. "Couldn't be better," I thought. "This has gone really well."

It was at that moment that the door burst open.

Nine

We didn't have a hope. "Nowhere to run, ain't got nowhere to go." If I'd heard Dad play that song a thousand times I'd heard it a million. We were caught between the door and the window and we might as well have been a mile away from each of them.

They burst into the room like cattle when you let them out of the crush. They came through the door so hard and so fast that the fourth man was hit by the door swinging back in his face. Every time anything really appalling happened in my life there always seemed to be a funny moment with it. Or a moment that would have been funny in a different situation. Like Kevin farting when we were captured. This guy went stumbling to the floor when the door hit him, but I only noticed it out of the corner of my eye, because there were more important things to worry about.

I grabbed Gavin and held him to me. Things got pretty wild. Homer was bigger than any of them and he charged straight through the crowd, towards the door. I don't know if he had any particular aim, maybe to get the door shut and barricaded and then deal with the guys already in the room. More likely it was just a reflex to go that way. Two of them tackled him then a third joined in. He flung the first guy off into a stand of antique saucepans, black cast-iron things. At that moment someone turned the light on, so I got a good view of the saucepans rolling over the floor and the man sprawled among them. But Homer was falling backwards as the other two wrestled him down. Then a third guy did a flying dive across the room right onto Homer's head and for a minute I couldn't see anything except a mess of writhing bodies. I let go of Gavin and picked up one of the cast-iron saucepans, a medium-size one. I took a swing at the nearest head but missed, and got the guy's shoulder instead. I think I hurt him though. More people came running in. Two of them grabbed my arms and that was the end of my contribution. By now the kitchen was almost full, mostly men in their twenties or thirties, but a few teenage boys and three or four women. Gavin, as soon as I'd let him go, had thrown himself onto the pile of wrestling bodies and was clinging to a pair of legs like a human leech.

They hauled him out of the way, but as they did, Homer rose up out of the ruck. It was one of the most awesome things I've ever seen. He had blood all over his face and his hair was red with it. But he towered above them. All he needed was a torch in his hand to be the Statue of Liberty. He threw two more guys off, one in each direction: just threw them like they were stuffed toys. A man came at him and Homer head-butted him with a dull thunk, like a breaking watermelon. He headed for the door again, kicking people clear with every step. I fought desperately to get rid of the guys holding me but I wasn't as strong as Homer, and they gripped my wrists so hard their hands felt like steel bands. A bloke jumped on Homer's back and tried to ride him down to the ground. He managed to get his hands around Homer's throat to pull his head back. With his huge paws Homer started ripping the hands off his throat, but in doing that he tipped backwards, and two young blokes realised that they had a good chance at last. They drove in simultaneously at his stomach and down he went again. This time he didn't come up.

I saw a couple of boots go in and some fists fly, but the next time I had even a glimpse of him was five minutes later when they started standing up and counting their own bruises. First I could see Homer's legs, and then one arm. Inside I was feeling hysterical but no way was I going to give them the satisfaction of knowing that. I had no idea if he was alive or dead.

When I did see his face I realised at the same time

that he had been neatly trussed up; his arms and legs tied behind him, like a sheep in the back of a ute. But I wasn't very interested in that. All I wanted was to see his eyes, for any sign of life. But his eyes were closed and his head had rolled to one side.

I mightn't ever know a more terrible feeling than the one I had then. I felt a bomb had gone off inside me. It was like my heart had been ripped in half in the middle of my chest. I seriously thought I was having a heart attack. I couldn't get my breath, and the pain seemed to grow all the time. The only way I was going to get relief was to see Homer's eyes open. I was dimly aware of Gavin on the other side of Homer, being held by two men, and across to my left Fi was also held by someone. But I had no real interest in them, just a terrible all-consuming desire to throw myself onto Homer's blood-covered body and breathe life back into him.

Then suddenly I was lifted off my feet and bustled out of the kitchen. I got my breath then, and started screaming, "No, no." They thought I was scared, but I wasn't really, just angry, and desperately worried about Homer.

I found myself in a long corridor, quite narrow and dark. They raced me along there at quite a speed. They were very angry and very excited and no-one seemed to be in charge. Half-a-dozen different people were yelling and every time we came to a room they'd hesitate and then one person would say something and someone else would say something else and away we'd go again. I guess they were looking for a safe room to store me in. Then someone, quite a young voice, suggested something, and they all laughed and it was like they'd made a decision, because now they pushed me along like they knew exactly where they were going.

To my surprise we went through a door into the cool outside. I could have wept with relief to feel fresh honest air on my skin again. I lifted my face and let the dew touch me lightly, like the rain of life. Still the men did not slow down. The shadow of a roof came over me and I realised we were in a large machinery shed, open front and back with a concrete floor. There were all the usual working vehicles you find on a big farm — tractors, headers, Ag bikes, four-wheel drives. They took me to none of those. I still didn't have a clue what they had in mind. They frog-marched me down to the end of the shed, where the cars were sitting. I hardly had time to take them in, but there was an old blue Falcon, a very old Renault or Citroën or something, and a fairly new grey Alfa. I wasn't given any time to think, but I suppose if I'd had the time I would have assumed they were going to drive me into town, with the other three, and hand us over to the authorities.

Then they opened the boot of the Falcon.

I still didn't understand. The boot? But they soon cleared up my misunderstanding. With a lot of pleased laughter and little jokes they signalled me to get in. I backed away, as much as my escort would let me. I couldn't believe they could be so barbaric. "No way," I said. "I'm not getting in there."

I got hit on the back of the head so hard it almost knocked me out. I don't know what hit me: not a fist, it was too solid for that. Maybe a block of wood. If they hadn't been holding me up I would have fallen. And I got no chance to recover. With a quick rush they virtually lifted me and carried me the half-dozen steps to the car, threw me in, then slammed the boot shut.

In the old days, BTW, before the war, Mum and Dad joked about how their friends used to hide in the car boot to get in the drive-in movies for free. Mum shuddered when she talked about it and said, "No way would I ever do it. If they charged a hundred dollars for the movie I still wouldn't have got in the boot."

I shuddered and shivered when I heard the story and thought, "Yes, me neither."

I don't think I'm exactly claustrophobic but I definitely don't like feeling trapped. Maybe it goes back to a terrible moment I had in Corrie's hayshed, years ago, when we'd been crawling through the tunnels left by the little gaps between the bales. I was way inside the haystack when suddenly I panicked and thought I'd never get out, I'd be suffocated in there. I started backing up, and of course eventually got out, but I'll never forget the terrifying few minutes of struggling backwards through the bales.

And if I did develop a few claustrophobic feelings, they weren't helped by my time in maximum security in Stratton Prison.

So for the first few minutes in the boot I lost it completely. Almost completely: I didn't scream or beg or go hysterical: There was still a little thing called pride that was powerful for me. But I went hysterical inside. The trouble was, I couldn't do anything with my hysteria. I sort of writhed and twisted about, biting on my knuckles. I shoved half my right fist in my mouth and bit into it so hard I expected blood to flow down my arm. The back of my head, where they'd hit me, was numb and felt like it didn't belong to me any more, like it had been removed by a surgeon but might be put back later with no anaesthetic — if I was lucky.

Somehow I had to calm myself. Even in the middle of going hysterical I knew that. Like a spoonbill searching the water in a billabong, I scanned my brain for something, anything, that might help. And gradually a memory emerged. It was Robyn's voice, and suddenly it wasn't a memory any more; she could have been in the boot with me. I remembered her telling me the story of Shadrach, Meshach and Abednego, and how they'd survived: when the King chucked them in the furnace and an angel or someone went in with them. The furnace blazed all around them but they didn't burn.

And it did calm me. I don't know if Robyn or an angel or even God himself was in the boot, but I was starting to suspect that whenever I wanted God, he was there. Only not necessarily in the form I wanted, or doing what I wanted. Very inconvenient and self-willed of him: I was fairly sure I knew better than everyone about everything, and when I say everyone I include God. But in the pitch black of the boot I clung to the image of a fiery furnace, and it wasn't the furnace of Hell either.

It was ironic to think of such a place, because the boot, as well as being cold, was the blackest, darkest place I have ever been in. For an experiment I held my hand in front of my face. Nothing. I couldn't see a glimmer of my own fingers. Nothing but that awful blackness, that seemed to be inside me as well as out, so much so that I couldn't tell where me ended and the air began.

My first fear was that I'd suffocate, that there simply wasn't a way for air to get in. Gradually though, I realised it was getting in somewhere. I'd probably been in here ten minutes already and although the air was getting stale I wasn't desperate for oxygen. Maybe there were some little holes where air entered, but as it was the middle of the night there was no light to show them.

As I started to get control of my mind again I tried to work out what I could do. It seemed like they weren't about to drive me straight into Wirrawee. Maybe they'd do that in the morning. They probably weren't too keen to go all the way in there in the middle of the night.

Somehow I had to get out of this boot before they handed me over to the authorities. By groping with my fingers I found the lock mechanism and pulled desperately at it, hoping there'd be some way of working it from the inside. But it was a tightly sealed little unit, and seemed impossible to open. I let go of it and sank back on the hard floor.

There was so much to think about. The sheer panic of being in the dark, with no room to move, and the air getting worse: that was enough. Yet they were almost little worries. On top of it were the real worries: what had happened to Homer and Fi and Gavin, what was going to happen to me when they came and got me out, or drove me into town, what chance did we have of escaping death? Not much point solving the little problems of being squashed and uncomfortable in the boot, when the death sentence waited at the end of it.

All I could think to say to that was, "Ellie, you can only deal with what you can deal with, and right now all you can deal with is this horrible black hole."

It was as much use worrying about Homer and death sentences as it was about the schoolwork I was missing, or the price of petrol in New Zealand, or the number of repeats on Bulgarian television.

Anyway my body was starting to take up so much attention that I had no choice: I had to concentrate on that. My legs were pushed into my chest, making my back ache. My head had some feeling back again but I wished it hadn't. Every minute or so a pain grew in there, then exploded like a huge flowering plant. I remember reading about some palm tree in Kakadu that flowered every seventy-five years then died. I felt my head might do exactly that. Right then I would have given every dollar I had — not that I had many, only $423 in the Wirrawee branch of the ANZ, which I'd probably never see again — for a couple of glasses of water and some fresh air. And a couple of Panadeine.

Twenty minutes later I would have given even more than my $423. It was indescribably awful. The first few minutes had been bad enough: the quick rush of terror at being locked in, the first violent anxiety. But a million times worse was the long slow stale horror of time passing in a black nothing. My eyes received no signals, my ears received no signals. If you sat staring at a TV screen with no picture and no sound, you'd go a bit crazy after a while. Now I was inside the TV, and my whole world was reduced to that.

The air was certainly bad: hot and heavy. It was like breathing cotton wool. It made my headache worse and worse, and although I kept wriggling around into new positions, there was a limit to the number of ways I could rearrange myself. My legs went to sleep and my back got more painful.

Worst of all was the fear that I'd go mad. If only they'd

told me how long they were going to keep me here. Then it might have been tolerable. But my mind played tricks. I felt like I was in infinite space for infinite time. One infinite I could have put up with, maybe. Not two.

I didn't really have any idea how much time was passing. Ten minutes, twenty minutes, half an hour, I still used those words but I couldn't tell if they meant what they used to mean. A minute could have been an hour. I felt like I might have been there one hour, or twenty-four.

At one point I passed out. Maybe it was sleep but it didn't feel like sleep. I woke up after — how long? — and immediately panicked. What if I hadn't woken up? I didn't get the impression these people had put me in here to die a slow and horrible death. But how did they know what would happen in a car boot? How did anyone know?

I started pounding on the lid as hard as I could. That wasn't very hard, because I couldn't get my arm up high enough. And I stopped again pretty soon. I knew I wasn't making much noise; all I was doing was hurting my fist and breathing in more bad air.

I lay there, twisted like a piece of ornamental wrought iron, panting and sweating, and thought, "I've got to do something. I've got to get out of here." Again I started to feel hysterical. I put as much upward pressure on the lid as I could, using my knees and hands. The metal felt soft enough, and I thought I was putting bulges in it, but there was no sign of the lock giving. I panicked myself again by wondering if I was distorting the boot so much that they wouldn't be able to open it, if and when they ever came to get me. But I gritted my teeth and thought grimly, "I'm not giving in."

I lay back again. There had to be a different way of doing this, a different approach. I needed to do some lateral thinking. As I lay there I felt the bulge of the spare tyre under me. Its hard rim had been cutting into my skin all this time but I hadn't thought about it, except to be annoyed by it. I remembered the spare tyres in our vehicles, how there'd always been a tool kit with them, usually under them. With Mr Roxburgh's new Volvo there'd even been a pair of white gloves, so you wouldn't get your hands dirty changing the tyre. I didn't think white gloves would do me much good, but in the tool kit there might be something I could use to tear a hole in the metal. At worst I might find a weapon, for when they returned . . . assuming I was still alive then.

I started groping underneath me, using my hands to work out what was there. It seemed like the spare tyre was held in place by a bolt with a thread, and a bracket that screwed down onto the bolt. I had no trouble getting the bracket off, but the problem then was to get the tyre out of the way. The Falcon boot was small, the tyre was heavy, I was exhausted, and the air was getting worse all the time. I started trying to raise it, lying above it and pulling it up with a short quick lift, using just my arms. The first three tries didn't work, just left me panting and feeling weak. I lay on top of the tyre for a few minutes. Then I gave it the big charge. A tennis player grunt and the knowledge that I wouldn't have the energy for any more tries: this was all I had left.

And it worked. I got it. I balanced the tyre on top of the bolt while I took a breather.

The only trouble was that it's difficult to take a breather when there's not much to breathe.

I pushed the tyre a little further to the side, as far as it would go, then shoved my hand into the pit and had a hunt. The tools were scattered around. Bad sign that: the owner was pretty sloppy. Dad would not have been impressed. I could feel a spanner, which wasn't a lot of use, and a foot pump, then a pair of pliers and a jack. And a tyre lever.

There was something very comforting about that tyre lever. My hands closed around it and gripped it. It made quite a good weapon. Anyone I hit hard enough with it would stay hit. With a good backswing I could rip a head open like a pumpkin.

I took another rest, then gritted my teeth and attacked the lid. I stabbed at the metal again and again. I had to take the risk that there'd be people outside, ready to pounce on me. I hit as hard as I could. I pounded until I was wet with my own sweat, wheezing like Fi's little sister, so drained of energy that I couldn't lift the lever again, let alone hit with any force.

That metal was tough stuff, tougher than it looked. I suppose though, the real trouble was that I was lying on my back, I had no room to swing and I was too tired to hit hard. For the boot it was probably like me being beaten up by Fi's sister: her little fists would rain on me with a gentle pitter-patter. "Gee the flies are bad today," I'd tease her. I had a horrible feeling that my bashes on the boot lid weren't much harder than the pitter-patter of the flies on the outside.

Thinking about that made me wonder about the flies. Would they be starting to buzz yet? Was it daylight? When I looked at the rear corners of the boot I could see some grey spots: fuzzy, but such a contrast from the complete black I had been enduring for so long that I felt some joy and excitement to see them.

I looked more closely. Then felt with both hands. On the right-hand side in particular the grey spots were part of the bulge that must have been the taillights. They seemed like they weren't very well fitted. That gave me an idea. I lined up the tyre lever again, drew it back as far as I could, and rammed it into the tail-light. It went all the way through. I heard the tinkle of broken glass and plastic hitting the concrete floor of the machinery shed. That sound, and the stream of soft fuzzy light suddenly pouring in, was like a beam of comfort. The light was followed by a stream of warm fresh air.

If you could kiss air I would have done it then. Instead I closed my eyes and let it blow into my nostrils.

There wasn't time to rest though. The little bit of oxygen gave me strength. I gripped the tyre lever and used it to widen the hole, poking out the rest of the glass and plastic. I was half — more than half — expecting that at any moment the boot would be thrown open and a savage hand would reach in and grab the lever and whack me with it. But I had to keep going.

When I'd cleared the little hole right out I started wriggling around. It was difficult to get into the best position. With daylight arriving I suspected that they'd be coming for me soon. I had to give myself the best possible chance.

I was contorted into an excruciatingly painful position, but I started squeezing my hand in. If only I were Fi! With her long slender arm there would have been no problem. She would have pushed it gracefully straight through. With me there was a problem, especially as the hole got narrower towards the end. I felt my skin being grazed, then pushed back, as I got it to the outside. But I didn't care about that. The important thing, the exciting thing, was that it was out in the fresh air. If anyone had been standing there I could have waved to them. They could have grabbed my hand and shaken it.

But that wasn't enough. I started reaching to the left. My fingers were moving across the smooth metal. I had to find the centre point, low down, the other side of the lock mechanism.

The biggest problem was the angle. If I could have bent my arm ninety degrees, so it was straight across the outside of the boot, the whole thing would have been easy. But limbs aren't that flexible. I had to come at the button from quite a way off. I don't have a very long arm and I definitely don't have a hinge on my elbow. My mind flashed the thought, "What if they locked the boot? I didn't remember any sound of it being locked, but I was in such a state that I mightn't have noticed anyway. And maybe you can't hear a sound like that from the inside. "Well," I thought, "if it is locked you won't be able to do a damn thing about it. Just keep going and hope God's on your side."

I stretched and stretched. My fingers scrabbled around, desperately searching for the button. I was staring at the inside of the boot, opposite where I thought my fingers were, as though I should be able to see them through the metal. I could feel nothing, just the smooth skin of the car. My hand, getting tired, slipped down without my realising it, until I felt the seam where the boot fitted into the body of the Falcon. I realised that was no good. I went up again, and stretched even further, as far as possible. The tip of my middle finger touched the button. It gave me such a shock it could have been electrified. But at the same time I felt awful frustration. I just couldn't stretch further. My arm was already as good as out of its socket. I could get an extra millimetre maybe, but I needed a couple of centimetres. I groaned out loud. "Come on," I told myself, "oh come on, you've got to do it." I reached and reached. I felt as if sinews would tear, bones would crack, joints pop. As my strength finally gave out I made a last desperate lunge. It was all or nothing. I hit the button as hard as I could. It was much stiffer than I'd expected. For a moment I thought I hadn't hit it hard enough. For an instant I felt total despair. But then as I kept pressing it scrunched all the way in. And the boot lid slowly swung open.

I couldn't move. It was a combination of everything: the paralysis of my body, the emotion of feeling fresh air again, the shock of the dawn light on my eyes, and the fact that my arm was stuck painfully through the little tail-light hole. Slowly I withdrew it, wincing as my grazed skin got grazed all over again. I looked anxiously out at the machinery shed. There was no-one in sight. I started to unknot myself, half-rolling half-crawling out of that hellhole. It took a full minute, but at last I was on the concrete floor. My head pounded, my back ached, my arm stung, and I couldn't stand up straight. But I felt wonderful.

I looked around. The place seemed innocently quiet. The house too was quiet. After the excitement in the middle of the night they were probably sound asleep. I hoped so. Trying to ignore the aches and pains I stumbled around to the front of the Falcon. No keys in the ignition. Damn. I checked the other vehicles. The same. Only the Ag bikes had their keys. I kept looking around, more and more desperately. I had to find something fast, not just something I could use to escape, but something that would help me get to the other three.

Then something weird happened. I was going past the last car, the old Renault, when I thought, "I could have sworn that car moved." Not move, like drive itself away, but shake and shudder, like its engine was running on a cold winter morning. I stopped and stared. Was I imagining this? I couldn't afford to stand around gazing at a car, but on the other hand anything unusual might help me. As I stood there, it happened again. It shivered. I walked towards it, nervously, worried that I was wasting time but knowing I couldn't turn my back on this. When I was just a couple of metres away I heard a faint thumping noise. My brain must have been numbed by the lack of oxygen from my time in the boot, because I still couldn't make sense of it. Then suddenly I understood. I leapt at the car. For a moment I couldn't open it, then I found a sort of lever-handle under the lid, which pressed to the left. Up it came, out came a breath of bad air, and there was Fi, blinking in terror, shrinking away, expecting violence and worse.

I didn't even wait to see the expression on her face change, let alone help her struggle out. I was already on my way to the other car, the Alfa. It had a boot with no button. I had to open the driver's door and find the lever down on the floor and jerk that up. Lucky the driver's door wasn't locked, because when I rushed back to the boot I found a white-faced trembling little kid.

"What kind of bastards are they?" I asked myself.

I helped Gavin out, as Fi staggered up to me. We had a bit of a hug, all three of us, but at the same time we knew we couldn't stand around bonding.

"I know where they put Homer," were Fi's first words.

"So he's alive? Is he OK?"

"I don't know about OK. But he was alive."

I didn't like the way she said "was."

"Where is he?"

Fi pointed to the left end of the house, in the original homestead. "There's a little room down the end of a long corridor. It's a bit like a cell. It might have been a pantry or something in the old days: there's no window or anything. They were going to put me in there too, then someone decided we should be separated."

"How do you get to it?"

"It's through that grey door. Then you'd turn, um, let me think, left, go down to the end, go left again, and that's the long corridor I was talking about. The door's facing you, at the very end."

I stood there, making my brain work, forcing it to accelerate to maximum revs. It still hurt from the hit on my head, but that was bad luck for my brain. After a minute I said to Fi, "You take Gavin and get out of here. I'll meet you at the bottom of the track to Tailor's Stitch. If we're not there by midnight don't worry about us, go on into Hell."

I gestured to Gavin. "You go with Fi. Homer and I'll meet you tonight."

They both paused, looking at me. I could see from their eyes what was happening. They were realising that I was right. They didn't want to admit it, but they were slowly having to face the fact that this was the way to go.

If all three of us got caught again it would be terrible — too appalling to think about. Unforgivable. And the cool hard fact of the matter was that Fi and Gavin weren't going to be a lot of use from now on. This was not the scene for either of them and I think deep down they both knew it.

"Quick," I said to Fi, "get going, they'll be coming out soon."

She looked at me, made a sad face, grabbed my hand, squeezed it, grabbed Gavin and off they went. I didn't bother giving them any ideas about what to do, how to escape. I had to give all my attention to Homer and myself. God knew, I'd need every last skerrick of concentration I possessed to get us out of this one.

About three ticks later a guy came out of the house, took a few steps into an herb garden, unzipped his fly and gave the lavender a good hosing down. My worst fear looked like being realised: the house was going to stir into life too early. Those few moments getting Fi and Gavin organised might have been fatal for Homer and me.

I stepped lightly to the left. I didn't have a plan, just a desire to get out of sight of the guy in the herb garden. Things quickly got worse. As that guy zipped up, another man came out yawning, then a woman. A teenager opened a door up the other end and came half out, then turned and started talking to someone inside the house.

When this place came to life, it really came to life.

I was right next to the motorbikes when they saw me. The man and the woman who'd just emerged both saw me at the same time. They pointed, cried out. The fact that I was beside the motorbikes decided everything from then on. Talk about coincidence. I looked around desperately. Right next to me was a big Yamaha Triton. Naturally the Whittakers would have the best. I took three steps to it, flicked out the kick-start, swung my leg over the bike and rammed the kick-start down. It felt good having a bike between my legs again. I felt a sudden surge of confidence. I don't think the bike shared it though; it didn't start. I kicked down again, and it roared into life. I swung it around. I don't quite know why I did that. Ahead of me had been the back of the shed, open to the weather, and beyond it the paddocks and hills and open blue sky. Once I turned it around I had nothing in front of me but captivity and death.

Ten

I rode straight at them. That at least gave me the element of surprise. I didn't have a clue what to do. I just wanted to scare them with the bike I think: get them out of the way a bit. I opened the throttle and roared down the slope.

The looks on their faces were pretty comical. They couldn't wait to get out of my way. Two of them fell over each other, into the lavender. I hoped they landed in the section where the guy just pissed.

Before I knew it, I was going full-on at the door, the grey door Fi had pointed to. It was open and I didn't seem to have left myself with any choices. I went through.

Inside felt weird, sort of warm and intimate, even

through the fumes of the motorbike. Weirdest of all though, was that I was riding a bike in a house. The Whittakers would never forgive me. The noise was scary: bouncing off the thick old walls, so I felt I was in an echo chamber. It didn't help my headache, not that I was thinking too much about that. Instead I was trying desperately to remember what Fi said. "Turn left, go down the end, left again." Trouble was, while I was thinking about this, I was manoeuvring the bike through a tricky arrangement of little rooms that Fi hadn't mentioned and which didn't seem to have any function: they just opened up into each other. They were a waste of space. A few mahogany tables and chairs were scattered through them, that was all.

Then a corridor appeared on the left, and I swung into it.

The moment I did a man came out of the first room on my right, about three metres ahead. And I was accelerating. He held out a hand, not to try to stop me, just as a reflex. He looked like he'd swallowed a hand grenade. I tried to duck under his arm but failed. I slammed against it pretty hard as he fell backwards. I got another stinging blow to the head, but I think he might have broken his arm, because I heard a crack and it seemed to go limp suddenly. He let out a hell of a scream. I just kept accelerating.

The noise in this narrow corridor was enormous. The old house was too solidly built to start shaking, but any lesser house would have vibrated like a kite in a gale. It was a roar; there's no other word for it. I hoped Homer, if he was alive and awake in his cell, would hear it and be alert, ready for me.

All too soon I was at the end of the corridor, braking hard, braking violently, swinging the rear wheel out and planting my left foot for the turn. As I made the turn I glanced up and saw the last thing I wanted. A young guy with the biggest eyes I've ever seen was lifting a rifle. His eyes were big because they were wide with fear and excitement and his determination to kill me. He was dropping to one knee to get off his shot. Impossible to miss at that range. I would have filled his sights; for him it'd be like looking at a whale through a magnifying glass. It became a race. Could I run him down before he got off his shot? I opened the throttle as wide as it would go. There was a hiccup, a gulp, before the carburettor got the message from the throttle. That moment seemed to last forever. I felt like I was in a vacuum, not moving, while the young guy continued to lift his rifle. I remember his shining eyes. Then I ran over him.

The motorbike was like a wild beast then. It was trying to climb over this guy, still at full throttle, kicking and bucking and falling sideways, while I struggled to stay on it and get control. I didn't think about the young man, except to be relieved that he was unconscious. He may have been dead, I don't know. I know his head hit the wall hard when I wiped him out.

In the end I had to walk the bike over him, and I lost valuable time. But at last that precious door, the door Fi described, was in front of me, about fifteen metres ahead. It was a solid, strong old white door, curved at the top, set into a thick stone wall. It had no handle, just a keyhole. And it had no key.

Until that moment I hadn't thought about how to get

the door open. I hadn't thought about anything much. Just acted on impulse. I suppose I sort of assumed it'd open magically for me. Or I'd crash the bike into it. Or something.

I pulled up and stared at the door, my brain going off like a fireworks display. I looked around for a tool I could use. Nothing. I looked behind me.

Yes, there was the answer. I didn't have time to put the bike on its stand so I leaned it against the wall and ran back to the guy on the floor. His rifle was under him. I tried to lift him but he was too heavy. So I grabbed the butt of the rifle and worked away at it, twisting it backwards and forwards then levering it up.

The fumes from the bike were filling the corridor so quickly that it was as bad as being in the car boot. Carbon monoxide mixed with petrol and oil. Sweat stung my eyes and my hair was getting wet. I had to wipe it away, to stop myself being blinded. But I got the rifle. I was a bit horrified to see that the safety catch was off. It could easily have fired while I was prising it out. But I left it off.

I ran back to the motorbike. As I did I glanced behind me. Someone turned the corner into the corridor at that exact moment. I couldn't see if it was a man or a woman, young or old, but I saw their rifle. I swung around and fired from the hip and they ducked back as fast as they'd appeared.

My problem now was that Homer might be crouched by the keyhole and he mightn't be able to hear my voice through the thick door. The noise of the motorbike didn't help. I couldn't afford to turn the bike off in case it didn't start again. I knew there was a risk that I was about to shoot my best mate, but I had to take the risk. I yelled through the door, "Homer, I'm going to shoot the lock," and I pressed the end of the barrel to the keyhole. I pulled the trigger. It only made a little hole but it seemed to have blown away the vital bits. I kicked the door open.

Well, I hadn't shot Homer, but I nearly knocked him out with the swinging door. I guess I did kick it pretty hard. The first sight I had was of him spinning backwards as the door struck his shoulder. He was a pretty frightening sight anyway: dried blood all over him, his clothes torn, and a horrible messy open wound on one knee. For a second I thought the bullet had got him, but then common sense told me he would be a lot worse off if I'd shot him at that range. Anyway I could see where the bullet had hit. It mightn't have done much damage to the door lock but it made up for that when it hit the back wall. Slabs of plaster were still falling as I stood there.

I virtually ignored Homer, just grabbed the bike, pulled it up, and got on. I didn't need to tell Homer what to do. I felt the bike sag as he threw himself on behind, then felt his big arms grab me round the waist. Even after all he'd been through the strength was still there. "Get the rifle," I yelled back at him, and I felt one arm release my waist, so I assumed he had it. I straightened the bike and took off. Instead of going the way I'd come I went the only other possible way, down a new corridor to my right.

It was a short corridor and a moment later we came burning into a huge area that seemed to be a breakfast room or something. I didn't exactly get time to study it in detail, but there was a big dining table and a bunch of old stuffed armchairs, and a wall full of books. Two or three people scattered as we charged in. To avoid one of them I did a quick turn around one of the armchairs. Homer wasn't expecting it so the turn ended up being pretty slow, with his weight working against me. As we did it though, he fired a shot. I accelerated, knocking over a small table. A collection of jugs and vases went flying. Even above the engine noise I heard the crash as they hit the floor and shattered. We burned out of that room with the rear of the bike fishtailing, threw a right, and charged through the proper dining room. The table was set for a meal and I realised, glancing sideways, that Homer was holding the rifle out and running it along the whole length of the table. Dishes and cups were spinning in all directions, but they all ended up in the same place: fragmenting on the polished wooden floor.

It was the same story in the lounge room. I had a strong feeling that behind me, Homer was enjoying getting his revenge. There was so much furniture scattered around the lounge room that I had to use my feet a lot to balance, to turn, to get around armchairs and coffee tables. It was like a slalom course, with Homer amusing himself by smashing everything within reach. I gripped the handles so tightly that I didn't know if I'd ever be able to get my hands open again. The exhaust fumes, and the continuous roaring of the loud engine in the enclosed spaces had my head throbbing and my ears going deaf. But even through my blocked ears I heard Homer's next shot. Mainly because he fired past my right ear. It happened so quickly that I nearly fell off the bike in shock. There was a flash and a blast and a burning blur of flame that scorched my neck.

Bloody Homer. I should have left him in his cell. That wasn't the kind of thing we'd been taught to do with guns.

I think he was just clearing the way. And a moment later we were in the kitchen. That took me by surprise, a bit, because I didn't think we were even near it. I'd gotten confused by all the different rooms, the twists and turns. But there we were, back on familiar territory. In fact our packs were still there, on the bench next to the sink. From my quick glance I thought they'd unpacked one of them but left the others still stuffed. Guess our visit had been a bit late for them to bother with tidying up. I braked sharply beside them.

"What?" Homer shouted.

"Grab them!" I said.

He hesitated, but I guess one advantage of being so stubborn and pig-headed is that people sometimes find it easier to go along with what I want than have a standoff. Homer grabbed one pack then another and shoved them in between us. With his wide arms he could hold them OK but two was all he could manage.

The stop for the packs was a bad idea though. There hadn't been time for it. At the other end of the kitchen was the door to the outside. That was our target. I revved the bike, planning to ride the length of the kitchen, then have Homer open the door. Suddenly though, it wasn't going to be that easy. Suddenly we were in big trouble. A guy came from the sitting room and another guy came from somewhere down the end, to the left. I don't know how he got in; I hadn't noticed a door there last night, but maybe it was an exit to the coolroom or the laundry.

The trouble was they were both armed and both shooting as they came. They weren't stupid, these two. It was like they were using the bullets as their shield.

It's hard to shoot someone when you're being shot at. We both ducked as low as we've ever been, and I accelerated along the side of the kitchen, hoping the big solid benches would give us protection. It all happened in a flicker. I wondered what we'd do at the end of the benches. It was lucky the Whittakers had such a big kitchen, but that luck was about to give out.

The shooting was wild. These guys had their guns on automatic and they seemed to have unlimited ammunition. Windows shattered to my right, in a continuous noisy waterfall of glass, and the containers and appliances on the shelves exploded. We were in as much danger from flying fragments of glass and porcelain as from bullets. It was like hundreds of mosquitoes screaming around the room. The noise was unbelievable, beyond pain. I've never been caught inside a computer game and never likely to be, but that's how it felt. I got stung on the cheek, thought for a horrible moment that it was a bullet but realised straightaway that it couldn't be, started to brake as we got to the end of the kitchen, still didn't have a clue what to do, then, almost like a dream saw the door open in front of me, gunned the bike, put my head down again, and went for it, not sure who or what had opened the door, not sure who or what would be on the other side, just knew it was our last and only chance. I felt a bullet whiz above my head as we went through, and suddenly, there we were out in beautiful daylight and open air.

And then found to my horror that I had to stop.

Just at the moment when I thought we had a chance. Just at the moment when I could see the soft blue hills in the distance.

Gavin again. That little bugger. We owed him our lives but it was a confusing moment. It was like he'd given us a glimpse of freedom, then snatched it away. It seemed cruel. I slammed on the brakes as Gavin slammed the kitchen door shut behind us. He was no fool, that kid. He knew what an extra second was worth. Then, like a regular little stuntman, he took a racing dive onto the bike, on top of the packs, between Homer and me. I realised I hadn't even needed to stop completely. We were still slowing down and there he was, wriggling around behind me. I didn't wait to see if he was OK, just turned the throttle up again. Maybe we still had a chance after all.

We must have looked a bizarre sight. Three people and two packs on one bike. I discovered how overloaded the whole thing was when I tried to make a fast turn to the left, and nearly lost it. Nearly put it down. The front wheel wobbled wildly and the back one slid away. I planted a leg and with sheer strength pulled it back up. But I knew we couldn't go far like this. It would have been OK in peacetime, just going out to a paddock. I'd often taken unbalanced loads on a bike. I usually had a couple of dogs, for a start and I sometimes came back with a sheep on my knees over the petrol tank. But here, even if we pulled off a miracle and got clear of the house, we wouldn't get far before the inevitable pursuers caught us.

I decided on one more risk. I saw two older men running around the corner of the building, fifty metres to my right, but they weren't armed. They were yelling to people I couldn't see, and they gave the general impression they didn't quite know what to do. I'm sure there were people at the other end of the house too, but the machinery shed, where I wanted to go, would be just out of their sight.

I skidded the bike around in another tight turn and accelerated into the shadows of the shed. Last time I'd been here, locked in the car boot, it had been a place of terror and darkness. I was astonished to think that was probably only ten minutes ago. Now our one chance of escaping this nightmare was in the machinery shed.

I pulled up next to the best bike left there, a Suzuki. Homer didn't need any instructions; neither did Gavin. Homer seemed to leap from one bike to the other. I've never seen him move so fast. As he started the Suzuki, Gavin chucked a pack in front of Homer, then jumped back on behind me. I appreciated the vote of confidence. In fact I was surprised by it. His tense hands gripped my hips. He couldn't grab much else with the swollen pack stuck between us. As soon as Homer's bike was running, I was off. I didn't wait for him. I mono'd my Yamaha through the shed to the other side, then, once we were in sunlight again, spun it round, put my head down, and slaughtered it.

Wow, did we move. Gavin had been hanging on tight before but now he gripped me like he was free-falling and I had the only parachute. We went along the flat faster than electricity. I glanced around and saw the dust furling out behind us, and Homer a bit further back, swerving and zigzagging. Which reminded me that I should be doing the same thing. We were going fast all right, but not as fast as a bullet. At least with Gavin's light weight on the back it was easier to keep the bike balanced.

As the flat started to run out I swerved to the right and up the hill. We kangaroo-hopped over a hundred metres of corrugations, then jolted at a crazy speed through a rabbit warren. An old fenceline lay ahead, but it was easy to find a gap. And through that was the black bitumen of the road.

I flung the bike to the right in a racing turn. I was kind of admiring my style when Gavin spoilt it by bashing me hard on the shoulder. It scared me. I thought he was warning me of something, most likely people chasing us. I didn't think they'd have been that quick though. I glanced around at him, reluctant to slow down or lose my concentration.

He pointed behind us, and as I looked at him a moment longer, trying to work out what the hell he was on about, he shouted, above the roar of the engine: "Fi."

I still had no idea what he meant, but I knew I couldn't keep going towards safety while Gavin was pointing in the opposite direction and yelling Fi's name.

I skidded to a halt. A second later Homer ripped up beside us. "What did you stop for?" he yelled. His face was all covered with dust. That's what happens when you come second.

"I think Fi's back there," I yelled at him.

Kicking down into first I swung the bike around. As I blasted away Homer, who was still turning, got another faceful of dust. I had other things on my mind though. Just when I thought we were getting clear of the Whittakers', we had to ride back into the jaws of the place. It seemed incredibly unfair.

Luckily we only had to go a few hundred metres. We rounded a small bare hill, and suddenly, from out of the bushes at the base of the hill came a wild-looking figure. She could have been a distressed angel, blonde hair all mussed up, distraught look on her face, arms reaching out. "I've lost Gavin," she said. Then she saw him. She didn't seem to know whether to embrace him or hit him. But there wasn't time for either. She hesitated but I yelled at her, "Get on Homer's."

I spun around yet again and took off flat chat. I didn't see Fi's reaction when she saw Homer's bloodied face and body, but I did catch a glimpse of Homer as Fi climbed on behind him. That sleazebag, even at a time like this he had a little smile when Fi's arms went around his waist. She wasn't hanging on too tightly though. It looked like she'd fly off at the first bad pothole.

Maybe she was safer that way.

We raced along the road for a couple of kilometres. I got the Triton up to 110 k's. I'd love to have stayed on the road longer, enjoying the smooth ride, but we had to assume the people at the house would have been on the phone to the authorities ten minutes ago, so the chase could be coming from two different directions. I kept searching right and left for the best place to leave the road, and finally found it when a big patch of rocks loomed up ahead. Rocks were perfect for us because we'd leave no tracks.

Homer and Fi had dropped a bit behind — their Suzuki wasn't as fast as our Yamaha — but they were still in sight, so they could see what we were doing. I didn't need to put on the blinkers to make my turn.

It was a tough gig, going up those rocks. There were plenty of patches of grass, but I wanted to stay off them as much as possible. The flat stretches of rock were fine, but quite steep, and of course there was no traction. I had to manhandle the big heavy bike up a lot of it. I think Gavin on the back was having some kind of reaction to all the excitement, which wasn't surprising. He sat there crouched over like a little jockey, not helping at all.

I didn't have time to do anything about him: all my energy and concentration were on getting up that hill.

We were about halfway up when the road started getting busy. A couple of four-wheel drives raced past, going towards the Whittakers'. I was more-or-less walking the bike at the time so I heard them coming and was able to get into the shadows and lean the bike against a tall boulder while I struggled to get my breath. Looking down the hill I saw Homer and Fi hiding behind another boulder. I wondered how Homer was going, with all his injuries. At least he had Fi to help him. Gavin seemed to have lost all his strength.

As soon as the cars had gone we resumed the long grunt. There was one big flat area, quite unexpected, all grass, and I left tracks on that. We accelerated across it, and from then on the going was better: not so steep, with smaller rocks. I went another two kilometres, then stopped again. I put the bike on its stand and waited for the other two. They got there about four minutes later.

"What do you think?" I asked.

"We've got to keep going," Homer said. He looked awful, grey and sweaty, although not so bloody now.

"They got such a good look at us at the airfield, and once they sit down and compare notes with the people at the farm . . ." He had to pause for breath. "It won't take them long to work out that we're number one on the most wanted."

"OK," I said, impatient about all that stuff. I'd already figured that out. "But which way do we go?"

"What about out around the Mingles?" Homer said. "And then across the bridge near Holloway. They won't be able to follow us that far, and even if they did, it wouldn't point them to Hell."

"Have you got enough petrol?" I asked.

"Yeah, should get us most of the way, if the gauge is accurate."

I didn't have the breath or the energy to argue. I pushed the bike off its stand. Gavin said, "I'm going with Homer," and jumped on his bike. Fi shrugged and got on mine. We blasted away again, over the last of the rocks and into the bush.

Some of that day was actually pretty good. Sure the tiredness got worse and worse. The physical exertion of the climb, after a sleepless night on an empty stomach, and the emotional exhaustion after such a series of horrible events combined to steal my legs of strength and my heart of courage. I kind of blanked out for a while — in fact for most of the morning — and rode in a coma. Fi kept prodding me to keep me awake. But there's something about the bush that calms you. I try not to get sentimental about it, because I know how cruel it can be, and I saw what it did to Darina, but all the same, sometimes it does make you feel better. We'd have visitors from the city, and they'd get all gooey and sentimental.

I remember two friends of Mum's looking out across the creek at a flock of ducks on the other bank, and saying, "Aren't they beautiful? What a peaceful scene." I just stared at the ladies in total disbelief. At the time the ducks were engaged in a screaming brawl, a full-on civil war, racing around with wings flapping, feathers flying, voices squawking, like they wanted to kill each other.

So it's no good kidding yourself about the bush, or about nature for that matter.

I knew all that, but I still couldn't resist the power of the place. At one stage we were riding through a eucalypt forest, trees quite widely spaced, no undergrowth. It was so easy, so relaxing. Tall white trunks, fawn bark peeling off them, little brown birds darting from one to the next. There were no bright colours to hurt the eye. Quiet, fresh, self-contained. It wasn't paradise — far from it — but it would do me.

Just after noon my bike ran out of petrol and we dumped it in a billabong. We shared the other bike for another hour. It carried two people and the two packs. We agreed that when Homer's bike ran out we'd shout ourselves lunch. We were being tough, making ourselves wait, but we needed to be a long way from the farm before stopping. I found myself waiting desperately for a cough or splutter from the Suzuki, hoping for a signal that it was nearly empty.

At last, at 1:15, it gave its last sad shudder and died. We chucked it in a patch of blackberries.

The silence felt weird. I'd become so used to the roaring of the motorbikes and it took a while to get used to the difference. We had a nice picnic though. Gavin watched wolfishly as we opened a pack. It had been so long since we'd stolen the food that I couldn't remember what we'd put in them. Sadly, it seemed like we hadn't brought the pack with my favourite cashews and the other nuts. We did find rice snacks, and the bananas and oranges I'd thrown on the top at the last minute.

No-one said a word. We knew time was precious, and we had no energy for conversation anyway. We ate kind of furtively, like we didn't have the right. In our own country! It was so unfair. Homer kept walking off through the trees, banana in his mouth, stopping and listening with head cocked while he ate, then returning for his next helping.

Within fifteen minutes I got them moving. I put one pack on my back, Homer took the other. We started walking north-west but gradually circled around, until at about four o'clock we saw the blessed outline of Tailor's Stitch, a high purple-blue ridge in the distance. The sight gave me fresh energy. I dropped back and walked with Fi and Gavin, to keep them company, to encourage them. They had fallen behind and I knew they had no reserves left. But I also knew that if we kept up a decent pace we could be in Hell by dawn.

Eleven

The weird thing was that everything in Hell was so normal: like, while we'd been locked in boots or chasing around on motorbikes with bullets flying, they'd been sunbaking and reading and playing. The only interest the ferals had in our adventures was when we treated Homer's injuries. They seemed to enjoy watching him flinch and bite his lip and swear while Fi and I washed his wounds.

He had a bad gash on the scalp, in among his thick hair. It seemed to be the cause of all the dried blood on his face. Most of his other injuries were cuts and bruises, especially on his right hip and shin. They must have hurt like buggery.

There wasn't much we could do about them, except admire the spectacular purple-blue-green-black colours.

True to form Homer was tough though. He might have grimaced and sworn, but every time we hesitated, worried about how much we were hurting him, he'd say, "Come on, get on with it, what's your problem?"

Gavin and Jack watched enviously. I could see the lesson they were learning. At one point I said to Homer: "Would you mind shedding a few tears, just so these guys can see it's OK to cry?"

Fat chance of that.

As soon as we finished Natalie wanted me to tell her a story, and Jack and Casey dragged me off to see this elaborate dam system they'd constructed in the creek.

It was pretty good as a matter of fact. I stood looking at it thinking how they'd both make good engineers when they were older, then went into a big downer by reminding myself that they were unlikely to survive long enough to have the luxury of becoming engineers or anything else. Becoming a corpse wasn't much of a future.

But for the time being they seemed quite cheerful. They showed me how they'd channelled the water through a series of locks. They could alter its flow by moving a few stones. "Clever little buggers," I thought.

I said to them, "All you need's a turbine and you could run electricity through Hell."

Their eyes sharpened and I think they had visions of the whole valley ablaze with streetlights. Casey was probably dreaming of a TV and video player already. I didn't like to tell them it mightn't be that simple.

Lee and Kevin were interested enough in what had happened and happy to listen to our endless post-mortems, but as always it was never quite the same, telling people who hadn't been there. Homer was in the middle of describing how I'd shot through the door lock, and Kevin was nodding like he really cared, but just as Homer got to the most dramatic part Kevin pulled off his sock and started inspecting an ingrown toenail. I mean, honestly, sometimes I thought there was no hope for Kevin.

I had made one decision while I was in the boot, and it was about Lee. Those terrifying hours had given me a slightly different perspective. I'd realised, curled up in the tiny dark space, that I didn't want to die without fixing things up with him. It wasn't worth throwing away a deep friendship just for the sake of pride. There were more important things in life. Sometimes being in the right wasn't the end of the story.

It was hard to get anyone away from the food though. As well as the two packs; which were certainly full, we'd killed a lamb and brought that in with us. We'd decided it was worth the energy needed to catch it and kill it and skin it and gut it, and then cover the blood and bury the unwanted bits so we left no evidence of our visit.

The trouble was that we hadn't thought about carrying it over Tailor's Stitch and into Hell. Fi and Gavin had been so out of it that Homer and I did all the work. At least we hadn't had to carry them: three times Gavin started asking us to piggyback him, and each time we cut him off before he finished the sentence. In a way I wish I could have carried him. It was the first time he'd shown weakness or softness or affection; the first time his tough veneer had cracked. It was the first time he'd asked me for anything. But like they say, war is hell, and no-one was available for carrying duties. He was the one who'd been so keen on coming on this trip, so he had to put up with the consequences.

Anyway, I kept looking for an opportunity to talk to Lee on his own, but I soon realised I had no hope while the food was spread out, attracting everyone's devout attention. It wasn't until I'd fought the human magpies off and got it organised and stored that I went after Lee, determined to track him down.

Within a few minutes I saw him on his way to the creek with a water bottle, so I followed him there. I found him crouched on the bank, watching the water run into and around the top of the bottle. Yet he wasn't making any attempt to fill it.

I deliberately walked loudly as I came up behind him, because I knew what a horrible shock it could be in this war if you didn't hear someone coming.

He didn't look around though.

I sat beside him and watched as he pushed the bottle a little deeper, making the bubbles gurgle. Then he lifted it out again, tipped most of the water away, pushed it back under and made more bubbles. I think he would have gone on like that for hours if I hadn't said anything. Seemed like he was content to squat there forever, watching the water eddy and flow.

"Lee," I finally said, "I have to talk to you."

He didn't respond so I just ploughed on. "I know what happened back in Stratton stuffed up our relationship. I hate that. I mean, to be honest, I hate what happened with that girl, but even more I hate how we don't talk any more, how we're not friends. I'd do anything to get that back. I know it'll never be the same, but if we both want it badly enough, we can get back the friendship. I just want to tell you that I do want it, really badly."

After a while I gave him a light punch on the arm and said, "So, what do you think? Are we going to be mates again?"

I was very tense, and maybe resenting that I was having to do all the work in this conversation.

Finally he did turn his head, and facing me, yet not looking at me, he said, "What do you think's stopping us being friends again?"

He spoke in such a level voice that it was impossible to tell what he was getting at.

"Well," I said, "I guess I've been pretty tough on you. I've had to come to terms with some stuff. I keep forgetting how much life can change in a war, and how we've all done dumb things that we're not exactly proud of . . ."

"So," he said, "the main thing for you is forgiving me for getting off with Reni."

Reni was the name of the girl he'd been with in Stratton.

I gulped at his question. I had a strong feeling that I was on dangerous ground. But I tried to be honest.

"OK, if you want to put it that way, maybe it is something like that."

Well I'd said it now. I dug one fingernail into each palm and waited. But he didn't blow up. He just lifted his water bottle, which was still empty, and walked away up the hill. As he went he said, "That's not the main thing. The main thing is forgiving myself."

Stupid me, I'd never really thought about that side of it. I'd been too caught up in my own feelings.

I sat for hours trying to work out where to go from there. I didn't have a clue.

I'd have brooded about it twenty-four hours a day if I hadn't got caught up in the project that was in the back of my head all this time.

Christmas.

I wanted to have a Christmas, especially for the kids. We knew from the start it would be the strangest one ever. The kids were thawing out a bit, but God knows, it was hard work. The biggest improvement came because of Gavin. They took their lead from him in almost everything, and after our wild times at the Whittakers' he had a better attitude towards us. He'd had a bad time in the boot of the Alfa, so I suppose he felt fairly grateful about being plucked out of there. But he was still a terror. He'd escaped from Fi within moments of leaving the farmhouse, without a word about his plans. He obviously resented being shunted away from the action. But he'd left her absolutely terrified, not knowing where he'd gone or what had happened. Where he went of course was straight back to the farm. From the way he described it, he'd waited like a fox outside a chook yard. He knew Homer and I were in there.

When Gavin told a story he was a joy to watch. He told it with his whole body. His arms outlined the circle of the house he'd started to take, his face showed how he went from fear to excitement to hatred, and back to fear. On tiptoes he demonstrated his light-footed route around the building, and the way he'd darted into shadows at the slightest sign of human movement.

The other kids watched avidly. So did we. I was fascinated by his ability. If Casey and Jack were going to be engineers, Gavin could be a great actor.

Gavin hadn't seen me grab the bike and charge at the two people. But within a couple of minutes of his arrival he noticed the movement inside: people running past windows and turning on lights. As the house erupted into chaos Gavin retreated towards the machinery shed. Suddenly people poured out of the house, gesturing wildly, sprinting in all directions. A couple of them had rifles. Gavin started stressing big-time. At last a moment came when the area outside the kitchen door was clear. That was all he needed. He went straight at the door, like a dart thrown full-strength. He flung it open. Coming at him was a large motorbike, ridden by two wild and crazy teenage homicidal maniacs . . .

He actually did a pretty good imitation of the two of us, which had Natalie rolling around on the ground holding her sides. I was rapt to see that. Natalie laughing was about as common as Homer crying, or Fi swearing, or emus flying.

I said exactly that to Fi a couple of minutes later, when we were in the toilet area. She was indignant. "I do swear!"

"No you don't!"

"Yes I do! Honestly, I swear lots of times."

"Oh Fi, I've never once heard you swear."

Although as I said that I had a vague memory of Fi saying "bloody" when we were organising the break-in to Tozer's, the night we were so nearly trapped in Wirrawee.

"I do, I do."

I couldn't help teasing her. She was so anxious to prove she was a rebel. The truth is, she was as much a rebel as I was a supermodel.

"OK, so when was the last time you swore?"

"At the farm, at the Whittakers'."

"I didn't hear you. Where are your witnesses? You've got to have witnesses."

"Well, it was to myself. No-one actually heard me."

"Oh! You can't count that!"

"Yes I can," Fi said, totally unreasonably.

The war had changed many or most things but Fi was still as innocent, as untouched by badness, as she had been at the start. I don't know how she did it.

As we washed our hands we talked about Christmas. We decided that today would be 22 December and we announced to the kids at lunchtime that Christmas was in three days. They stopped ripping into their cold lamb and biscuits and looked at us goggle-eyed.

"How can we have Christmas here?" Jack wanted to know.

It was good to get a reaction from Jack. He was still very withdrawn, hardly talking to the other kids, let alone us, although he seemed to think Big Daddy Homer was worth a bit of attention. Poor misguided child.

"Of course we can have it here," I said brightly. "We'll have a tree, and decorations, and we'll sing Christmas carols. And Kevin and Lee are going to go out tomorrow night and get us another lamb, we hope."

"Will Santa Claus come?" Natalie asked.

"Sure will. Santa never lets you down. But the kind of presents he brings will be special bush presents, that he made for the war. No stuff like the old days. No Barbie dolls or videos or roller blades."

Casey and Gavin looked interested, but suspicious. Judging from their faces the general attitude seemed to be "OK, if you can pull this off we might be impressed, but we'll believe it when we see it."

That psyched me up all the more to make it work.

Fi and I spent the afternoon making decorations, helped by Casey and Natalie, who were more hindrance than help. Jack actually dropped by for a little while and did some, while trying hard to look cool about it. I was pleased he'd made the effort.

We made wreaths out of fencing wire from the chook yard, using ivy, lavender and wallflowers from outside the Hermit's hut. Then we did a dozen posies with red berries.

Homer and Kevin and Lee went off to the Hermit's hut to organise the presents. We'd given them suggestions, and we'd ransacked our few possessions to find things we could donate. Considering the ferals had taken so many of our valuables in Stratton we didn't have a lot left. To make it more difficult, it had to be stuff the kids hadn't seen before.

I wanted to give Fi and the boys something too, and I spent a lot of time thinking about what it could be. For Lee I eventually wrote a poem on bark. Bark's great to write on, as good as paper really. I did a bark sketch for

Homer, a picture of his house. For Fi I made a pair of earrings out of wire, with two owl feathers hanging from them. Kevin's present was a burl bowl that I'd deepened a bit with sandpaper, but it was already such a good natural shape that it hadn't needed much work.

It was a busy couple of days. Halfway through it I realised that there'd been a small miracle. Everyone was so busy, so caught up in the Christmas preparations that it was like the war had gone away. No-one even mentioned it. We were so involved in our little secrets that we didn't have time to think about the bad and ugly stuff of the last twelve months. I thought proudly that my Christmas idea had already proved itself. Even if the day was a complete flop it didn't really matter: our Christmas gift had arrived early.

Sure we kept checking Tailor's Stitch for more signs of unwelcome visitors, but everything seemed quiet up there. We had two and a half days of peace, and that was the most precious present any of us could have asked for. All those Christmas cards talking about "peace and goodwill" weren't so stupid after all.

The kids did get genuinely excited. By the time our Christmas Eve arrived they were off their heads. Even Jack, who was about as emotional as a lump of Blu-Tack, got the verbal trots. Well, by his standards. When I said goodnight to him he asked if there'd be any lollies tomorrow, and went into a long boring description of all his favourite sweets from before the war. Natalie checked for about the fiftieth time that Santa could definitely find us down here in Hell, and for the fiftieth time I assured her it wouldn't be a problem, as long as she realised Santa brought different presents for kids in the middle of the bush in the middle of a war. I thought it amazing and touching that in spite of their terrible experiences, Natalie devoutly believed in Santa Claus.

We had to wait hours for the little buggers to get to sleep. I started to understand how aggravating Christmas Eve must have been to our parents. I don't think Gavin or Jack were too into Santa, but they just wanted to stay awake for a stir, and Casey was willing to be persuaded either way.

Anyway we finally got to put out our pathetic little pile of stuff. It sure didn't look like the ads on TV. No tinsel, no glamorous paper, and definitely no BMX's.

In the morning I made them all go to church before anyone was allowed to open their presents. It's what we'd always done at home, and I suppose the longer the war lasted, the longer it seemed important to keep up our customs. So we gathered down by the creek, some of us reluctantly and some quite enthusiastically.

"Are we going to have some of that God stuff?" Jack grumbled. The water gurgled softly in the background, and I read a bit from Robyn's Bible, and we sang "Silent Night" and "While Shepherds Watched Their Flocks," and "Hark the Herald Angels Sing." I don't think it was too exciting for Gavin but the rest made an effort. The thin little voices of the kids mixed with Homer's gruff growl and Kevin's out-of-tune baritone. No-one actually remembered all the words. The first verses were easy: after that it got a bit patchy, but between us we got most of it together.

And then it was pressie time.

To my amazement it went OK. The kids seemed to accept that the rules for Christmas in Hell were completely different to the old days. No-one complained that there was nothing made of plastic, nothing needing batteries, nothing they'd seen advertised on TV. Considering how much whingeing they did most of the time I was pretty happy.

The three guys had done a fantastic job in their toy workshop. For example they'd made sock puppets for Natalie, out of a pair of Homer's old Explorers. They'd sewn button eyes and foam noses and cloth mouths to them, and created funny faces. They were a huge hit with Natalie. Jack got three wooden trucks, with button wheels and wire axles. I think Lee made them. For Casey there was a set of five knuckles they'd picked up from sheep skeletons, in a beautiful little box.

As well as all that stuff, I'd sat up at nights making four wooden crucifixes, which I strung onto bootlaces. This was quite a big deal for me. I did it for Robyn's sake, mainly, but for myself too. The longer this war lasted the more religious I was getting. Looking up at the stars at night, watching those faithful lights, made it harder and harder to believe there couldn't be a controlling force behind it. So I made the crucifixes as a way of trying to call up a bit of extra protection for the kids. I was getting fond of the little critters, even if some days they were lazy and selfish and irritating and irresponsible. After all, Gavin had saved our lives.

The only one who seemed a bit disappointed was Jack, who turned to me with a mournful look and said, "But aren't there any lollies?"

I just shrugged. He was such a sweet tooth. He turned

back to his toy trucks but I had the feeling his day had been spoilt.

Kevin gave me a small didgeridoo, with an apology, because he knew I couldn't really use it at full volume until after the war. Lee gave me a rock, a green-grey colour that changed every few minutes, as the light changed. Fi had made me a wreath with gum leaves on one side and on the other dried grass and green twigs, reflecting the colour of the gum leaves. Homer gave me a pendant carved from bone, a bit like some of the beautiful Maori things we'd seen in New Zealand.

Even Casey and Natalie gave me a present: a bracelet made from plaited grass and twigs, using different colours. I think Casey had done most of the work. It was a nice bracelet; Casey was a talented kid, and she'd done a good job for someone with a broken arm.

They had another one for Fi, and similar for the boys, except theirs went around the neck. Unfortunately Lee's fell apart as soon as he picked it up, but he covered it quickly and no-one else noticed.

Jack and Gavin weren't so organised. They didn't have presents for anyone. I don't know whether it was because they didn't think of it, or because they still didn't feel very positive about us, but they looked a bit embarrassed when Casey and Natalie produced their gifts.

For lunch we had a feast. When I'd dug into the two packs from the Whittakers' I'd found that a few treats had survived. I'd snuck them into my tent and hidden them. The meal started with another surprise though. Kevin and Lee had gone off to get a lamb and returned with four chickens instead. They'd raided my place, and come back triumphantly holding a chook in each hand.

A couple of them were old boilers but the other two were youngish. The boys had taken quite a risk, although our chook shed is a long way from the house. They'd lifted its fence at the bottom and dug under it, to make it look like a fox had tunnelled in there.

They were very full of themselves, very cocky, probably from hanging around with roosters. "We're just lazy," Lee said. "We couldn't be bothered carrying a lamb all the way back here."

I think they wanted to prove something, after the drama we'd got into at the Whittakers'.

It was early in the morning when they arrived and I was the only one up, so we took the chooks off into the bush and plucked and gutted them. It was a long boring job and we didn't do it very well, leaving an awful lot of the little end bits of the feathers in them, but face it, no-one was going to be too bothered by that.

We'd made a meat safe ages back, with a bunch of flyscreen I brought in when we were still using the Land Rover. I'd built a frame from light tree branches and nailed the flyscreen to it, then stitched some old towels to the wire. I put a tray on top of the safe and ran the towels up into that. Then I stood the whole thing in the bottom of a drum, and ran a little pipe out of the drum so the water dripped into a bucket. The physics of this is a bit beyond me, but I think the water condenses or something and that makes it cool. Whatever, as long as we remembered to keep filling the tray at the top, the inside of our meat safe stayed nearly as cold as a fridge. Admittedly it did run dry a couple of times, especially one day when there was a hot wind, but the chooks stayed in good shape and the lamb was still OK after three days.

Our secrecy had worked, and I thought it was worth the trouble when I saw everyone's faces as we unwrapped the chooks from our underground oven. For the first time in Hell we had a choice of food: lamb or chicken, although of course we all ended up going for the chicken. It was so long since we'd smelt that irresistible golden brown aroma. I closed my eyes as I sniffed it and for a moment thought I was back in the Wirrawee Supermarket.

As well as meat, Kevin — who'd become our vegetable specialist — had brought back beans and carrots. I think the kids must have been starved of whatever vitamins are in beans and carrots, because they actually wolfed them down. I couldn't believe it.

Then I produced my coup de grace, if that's the right word. Half a packet of Oreos, and a bag of little Mars Bars. The writing on the outside was not English but Mars Bars taste the same in any language.

I was watching Jack as I produced them. I've never seen so much pure joy. It was like someone switched on a light behind his face. It shone through his eyes, his mouth, his skin. At that moment I definitely forgot the war, and I think he did too.

"Oh," he breathed, "are they really for us?"

I don't know who he thought they were for, the possums maybe.

My best Christmas present was yet to come though. Fi and I had done most of the preparation and cooking, in true female tradition, and in true Christmas tradition we graciously made it clear to the boys and kids that we expected them to do the cleaning up. Preferably before the flies, who were as keen as anyone to have a good

Chrissie and who had swarmed over every bone and scrap of food that was left.

To my surprise though, Lee got up, grabbed a pile of the weird bits and pieces that we called plates, and said, "Ellie and I'll do it. Come on Ellie."

I hesitated, bit back the sharp comment I was about to make, and stood. I joined Lee in piling the plates. As we marched away to the creek with our arms full, followed by a swarm of optimistic flies, Casey actually wolf-whistled. Little brat! I was glad I had my back to them, so no-one could see my red face.

Down at the water we started soaking the plates and scrubbing them. Neither of us spoke for a while. Casey's wolf-whistle had made me self-conscious. It seemed like no time before we were down to the last plates and I was getting worried that nothing would happen after all. I cursed Casey.

Finally however, as I was looking down at the water, watching the shreds of lamb wash away, I heard a nervous cough, and looked up into Lee's brown eyes.

"Ellie, I just want to say . . ."

He paused. I stood, staring into those eyes, hoping he'd go on, hoping he wouldn't lose courage.

After a moment, he managed to finish the sentence.

". . . I know I haven't done the right thing by you."

I'd been red before; I must have been crimson by now.

"I've made you suffer, for something that wasn't your fault. The whole thing was totally me being selfish and stupid."

"Unbelievable," I thought. "When Lee apologises, he really apologises."

"So," Lee went on, "seeing it's Christmas, I thought it was now or never to say sorry."

I almost smiled, because it wasn't really Christmas at all, just our choice of a day to call Christmas. But it didn't matter.

I sat on my haunches and sighed. A great weight rolled off my back. I gave him a little grin and said, "Thanks."

I could guess what it cost him to say what he had. All the guilt and sadness I'd dammed up seemed to flow away in a quick flood. Somehow, all this time, there'd been a guilty voice in my head trying to tell me that Lee going off with the black-haired girl was my fault. The voice wouldn't shut up, even while another voice inside me told me not to be stupid.

Our conversation didn't end with me throwing myself on him and the two of us making passionate love there by the creek. Sadly our life in Hell wasn't much like Hollywood. I felt so awkward, I guess because it was awkward listening to Lee being humble and embarrassed. I didn't say much more. We went back to the others. I know my mood was different though, because for the next hour and a half I played crazy games with the kids, stuff like hide-and-seek and pin-the-tail on Homer and British bulldog, which I normally wouldn't have done in a pink fit. Then we went down the creek, and played pooh-sticks, which Gavin always won.

One quite strange thing happened though. When I went to put away some food we hadn't used: the nuts and the cooked rice and a tin of corn, I found a lot of it missing. All the almonds and macadamias for a start. It was weird. At first I thought someone had just developed an urge for more food, but it was against all our rules for people to help themselves, even on Christmas Day. And when I asked around they all denied it. Then I thought, "Bush rats, possums, magpies?" But I knew it wasn't them. The nuts had been neatly plucked out of a pile of stuff; no mess left behind. It had to be a human magpie. It was infuriating, because if we couldn't trust the people in Hell, life would get very complicated.

Twelve

Honestly, kids. Sometimes they made me feel like a parent. I found myself stuck with the role of story-teller, and the stories they seemed to want over and over were the ones of my childhood on the farm. It reminded me painfully of when I was their age, on long car trips, or at the kitchen table, or in bed, asking for the stories of my parents' early days. How Mum stood her little sister against a wall with an apple on her head and threw darts at her, until their mother found them at it. She made Mum stand against the wall while she picked up the darts and walked to the other end of the room, then she took aim and made like she was going to open fire. How Dad, at the age of nine, put a wallet on the road with a fishing line attached to it, then hid in the bushes and waited. Every time a car stopped and someone got out to pick up the wallet Dad jerked it away with his fishing line. How when Mum's team lost a game of hockey she persuaded all her teammates to spit on their hands before they shook hands with the opposition. How Dad had his first cigarette, with his mates, and was trying so hard to be cool as he got it out and lit it, but then spoilt the effect by putting the lit end in his mouth. How Mum and Dad met when Dad went to sleep in the back of Mum's ute at a B&S.

So I found myself telling my own stories. It was strange: as I did it I realised how much we get shaped by our stories. It's like the stories of our lives make us the people we are. If someone had no stories, they wouldn't be human, wouldn't exist. And if my stories had been different I wouldn't be the person I am.

My stories were often simple things but often they were the ones the kids liked most. For example they loved hearing how in Grade 5 we had a craze on Perkins Paste. It was incredibly trendy to have your paste nice and runny. We'd go down at recess and add water to it, and then when the teacher read to us we'd take out our pots and stir them. It got even more exciting when Fi had the brilliant idea of adding texta to hers, and within a day everyone had lurid shades of colour in their Perkins Paste. Totally bizarre, but that's what we did. I can't remember who started the craze or how it ended, but it kept us entertained for weeks.

The farm stories were their favourites though, and they were usually about animals: like the heifer who hung herself. She caught her hind hoof in a rabbit hole and fell over a bank. The story about our cattle dog who got kicked by a bull one day at the saleyards. He flew twenty metres across the yard, got up, shook himself, came in again, got kicked again, flew another twenty metres, got up, slunk away to the truck and never went near another beast as long as he lived. Needless to say he didn't live very much longer, but I didn't tell the kids that. Sometimes you have to be ruthless on a farm, but I thought they'd already heard and seen enough of death.

The time we had a cat bitten by a snake. She was paralysed in the back legs, and we had to feed her with a dropper.

The time I came home from school and found a snake asleep in the kitchen sink, enjoying the stainless steel, so warm from the sun shining through the window.

These were town kids, city kids, all from suburbs of Stratton. As time went on — especially after Christmas Day — they started to tell me their stories.

Casey grew up on the edge of Stratton in a house her father and mother built, staying in a caravan for three years while they built their dream home. She had a brother and a sister and a pair of guinea pigs, named Black and Blue. For a few days after the surrender Stratton was left alone but then the soldiers came. After another week everyone was loaded into trucks and trains and taken away. In the chaos Casey was separated from her family and put in a cattle truck. When the trucks stopped at a railway crossing just out of town she slipped through the side and ran back, looking for the truck her family were in. But the convoy started again and rolled away before she could find them.

Jack lived in a block of flats which we worked out were part of a public housing development near the centre of Stratton. He was an only kid and his parents were divorced. He lived with his dad. One day, after the soldiers had taken over the city, his dad didn't come home. Jack had no idea what to do as they didn't really know anyone in the housing development, and his dad didn't like him mixing with the neighbours. So he fed himself and fell asleep on the sofa. The next thing there was noise everywhere outside. The soldiers had arrived to take people away. Jack was terrified. He hid in a big trunk in the bedroom, and although they broke the door down they were only in the flat a minute. When Jack finally emerged the blocks of flats were deserted.

Gavin followed these stories, including mine, with fantastic accuracy. When it was his turn, he described the soldiers coming to his house. His face burned with anger as he remembered. He told us how one of them hit his little sister because she was too slow getting in the truck, and he charged across the clearing to show how he'd attacked the soldier. Then he sent himself sprawling into the dust, as though the soldier was knocking him down all over again. A moment later he went into such grief as he explained how the truck drove away without him that I didn't know if he was acting it out for us, or going through the real mourning for his family. Probably both.

Gavin only had a mother and sister; his father died in a factory explosion when Gavin was three years old.

The saddest thing about the kids' stories was that Natalie had so little to say. She had already forgotten most of her life before the war. She couldn't remember her parents' first names, for instance. She knew her surname was Keast and she knew she'd lived in Summer Crescent, but she couldn't remember the number. She couldn't remember the name of her school, or her teacher's name, or her friends' names, or her telephone number, or anything about her aunties or uncles or cousins. She knew she'd been in Grade 2 in her last year of school, that her nanna and pop had a horse, that she'd broken her collarbone once when she fell off a swing, and that her favourite toy had been called Night-night Nellie because she took it to bed with her each night. There wasn't a lot more.

It scared me to realise how shadowy our memories can be. In English we'd read a book called *Night* and Mrs Kawolski told us how the author once said that the opposite to identity is Alzheimer's Disease. Now I wondered if the opposite to identity was war. By separating us from our pasts, by tearing out all the previous pages of our lives, war had left us with nothing. I felt my life began last January and what went before was a vague dream, growing vaguer every day. And if it was like that for me, how much worse was it for Natalie? She had barely begun her life, barely begun to grow into a human being, and already her world was being dismantled around her.

I was keen to get them to tell me what happened in Stratton during the last year but it took a long time before they'd say much about that. I never did get a story with a beginning, a middle and an end. Instead there were fragments, bits and pieces, random comments that I gradually put together into a history.

None of our four kids had been in the group from the start. They'd all survived on their own for different periods of time, before getting caught up with the gang of ferals who'd mugged us in the alley. It seemed like they'd had as many as twenty in that group for a while. But the numbers kept changing. People came and went. Some were arrested or killed. Three got sick and died.

A kid called Aldo had held them together. I got the impression that he was a real dictator, but he must have been quite a personality. The kids complained that he was "bossy" but they obviously admired him, and I couldn't help thinking that their survival might have been due to Aldo. Without a strong leader I doubt if they would have lasted five minutes. Aldo was full of ideas for getting food, for avoiding the soldiers, and for protecting themselves with booby traps and sentries. Gavin had been one of his main men but our other three seemed to have been very small-time in the organisation.

And despite Aldo's efforts they'd been through some awful times. They'd all had illnesses, and it seemed like no-one cared for them much when they did. Ordinary things that would have been easily fixed in peacetime, like colds and coughs, dragged on for weeks. They had endless bouts of gastro; in fact it sounded like two of the dead kids had died from that. They got infections. Casey told me how a cut on her leg was infected for weeks: her leg swelled to twice its normal size and got red and hot, until she had fever and delusions. I think she must have been quite lucky to survive that. The other kids had similar experiences.

They told wild stories about one boy who they obviously hated, but who sounded like he was a bit mad, probably because of the war. He stabbed another boy with a pair of scissors, and Aldo kicked him out of the group, but he kept hanging around for weeks, saying strange things to them when they met him on the streets. Then he disappeared, and they never saw him again.

I suppose really they'd done quite well. Face it, anyone who'd survived this long had done well. They knew that being kids gave them a slight edge, because the soldiers weren't going to waste a lot of time and energy chasing kids. As long as they didn't give the soldiers too much grief they had a better chance than adults of escaping capture.

At first they did get help from various adults they ran into but it wasn't long before those people became rarer and rarer. Then a man who befriended them tried to rape one of the girls and after that they didn't trust adults. They mugged a few people and stole odds and ends, but by the time we came along they hadn't seen anyone outside their own group for months. A few times they found food left in really obvious places, but when they ate it they got sick, and they were sure it had been poisoned: a deliberate attempt by the enemy to finish them off. That's why they ignored the food I left for them.

The one thing they found extremely embarrassing was the attack on us. Every time I mentioned it, even in a joking way, they went red and mumbled and suddenly found something important they had to do. One thing for sure, we didn't get any of our stuff back. I knew I'd never see my watch or ring again.

So we swapped a lot of stories and played a few games, but time passed slowly, and not long after Christmas it became obvious to all us big kids that boredom was getting to be a problem for the little kids.

I think it was Fi who suggested we start a school. We were sitting around the fireplace, where we always seemed to meet, even though most of the time there was no fire.

There was no fire that night. The kids had gone to bed ages before. We let them stay up pretty late usually, but they'd been driving us crazy all day with their squabbles and whinges and questions.

We got the giggles as we talked about having a school. I don't think any of us ever imagined ourselves as teachers. Not in recent years anyway. In primary school we'd often played schools, and through my Grade 3 and 4 years it had been my favourite game. My ambition was to be like Mr Coles, my Grade 4 teacher. I'd grown out of that ambition.

But now we thought it'd be pretty funny if we ran a school. We started making up stupid rules, like uniform policy and library behaviour and how to queue for the buses. Homer wanted to have detentions and letters home for being naughty. Fi wanted parent-teacher interviews. Kevin insisted the kids should line up to go in, stand when we entered the school area, and say "Good Morning Mr Holmes" in a singsong voice at the start of the day.

Once we'd got over the giggles we did give it some serious thought. It seemed like a pretty good idea. Not only because it would help them remember their lessons and learn new stuff, but also because it would help them realise that there might be a future, after the war. They didn't have to give up.

When we suggested it to the kids in the morning, over breakfast, to our astonishment they were really keen. We nearly fell over. Later in the day though, away on my own in the bush, collecting firewood and thinking about life, I could understand why they might be so willing. They'd spent a year living like animals, learning nothing. I think they were longing for normal life again, but they were also longing to learn. After all, it's natural for humans, isn't it? To want to learn. Being curious, wanting answers: that's the way we are. Just because school's boring so much of the time, that doesn't mean kids don't want to learn.

So we started the very next day. The kids wanted to treat it as a big joke at first but when they saw that we were serious, they picked up the pace. We knew we had to treat it seriously from the beginning, because if we didn't, the kids would stuff around. Fi and I taught them English, Kevin taught them Science (which he was actually quite good at), Lee did the Art and Music, and Homer ran the Maths (which he was actually quite hopeless at).

It was surprisingly hard. I thought Lee had the toughest job, because there was a severe shortage of materials for his subjects. But Lee, no doubt about him, he was creative. For musical instruments he had the kids make pipes out of wood, and hollow tent poles, as well as using stuff like water bottles and of course the good old gum leaf whistle. He said you could make music with anything, and I guess he proved it. Gavin picked up on rhythms pretty well, and I'd often come across him pressed up close to one of the other kids, using his hands and body to feel the vibrations.

As Jack told us, Gavin did have some hearing: one night in a thunderstorm, when there was a bigger than normal boom of thunder he said, in his quaint voice, "That was loud," then rolled around laughing at the look on my face. He'd said it to get just that reaction.

Lee taught them theory too, and basic rhythm stuff,

like clapping back a rhythm to him. It was quite fun and I often joined in. I have to admit, the kids were better than I was. Once the sequence got complicated I'd lose it. I'd go "Clap-clap, clap-clap, clap," instead of "Clap-clap-clap, clap-clap," and they'd look at me pityingly and Lee would roll his eyes.

Lee's biggest problem was volume. We couldn't let the kids make much noise, so all the music had to be played in whispers. I gave my didgeridoo, my Christmas present from Kevin, a few trials, and although it sounded like farts and burps at first, I did get some quite good sounds out of it.

After a session with Lee, clapping and humming and singing, and playing home-made didgeridoos *pianissimo,* it was time for Science with Kevin. He got them planting seeds and collecting insects and doing experiments with levers and pulleys and inclined planes. Kevin was a revelation. The rest of us bumbled around and made a lot of mistakes, especially by underestimating or overestimating what the kids could do, or trying activities that were too corny or too complicated. Kevin seemed to know instinctively what would and wouldn't work. Before long we were asking his opinion about our lessons, getting his advice.

Most of the time I liked teaching English, although some days I wasn't in the mood, and on those days we got pretty slack. I guess Fi kind of took her lead from me so if I was in a slack mood she didn't take over and fire the troops up with enthusiasm and energy. On those days we were more likely to sit by the creek chucking pebbles at sticks, trying to sink them. But generally I'd say we worked quite hard. Casey had trouble writing because her arm was still in its splint, but I think sometimes she said it was hurting just so she could get out of work. Natalie's reading was rusty but she slowly picked it up again. Fi and I wrote stories for her, then we got the smart idea of having Gavin and Jack write stories for her too, because they really liked Natalie and spoiled her outrageously. They hadn't been too keen on writing before that, but they thought they were pretty cute doing those stories.

Some of the stuff they wrote was sad though. I got a much better understanding of their life in Stratton when I read their stories. Jack wrote one that said, "Once upon a time there were some kids living in a house and they ate yucky horrible awful food like soft apples and marmalade and heaps of sardines and then one day the soldiers came and shot two of the kids and then another day some nice big kids came and took the other kids away to a hidy place in the bush."

That was the whole story. I already knew they'd found a carton of sardines in a shop, but I didn't know about the two children being shot.

Gavin wrote, as though it were the wildest fantasy, "There was this magic land. A boy and a girl lived there with their mum. They lived in a nice house with a swimming pool and a TV. One night they had roast chicken for tea, then they had ice-cream with banana flavouring. Then their mum gave them a big kiss and a hug goodnight and they went to sleep in a nice bed."

It seemed like when they wrote stories for Natalie they let down their defences.

I was glad we had a good pile of paper, which was only

because I'd brought heaps with me for myself, but it was scary how fast we used it.

We went on like this for four weeks after our Christmas. Time started to drift again. I measured it by a couple of things: one was our weekly trips out of Hell to get food. We'd had a conference after the near disaster of the trip to the Whittakers', and decided meat, fruit and vegetables would be the safest way to go from now on. In practice that meant grabbing a lamb out of a paddock — a different paddock each trip — and raiding orchards and gardens in the middle of the night for fruit and vegies. It wasn't much fun, digging up spuds at three in the morning, in such a way that no-one would notice we'd been there, but we kept ourselves quite healthy and well fed on that diet. The kids certainly looked a lot better after a few weeks of it. They started putting on weight, and playing with more energy, and even working better at their school lessons.

The other way I measured time was by our calls to Colonel Finley. Once a week, by arrangement, we trudged to the top of Wombegonoo and contacted New Zealand. They were brief calls, because we didn't want to waste our batteries, and because we were worried about being tracked down by our radio frequencies, and because there wasn't much to say. We didn't have the honour of talking to Colonel Finley himself any more, but the operator passed on his messages, which were worded in different ways but always amounted to the same thing: "Stay put, we'll advise."

It seemed that somehow we'd become soldiers under the Colonel's orders, which suited us just fine, because it meant that as long as he was telling us not to do anything we could relax in Hell without feeling too guilty.

When time stopped drifting it wasn't because of any orders from Colonel Finley. There were some things he couldn't control all the way from New Zealand.

Homer and I climbed out of Hell at eight o'clock one night for the radio check. There had been a time when all of us, kids included, would go up there, full of excitement, trying not to chatter too loudly. Now however, with the novelty worn off, there wasn't a rush of volunteers. I always enjoyed the view from the high peak of Wombegonoo though, and it was a nice night for a walk. I was actually relieved the kids had lost interest, because when they did come it was too hard to keep them quiet. They were a lot more relaxed these days, and they seemed unable to believe there could be any danger from soldiers out here in the bush. I had once felt that way myself, but I'd been on maximum alert since Lee showed me the warm fireplace at the enemy campsite.

Whenever we went up to Tailor's Stitch now we took weapons, from our little stockpile of rifles and shotguns. Unfortunately our ammunition supplies were still almost non-existent. We hadn't picked up anything from the Whittakers'. On this trip I actually forgot to take a rifle, until Homer caught up with me and handed me one.

I'd left early, calling to Homer as I went, "I'll meet you on the top."

I wanted some time and space. Hell seemed pretty crowded these days, with the four kids. They were at me day and night, wanting to play, wanting to show me their stories or homework, wanting to jump all over me.

So I got to the top on my own and sat on a rock above the tree that marked the end of our track. By God I saw a sight then. The top of the full moon was just appearing and I sat and watched it like it was the greatest show on Earth. It was, too. I can never get over how huge the moon is when you see it at close quarters. I don't know much Geography, but I guess the moon must be heaps closer to Earth when it's rising, and that's why it's so big.

There were hundreds of clouds around, all white and see-through, so even though they formed a kind of patchwork over the moon, it lit up the landscape enough for the trees and rocks to cast shadows.

On the other side of the sky was a bright star that I guess was Venus. I know they call Venus the evening star, because it's the first one out, and the brightest. This star certainly was bright. It hung quite low, shining through the clouds like it was powered by neon.

I didn't hear Homer until there was a slither of loose stones behind me. I turned around and he grinned and gave me a rifle.

"It's not bad, is it?" he said, nodding at the moon.

"Sorry," I said, embarrassed that I'd forgotten the rifle.

"Oh well." He shrugged. "I wouldn't have bothered if I knew I had to bring it all the way up here. I didn't realise how far ahead you were. I kept thinking I'd catch up with you at any moment."

By now the moon was well clear of the horizon and it was getting close to our call-time. I stood, lifted the rifle with one hand and picked up the radio with the other. We walked up to Wombegonoo, not taking any special precautions, but not being stupid either. These days we moved silently and cautiously as a matter of course. And on such a clear night any sound seemed magnified twenty times.

The last bit was a scramble up rocks, where it was almost impossible not to make a noise. To tell the truth, we weren't trying that hard. Our Christmas celebration, and the nice weeks we'd had since then, had us too relaxed. Sometimes I almost forgot there was a war on.

I shudder to think what would have happened if we'd gone up Wombegonoo a few minutes later.

I put up the aerial and once again got through with a minimum of fuss. We'd had a good run with radio calls lately. Certainly we'd had none of the weird static that messed us around when we were hanging out in Stratton. A woman, the same woman who nearly always answered these days, came through so loudly I hastily turned down the volume. This woman felt like an old friend, even though I didn't know her name.

I began our report, which was really just a matter of saying we had nothing to report, when suddenly Homer lifted slightly beside me and leaned forward, quivering like he was made of brand-new fencing wire. I stopped talking and gazed anxiously at him.

"Shut down," he hissed, without looking around.

I should have turned the set off straightaway, but if there was danger I wanted New Zealand to know, only because I couldn't bear facing it on our own. Sure they were a long way away, safe and sound, but it might be some consolation to know they were thinking of us.

So I whispered into the radio, "We're in trouble," then slammed off the switch. I shoved the set into its little pack, and slung it over my neck. Then I had a second and better thought. Taking it off again I rammed it in a hollow under a rock to my right, just hoping I wasn't pushing my hand into a snake hole.

Homer was leaning forward even further, then he crouched and slid down the hill a couple of metres, reaching for his rifle. That scared me. I picked up mine. I wished I knew how many rounds of ammunition were in it. I suddenly remembered the time Gavin shadowed us, so I slid after Homer and tapped him on the shoulder. He didn't look around.

"It might be Gavin again," I muttered. He just nodded, and moved a couple more metres. I still didn't have a clue what had caught his attention. But I brought my rifle up to my shoulder, slipped off the safety, and followed.

We'd gone maybe ten metres, taking a good five minutes, Homer with his rifle raised too, when at last I saw something. It was a shadow moving from one tree to another. It only took a second. By then though, my nerves were stretched by the five minutes of suspense, and I nearly dropped my .22. I knew one thing straightaway. That shadow hadn't been Gavin. He wasn't that tall. It could have been Lee or Kevin but it wasn't. My message to New Zealand had been deadly accurate. We were in big trouble.

I got in next to Homer. "How many do you think there are?"

"I've seen three."

"I've only seen one."

We waited another couple of minutes, unsure of which way to go, what to do. Then I saw another shadow, away to my left, getting around behind us. My insides turned to water. I felt like I had an elephant in my stomach. I felt like I had two elephants in my stomach, and they were mating.

"I think they're surrounding us," I whispered to Homer.

"Shit," he said.

We gazed desperately to right and left.

"We've got to do something," I muttered.

I meant that we had to take the initiative, like when Gavin followed us. It was something we had to keep remembering in this war. If we stayed where we were we'd be finished off as easily as rabbits in a ferret net.

We started wriggling forward, side by side. The whole thing had an air of unreality, and in the back of my mind I still half-wondered if Lee or Kevin might be playing a joke. Of course they wouldn't be so stupid, when they knew we had rifles. But there wasn't time to think things through like that. I had to concentrate on scanning the hilltop around us. Nothing else mattered.

In the light of the full moon it was like alien territory. There were no trees up here and hardly any vegetation. There was moss, sure, and the odd plant, but you couldn't see much of them at this time of night. Virtually all the landscape was rocks, large, medium, small. Grey, black, white. I'd always thought it was very beautiful but suddenly it seemed like a bare and lonely place to end my life. I guess that's why I stuck so close to Homer.

We got to the edge of the summit, where the ground started to dip a little. Right up to that point nothing had happened; we were still in the unreal world where time and space didn't seem to function.

That all changed in an instant. A shot smashed through the silence and the darkness. It came from the left, slightly behind us. I was so close to Homer that I felt his body stiffen and rise off the ground. For a terrible moment I thought he'd been hit. But if he had, the bullet would have gone through me first. It was sheer shock that made him lift like that. I probably went up as far as he did. It was horrifying. The noise was so horrifying, crashing through the silence like thunder. You could feel the air split in half.

I'd seen the flash of the rifle and as I flattened myself on the ground I slithered around and lined up where I thought it was. I waited a few seconds, and as soon as I saw a slight movement, almost exactly where I was watching, I fired. My ears rang with the noise. I heard not the slightest sound from the boulders, but after a moment a dark shape fell slowly forward, like a tree that you've felled but which is slowed in its fall by the branches of other trees.

The man hit the ground, still without a sound. For a moment, as I realised what I'd done, there was silence. It was like the Earth stopped revolving. Even the breeze died. "Good shot," Homer whispered. It seemed a funny choice of words. I'd just killed someone.

And then suddenly it was fight time. Everything lit up. Bullets flew. I flattened myself still further. A rock-picker could have gone right over me. It wouldn't have touched a hair of my body. The bullets whizzed everywhere. They sounded like jackhammers. These guys must have had their weapons on automatic, the way they let fly. It went on for thirty or forty seconds. I felt my teeth rattle with the vibrations of the air around me. A lot of the bullets were phosphorescent or something because they burned through the air like fireworks, whooshing overhead and leaving a blue-white trail. I'd never seen those before.

I realised in the middle of it that Homer was on the move again, without even telling me. He wriggled away towards a group of low flattish rocks. "Thanks Homer," I thought crossly, following him. I knew I was grazing myself, dragging across the ground, taking skin off, bumping and scratching. But that didn't seem too important. A bullet would do a lot more damage.

As suddenly as it began, the uproar ended. It was like someone threw a switch. My ears rang, but not from any new noises, just the after-effects of the firing. The fresh mountain air stank of gunpowder. A cloud of white smoke drifted away over the valley. Homer and I, both panting with fear, huddled into the tallest rock.

"How many do you reckon there are?" he asked me.

"No idea."

He didn't say anything, so I whispered, "Let's try down the steep side."

"OK. But I'm sure there's at least one over there."

"We'll have to shoot our way out."

"I know."

I gave his hand a quick squeeze and we started sliding across the knobbly ground. It was so difficult doing it and holding the rifle ready at the same time. I realised I still hadn't checked to see how many rounds were in the magazine, and cursed myself for being so careless. But it was too late now. I had to pray like mad that if I pointed it at someone and pulled the trigger, it would go off. The worst sound in the world for me would be the click of the firing pin, with no explosive blast to follow it.

A shot like a whiplash came from our left, and an instant later Homer fired straight ahead. He hit someone, because there was a terrible scream, and then a series of short sharp screams that went on and on. It was like a car's burglar alarm. We both realised the noise might give us some cover, because it was so distracting. So we hurried forward, moving about ten metres in a quick rush. Then the sound stopped in mid-scream. There was a horrible gurgling noise that made me feel like I had ants running up the back of my neck. But I couldn't think about that. I swivelled to the left, looking for the person who had fired from over there. I saw nothing. It was too dark in that direction. A glance behind showed Homer was covering the area to our right. At least I could concentrate on whoever was in those shadows. I peered and peered, screwing up my eyes, but I still couldn't see any suspicious moves. I was getting desperate. We couldn't afford to get pinned down for long.

Homer tapped me on the ankle and signalled that we should go forward.

We started our next wriggle. But the guy I'd been trying to pinpoint opened up on us. We lay there as a stream of bullets howled above our heads. The only shelter we had was rocks that looked about ten centimetres high. OK, thirty centimetres maybe. Anyway, they were low. Twice I felt like bullets actually touched my hair.

What was worse was that they were ricocheting, which meant they could go in any direction. Almost as bad were the fragments of stone. These guys were rearranging the landscape. Rocks exploded both sides of me. Chips whined all around us. I got hit by a couple, and even through my clothes they stung. I was lucky that was all they did. One of them going at full velocity would go through soft flesh like a bullet.

The moment the man stopped, Homer and I were both up and firing at him. Homer nearly shot my head off. Luckily he missed. But we both missed the man too. He fired two shots back at us, then I saw him at last, running to a new position. This time I could see where he'd gone, behind a tree down the ridgeline a little. I whispered to Homer, "Have you got much ammo?"

"Yeah, still got a bit."

"Did you see where he went?"

"Yeah."

"Can you pin him down?"

He hesitated, then nodded. He raised his rifle to his shoulder and opened fire on the tree. I went for my life — literally — over the chopped-up ground. I didn't even look at the tree until I thought I'd gone far enough. All that time Homer kept banging away. Panting like I'd run a couple of k's I got in behind a ridge of higher ground, and peeped over the top. Now I could see the man, a black smudge against the tree trunk. I couldn't miss at that range. And the rifle fired when I squeezed the trigger. I definitely wasn't out of ammo. I think I got him through the head.

I felt then that we might have a chance. Three down: how many could they have altogether? Surely not a huge number, way up here, so far from anywhere.

I heard a shuffling behind me and looked around. Homer had arrived. "You got him?" he half-asked, half-said.

I nodded.

"Good on you."

I tried to think. We had to make a critical decision. If we went further down the ridgeline and soldiers were behind us or in front, we'd be totally exposed, because we'd have no cover down there. On the other hand if we went back up on the summit we might walk into another ambush, or get surrounded again. That's where the rocks were though, and they gave good cover. The temptation was to head downhill, because ultimately, it led to safety. But if we tried to get there too early . . . Patience might save our lives yet.

I said to Homer, "I think we should go back up into the rocks."

He looked doubtful. He was as unsure as I was. I said, "They won't be expecting it."

That clinched it. Homer always loved doing the last thing the enemy expected. We started sliding back up the hill. Then I had a better idea. "Wait," I hissed to Homer, who was two body lengths ahead of me.

I made a fast move to the right, sliding part of the way, crouching and running part of it. It was tough: every moment I expected my head to be blown off my shoulders. But I was at the tree sooner than I thought.

The man was dead all right. I'd got him with a head shot, like I thought. One side of the skull was still untouched, but the rest was simply blown away. There was blood and stuff everywhere, against the trunk of the tree and over the rocks and ground. I didn't look at it much. Somehow he'd fallen so that the butt of his rifle was under him, and I had to lever the barrel backwards and forwards a few times before I could get it out. It was like the man I'd run over in the corridor at the Whittakers'.

But I did get it. And for the first time in this battle I

felt a little confidence. I knew this type of rifle. Iain and the Kiwis used the same ones. They were called M-somethings, I think. The magazine was plastic, and had at least twenty rounds.

My hands were sticky with blood from the butt. I wiped them on my jeans, and set out on the return journey to where Homer was waiting.

I nearly didn't make it. A wall of gunfire started blazing at me, from downhill. At least we'd been right, deciding not to go down there. I wasn't thinking about that though. I dived like a Rugby player, both hands still holding the new rifle, and flew through the air. Counting the bounces I must have gone six or eight metres, because I sure did bounce: over a series of small rocks, and coming to rest beside Homer.

I nearly bashed him with the gun.

The moment there was a break in the fire we took off again, this time ducking and weaving and zigzagging madly to get to the cover of the bigger rocks. We both aimed for the same little hollow, which wasn't a good idea, as there was barely room for one. We arrived there together and somehow squeezed in, gasping and shaking.

"I think there's three of them," Homer said.

"Oh God," was all I could say.

But after a minute I said, "I'll go higher, see if I can get a view from up above. Once those clouds blow away, there might be quite a bit of light."

"All right. Be careful. I'll go up that side, and cover you."

"Don't shoot me by mistake."

I set off up the ridgeline, bearing to the left. I got

about halfway before the firing started again, and again it was full-on. I went to ground, waiting for it to stop. It was just too dangerous. I didn't know if they'd seen me. The firing seemed to be pretty random. Bullets were flying everywhere. Only at the last moment before it stopped did I realise what it was really about. I caught a glimpse of a guy running across the hill above me, from left to right. Of course. They were providing cover for one or more people up there, so they could get in better positions. I called to Homer, "Look out, they're above us."

"Thanks," he called back.

I felt I had to keep going up. Absolutely the worst thing would be to stay in one spot for any length of time. Grimly, wondering what I was letting myself in for, I snuck a little further. The shots from below had stopped again and no-one had fired from their new positions above.

From my right I heard Homer's rifle speak, once, twice, three times. It was easily recognisable, a light little crack compared to the continuous bangs of the military weapons. It was an encouraging sign, that he had found a target. I hoped he'd hit it.

I got to a little knob of high ground and at last got a useful view, although not of the people down the ridgeline. I searched for them but couldn't see anyone in among the trees.

After a minute I glanced to my left. I'm glad I did. To my intense surprise I realised I was looking straight at a nice ambush prepared for Homer. Somehow they hadn't heard me coming. I scanned the area like I had a TV camera in my head. There were only two of them —

that I could see, anyway — but they were perfectly placed. Or they thought they were.

Just as they hadn't seen me, Homer hadn't seen them. Feeling like I was in a spell, almost unable to believe they hadn't noticed me, I peered at the closer one over the sights of my rifle.

I had to gamble that there were only two. But suddenly they both moved forward a few metres. Now I didn't have good shots at either of them. With one, I could just see the top of his head. With the other I could see an arm, and a bit of one leg.

It was no good waiting any longer. Homer was a second away from being blown to bits.

Was I ever grateful for my new rifle. I lined them up again, felt for the little switch on the left-hand side of the receiver, swivelled it down to "continuous shot" and pressed the trigger. It was a beautiful rifle, light, but I realised after a few rounds that the rebound was making it drift up, and I was shooting high. A few seconds later it did it again. I turned the switch back to "3"s, and that seemed to suit it better. It held its line pretty well now.

It was their turn to come under heavy fire. I just hoped Homer wasn't getting hit by ricochets. But in fact the next time I saw him was when he shot at one of the men. He sure had reacted quickly. He'd moved right up to a neat line of rocks near the very top of Wombegonoo. From there he popped up, fired one shot, and bobbed down again.

I think he wanted to advertise his presence, and it worked. Now the two men started to panic. They suddenly realised that instead of pinning Homer down and picking him off at random, they were themselves caught in a crossfire. I could hear them shouting at each other. Then one of them bolted, charging straight down the hill, carrying his rifle, but with one hand over his head, as if to stop a bullet hitting him. I swung my rifle around, lined him up and hesitated. But I didn't have to do anything. Homer wasn't as squeamish as me. He dropped the man with two shots, fired so close together it sounded almost like one. Crack, crack.

Everything up until then had happened fairly quickly. There'd been periods of stillness and silence, like when I'd shot the first guy, but not for long. Now everything happened so fast my head spun. It started with one of the worst moments of the entire war. The last soldier up here near the summit threw his rifle out from behind his rock. I'd never seen anyone do that before but I realised what it must mean: he was surrendering. A moment later he came into the open with his hands stretched in front of him. Almost like he was holding them for someone to put handcuffs on his wrists. I don't know why he didn't put his hands up in the air, like they do in movies. If he did he would have saved his life. Homer, coming down through the rocks, swiftly and silently and bravely, saw the man from behind, saw him emerging from his hiding place towards me, and thought he was holding a weapon in front of him. Homer shot him down from behind before I even realised he was there.

It was a terrible thing but I can see how it happened. It wasn't like Homer had five minutes to weigh up the situation, consider the evidence and make a decision. He had a millisecond. Even as he pulled the trigger he knew he'd made a mistake, but guns don't know about mistakes. Guns don't believe in mistakes.

Another millisecond later, before I could even think about the man dead on the ground, and the massive river of blood flooding from his body, the soldiers down the ridge launched a full-on attack. With their rapid-fire rifles they protected themselves behind a curtain of bullets. It completely intimidated me. They attacked in a different way, advancing up the ridge, out in the open, firing non-stop. By now I guess they'd figured there were only two of us.

Homer was as intimidated as I was. We both dived into the nearest cover: for me a shallow depression, for Homer a little rock crater, almost rectangular. I lay there, heart still pounding from the shock of seeing the man surrender and then get killed, the shock of seeing so much blood, more blood than I'd ever seen from one person before, my heart pounding all the harder as I realised that this was the crisis. There was nothing we could do except maybe stand up and die in a death-and-glory shoot-out, hoping to get one of them before they got us.

To make things worse, Homer was too far away and there was too much noise for us to plan anything. If we could have stood up together we might have even got two of them but I was sure, judging by the heavy fire, that there were more than two. It seemed we were both going to die alone.

The firing was so continuous and intense that I couldn't even peep over the edge to see what was happening. I knew they were approaching at a pretty fast bat. I got my rifle ready. The racket became deafening. Smoke drifted across my head. I looked up, expecting at any moment to see the top of a cap, then a head, then a gun barrel that would blow my life into oblivion. I caught a quick glimpse of the night sky, a smattering of stars, and thought, "Well, I guess that's a good last sight to see."

Better to die here, in my beloved bush, on a mountain, than in a gutter or a dump-bin.

Then behind the wall of noise, quite a way off, sounding thin and light, I heard a series of other shots. And suddenly my ears rang with silence, where a moment earlier they had rung with noise. The smoke drifted but there were no more shots. As I lay there, trembling, wondering what was happening, whether this was another trap, a new noise did start up. It was a series of coughs, four in a row, going from strong to weak, then starting again, strong to weak, four at a time. They could be heard clearly in the still air.

I heard a different voice.

"Ellie! Homer!"

I peeped over the edge of the shallow hollow. I was ultra-cautious, because it seemed too good to be true. The first thing that caught my eye was a body: a soldier about ten metres from me. He was the one doing the coughing. As I stared at him, his head fell quietly to one side, his mouth slowly opened, his eyes opened like he'd seen something very surprising, and I realised he'd coughed for the last time. I looked beyond him. I saw three people I'd almost forgotten about. They looked beautiful, walking up through the trees, out of the mist, or the smoke, whichever it was.

Lee and Kevin, and in the distance behind them, Fi.

Thirteen

Our gunfight had raged so long that it gave Lee and Kevin time to grab weapons and the last of our ammo and come belting up out of Hell. I guess it would have been the last thing on the minds of the enemy patrol, that in this wild and remote spot we'd have reinforcements coming up behind them.

The whole area was a mess. We found eight bodies altogether. Some were intact: just lying there, no blood even. Some weren't.

After we'd checked it all out we met halfway between the summit and the top of the path into Hell. We had a conference that we knew was hugely important. We had to make some decisions, based on guesses, but they had to be right.

No sooner had we started than Gavin arrived. I don't think any of us were surprised to see him.

"The others were too scared to come," he said, "but I wasn't."

In some ways he was tougher than us. As he passed one body he gave it a kick in the side. Homer grabbed him fiercely. "Don't do that," he said.

Gavin just shrugged.

"Well?" Lee asked me.

"My mother told me not to sit on cold things," Fi said, tucking her legs under her, "or I'd get something horrible, I can't remember what."

We were sitting on a ring of cold rocks. Fi was shivering continuously.

"Haemorrhoids," Homer said.

Seemed like everyone was trying to distance themselves from what had happened, but no-one more than Fi. There was a blankness about her that I hadn't seen too often. She was trying to be funny, to make a joke, sure, but it didn't work. Her heart wasn't in it. She could have been a thousand k's away.

We couldn't afford luxuries like distance. We had to concentrate.

"They would have been a patrol, either doing a general check of the area, or looking for us in particular," I said. "We know people were camping up here a few weeks ago. I guess it was these guys."

I looked around at their faces as I tried to think this through. It wasn't easy while I was still shaking from the narrow escape we'd had, the number of soldiers we'd just killed. But trying to keep my voice steady, talking carefully but urgently, I kept going.

"I've seen some of their packs, down there," I said, nodding at the trees. "It looks like they've got a heap of stuff. That suggests they were up here for a while. We've got that much in our favour. Sure they'll have radios for reporting to someone, but by the time those people realise they haven't heard from them for a day or two, and then get someone all the way up here to look for them, and, most importantly . . ." I paused, as I suddenly realised how we could buy time, "by the time they find the bodies, I reckon we've got at least three days."

"Not that long," Homer said.

"Yes, that long," I answered him. "And we can get longer."

I glanced at the line of thick cloud away on the horizon. "What I'm thinking is, if we carry all the bodies down into Hell and bury them, and if that cloud brings a good shower, we could make a big difference. If the rain washes away the blood and stuff, and wipes out our scent — I'm saying that in case they bring dogs up here — then what have they got? A few thousand square kilometres of mountains and somewhere in them an entire patrol disappears without a trace." I tried to laugh. "It could become the great mystery of the war. It might start rumours. Like the *Marie Celeste*. In years to come people might refuse to come up here in case it's haunted. It'll be the Bermuda Triangle on land. That'd be excellent for us."

They had listened in silence, and the silence continued after I'd finished.

Finally Homer said, "That sounds fair enough. But I think we should call New Zealand and give them an idea of what's happened. They might have some advice."

We were all keen to do that, again more for the reassurance of adult support.

We went back to where I'd hidden the radio and pulled it out. When we made contact it was with the same woman.

"We've had a big problem," I said. "We've been attacked. I don't think this is safe any more. We're not sure what to do from here. Or where to go. Over."

She just said, very crisply, "Can you call back in thirty?"

"OK. Over."

We busied ourselves on the big clean-up, taking the

dead soldiers' packs and rifles to the top of our track and using belts and straps to make a couple of stretchers. We knew that when the sun rose we'd have to pick up the hundreds of empty shells scattered around the landscape.

The clouds were getting closer and looking heavier, so that was one good thing.

We'd barely started the stretchers before it was time to call New Zealand again. The voice that came out of the radio receiver was a big surprise.

"Good morning Ellie," Colonel Finley said.

Everyone crowded around the set. We were very excited to hear the man who had such a big impact whenever he entered our lives.

"Oh, Colonel Finley, we're glad to hear your voice. We've had a lot of trouble. We nearly got caught by a patrol. I think they knew roughly where we were hiding. We had a full-on battle. Over."

"Any casualties?" That was unusual, Colonel Finley asking about our health before anything else.

"Not on our side. Total casualties on theirs."

"How many? Over."

"Eight. Over."

There was a couple of seconds of crackle: thinking time I guess. Somehow I felt my answer had been important. I think maybe the knowledge that we had taken out a patrol of eight soldiers convinced Colonel Finley yet again that we were seriously successful at what we were doing; we weren't just kids who got lucky once in a while.

"Do you think you'll be safe for another twenty-four hours?"

"Yes. We're taking steps now that we think will give us three days, maybe longer. Over."

Now his voice came back swiftly, decisive and firm again.

"All right. Call me at 2100 your time tonight. Things are getting interesting over there. And I may have some news for you."

With that mysterious comment he cut us off.

We looked at each other, wondering what he might mean. But there wasn't time to discuss it. We had a lot of hard work ahead. Homer and I finished the stretchers, while the other four took all the stuff they could carry down into Hell. Fi stayed there to start digging a mass grave. Gavin woke the other kids, who had managed to fall asleep in spite of the gunshots echoing around on the ridge. He brought them up to Tailor's Stitch, so they could start picking up the empty shells. Most of them could be seen, glinting in the moonlight, but we'd have to check and recheck that we'd found them all.

That left Homer and Lee and Kevin and me to do the gory disgusting job of collecting the bodies and carrying them down the track, on our rough bush stretchers. It wasn't the first time we'd carried a body into Hell but it wasn't an experience I wanted to have too often.

We started a couple of hours before dawn, knowing we needed to clean up the whole place before first light. If they sent helicopters over, the evidence had to be well and truly gone, and we had to be out of sight.

The clouds rolled in fast, and we found ourselves in a white-out. It wasn't raining but the light moisture of the mist sprinkled our face, and before long my skin and clothes were quite damp. I kept pushing my wet hair back from my face. The weather wasn't much help — it would stop helicopters but it wouldn't wash away the blood. And the dampness made the rocks slippery, which was quite dangerous, as the stretchers were heavy and some of the downhill sections going into Hell are pretty steep.

It was a horrible few hours. When I remember how in the old days kids played war games on computers as though they were a good fun-filled way to pass the time, I just wish they could have seen us rolling those mutilated bodies onto the stretchers. I never heard of a computer game that included that in its graphics. I wish they could have seen us slipping and swearing and sweating as we negotiated that path, sobbing with weariness and grunting at each other because we were too tired to talk. I wish they could have seen the shallow grave where we left the eight soldiers to rot, under a thin layer of soil and rocks, deep in the bush in an alien country, thousands of kilometres away from their homes and families.

Once again we had killed others so we could stay alive. I was tired of tearing myself apart trying to figure out whether that was OK. Nowadays I just pulled the trigger, justifying it on the grounds that it was human nature to do everything possible to keep yourself alive. And of course we'd accidentally done one thing very right. We'd killed the entire patrol. There were no survivors. That meant no-one could go back to dob us in, and we didn't have any prisoners to worry about. Long ago in Stratton Lee had pointed out the advantages of a one hundred per cent kill. It was the most cold-blooded thing I'd ever heard, but he was right.

The temperature dropped sharply, and by early afternoon it was really cold for summer. The bulk of the mist had rolled on, but wisps of it still hung around. We finished our work. We'd been able to do a thorough job, with no fear of being seen from the air or the surrounding mountains. We'd even got rid of most of the rocks that were chipped by bullets, chucking the small ones over the edge and rolling the big ones so the damaged side was hidden.

I headed off to bed, stopping only where the others were checking the packs. I watched for a few minutes, but it was a fairly disgusting job. The kids, used to being scavengers from their days of living rough in Stratton, were excited by it. To them it was like a second Christmas, so soon after the first one. It didn't seem to bother them that we didn't share their good spirits.

Perhaps it would have been all right if there hadn't been personal stuff in the packs. But I couldn't handle the sight of photos and letters and good luck charms. The only good thing was the amount of food, if we could bring ourselves to eat it. The packets of rice and soup and noodles and dried fish were further proof that the soldiers were planning a long stay. It could well mean noone would come looking for them just yet.

There was some ammunition, although I think they'd used most of it in their fight with us. There were two radios, but very different from our little gadget, and probably not safe for us to use, in case they sent out automatic signals or something. At least they were deep in the packs, so we knew they hadn't been used to send out calls in the middle of the battle.

The rest seemed to be the usual clothes and stuff.

I chased the kids away. It was like trying to keep flies off a leg of lamb. But once I'd convinced them they weren't welcome, and then got the food safely stored, I crawled to my tent for a few hours' sleep.

No luck there. Casey and Natalie were playing some complicated noisy game with a stack of empty cans, and cooking tools that seemed to be doing rude things to each other. I sighed in frustration and went to one of the boys' tents instead. At least it was deserted, and peaceful.

I crawled onto a bedroll and put my head on the pack that was there for a pillow. It was awfully uncomfortable and hard. I tried to rearrange the lumpy shape into something better but it was like a cushion of rocks. And it smelt a bit funny too. Curious, I opened the top flap, to see exactly what was stuffed into it.

And I found a little treasure trove.

Ryvitas, cans of salmon, dried apricots, Cup-a-soups, cans of corn, Violet Crumbles, rotting apples: it all came pouring out, over my astonished fingers, in front of my astonished eyes.

"You mongrel," I thought. "All that food we were going through too fast . . . even the food that went missing on Christmas Day. We've been risking our lives going out over Tailor's Stitch and you had enough to feed us for a week."

Food-stealing, in the situation we were in, was a major crime. I was furious.

I still didn't know if it was Gavin's or Jack's pillow I was exploring, but I soon found out. There was a shadow at the entrance to the tent; I looked up, and saw a quivering

Jack, standing looking at me. A moment later and he was gone, without a sound. It was like he'd been nothing more than a shadow.

Forgetting my tiredness I raced after him. He went like a whippet. Homer, coming along the path, stood in surprise as Jack swerved around him, then, seeing me in hot pursuit, assumed it was some trivial fight, and called after Jack, "Go, mate, you can do it."

Rather than swear at Homer I saved my breath; just glared at him as I brushed past.

Jack was faster than me over the flat, but that's not saying much: a rabbit with myxo would be faster than me over the flat. But once he started climbing the rocks I caught him easily. He was too short and didn't have enough reach to get up the steep bits. About a quarter of the way up I got him by the shoulder and wrestled him into a little hollow in the cliff. We lay there glaring at each other.

"Why'd you steal our food?" I hissed at him.

He looked away, his lips pressed together like they'd been supa-glued.

"Were you hungry?" I asked. "Didn't you get enough to eat? Why didn't you tell us?"

But I knew as soon as I said it that he hadn't been starving. If he'd been hungry he would have eaten the food as fast as he collected it.

My anger started to fizz out. "Why did you do it?" I said, feeling more helpless than hostile now.

I couldn't understand Jack. He was such a reserved kid.

He still wouldn't answer, but I saw his shoulders drop a

little, now that my voice wasn't so angry. His face seemed to relax slightly. I took full advantage and pushed harder.

"Don't you realise every time we go outside for food we risk our lives? We could have saved ourselves an entire trip, with the food you've got there."

Now he just looked sulky.

I couldn't think of anything else to say. I knew I was already sounding like a nagging parent, and if I kept going, I'd sound even more like one. After a while I almost forgot Jack was there. I lay back and studied the sky. The mist had gone but a new front of clouds was blowing in. There was a baa-baa lamb and a moo-cow and a choo-choo train. Was that the way these kids would see them? Or would they see a bomb blast, a smear of blood, a corpse? I tried to imagine the world through Jack's eyes. It wasn't easy. All my life adults have been decent to me. Sure, a few teachers got up my nose, and Mr Nelson was a pain in the butt, and my parents could be extremely annoying when they wanted. But nothing bad had ever really happened to me.

Before the war started I'd trusted people. I'd had years of experience at it. Jack, on the other hand, didn't have a clue. His life before the war sounded pretty crummy. He hadn't told us heaps about his father or the high-rise flats, but I picked up enough to know that almost everything had been the complete opposite to me. For example, when I was a kid, it never crossed my mind that the next meal mightn't be on the table. I'd never gone to bed hungry. I had a feeling Jack hadn't been that lucky.

In the middle of one of our meals he said, "We didn't have anything except chicken noodle soup to eat, for four days once." I made some comment about the war being tough on everyone, but he said, "No, this was before the war, with my dad." Then he realised by the way everyone suddenly looked at him that he was making himself conspicuous, so he shut up fast and got stuck into his roast lamb.

So as I lay there I started to get a feeling for how Jack saw the world. Maybe it had always been him and his father, on their own. As far as he knew, it was going to be him against the world for the rest of his life. At the age of nine that must look like a pretty tough gig.

Solo man, that was Jack. He didn't trust anyone, probably hadn't trusted anyone for a long time.

If there was food around, I could imagine how he'd want to get himself a guaranteed supply, a stockpile to keep himself alive. It probably never crossed his mind that he could rely on us to look after him, to feed him, to keep him safe. We didn't mind doing it, but I guess he thought we had some other agenda, or that we might be here today and gone tomorrow.

I was getting a headache trying to think like Jack, trying to get inside his skull. Feeling more tired and weary than any time since this war started, I got up and held out my hand. He looked at me suspiciously and wouldn't take it. We walked down the track, Jack following quite a way behind.

As we came into the campsite Homer, who was arm-wrestling Gavin, called out, "You got him, huh?"

"I guess I did."

"What did he do?"

I glanced back at Jack, who had stopped dead in his tracks. I knew how much he admired Homer. He was staring at me, and his face was about the colour of some of the corpses we'd buried.

"He bet me he could beat me up to Chicken Rock," I said.

Jack turned and walked away.

My tent was empty now so I had my second attempt at a sleep, on my own bed this time. I actually slept quite heavily. I woke to the best noise I could possibly hear: the steady drumming of rain on the tent fly. Even as I lay there it got louder and harder. There was a bit of wind: the fly stretched and strained, and pulled at the pegs, but nothing we needed to worry about.

Beside me Fi was snoring lightly, and between us Natalie and Casey lay sprawled in their own restless sleep. These days it seemed like they spent more time in our tent than they did in their own. It was musical tents around this place, musical chairs.

I lay back and closed my eyes again.

If Homer hadn't woken me a few hours later I would have slept through the radio call to Colonel Finley. Homer looked exhausted, and I was angry with myself, and embarrassed, when he told me he'd been up on Tailor's Stitch the whole time I'd been asleep, keeping watch. He'd taken over from Lee, then come down to get me for the call. I couldn't believe I'd neglected something so obvious. Your judgement goes straight out the window when you're tired. Of course we needed sentries: from now on we could never again count on being safe in Hell. All our objections to sentry duty, which we'd gone through when we first sussed out the enemy campsite and their warm fireplace, counted for nothing now.

In fact we would need quite a complicated system of

sentries, so that if a patrol came along Tailor's Stitch the sentry could notify us without exposing themself to danger.

We woke Fi but she didn't want to come, and Kevin was the same. Lee was already waiting. Grumbling at myself and apologising to Homer I stumbled along behind the two boys, up the path, trying to shake off the weariness but without much success.

I didn't shake it off until I was at the top of Wombegonoo, and heard Colonel Finley's calm voice speaking quietly from across the Tasman. He woke me up.

"Do you still consider you can hold your position safely for another forty-eight hours?" he asked.

I nodded.

"Yes," Homer said. "Over."

Now that the rain was falling steadily I was quite confident. The bloodstains, and our tracks, would be wiped out. For a hundred years or so, maybe longer, only the Hermit and us had found a way into Hell. I didn't think that enemy soldiers, not knowing the ways of the bush, would get down into it too quickly. We could hole up there for a while.

"All right," Colonel Finley said. "We're heading into a critical time. I want to ask for your help again. But be aware that I'm talking about active and dangerous service. And I need an affirmative response before I go any further. Over."

"You've got it," Homer said.

"Are you sure you don't want to consult among yourselves and call me back in an hour? Or later?"

"No," said Homer. "Over."

For once I didn't mind Homer making decisions on

my behalf. In fact I nodded encouragingly at him. Admittedly we were on shaky ground making these promises while Fi and Kevin were blissfully asleep in Hell, but we knew they wouldn't go against us.

"All right. The drop-off point, where you landed when we sent you back from here, is that still secure? Over."

"Yes. As far as we know. We haven't been there for a couple of weeks. Over."

"All right. At 0300 tomorrow you can expect a visitor. He'll be with you for twenty-four hours only. Understood? Over."

We looked at each other in astonishment. My first thought was that so soon after Christmas we were really getting a Santa Claus. Amazing.

"OK," said Homer.

"I want you to check the site at 2300 hours tonight and confirm by radio that it is secure. Your date of birth will be the password. Again at 0100 and 0245 you are to confirm that it is secure. Use Ellie's date of birth, then Lee's, for those two calls. Understood?"

"OK."

"Is there anything you want? Over."

"Chocolate," I yelled into the transmitter. "And avocados. And Iced Vo-Vos. And tomatoes."

I think Colonel Finley got worried that he'd created a monster and we'd go on all night, because he ended the call pretty quickly. But the funny thing was that after my little outburst none of us could think of anything else. Half an hour later, going back down the track, we were still trying to think of things we'd have liked. It helped take our minds off the pouring rain, but none of us came up with anything too brilliant.

"Marshmallows," Homer said.

"Some new books," Lee said. "I'm sick of *Red Shift.*"

"A watch," I said.

We didn't leave a sentry up on Tailor's Stitch right away, because in this weather we thought we were pretty safe. And we were so excited by the call to Colonel Finley — excited and nervous — that we wanted to get together with Fi and Kevin and discuss it, not be left up on the ridge on our own in the cold, straining to see death approaching in the dark.

Epilogue

I've been flat out writing, literally flat out, because I've been in my tent most of the day, lying on my right-hand side first, then my left-hand side, then my back, then starting again on my right-hand side.

Next to me is a little bunch of flowers that I found on my bed. I think it was a present from Jack. Half the flowers in the bunch are weeds, but it's about the most precious gift I've ever had, so I'm not complaining. Every so often I pick it up and have a sniff.

It's not all that comfortable, lying here like this, but somehow I need to do it. I don't want to go out into the bright sunshine that's been burning away since ten o'clock. I don't even want to sit in the open air. Not for the first time I've been thinking of Andrea, the counsellor I saw in New Zealand. I'd love to see her again right now, but I don't imagine she'll be the mystery visitor dropping out of the sky.

To be honest I don't know what I'd say to her at the moment. I need a few months to work that out. Some of it would be to do with the war, some of it to do with what Fi said to me that time we were climbing the spur.

Sure I've made up with Lee, and Fi and I seem to be getting on OK again, and I'm trying to be nice to everyone, but I've got a funny feeling Fi was talking about a bit more than that. What scares me is that she was talking about changes so big and deep and powerful that I can't undo them. Because I've got half a feeling that I've changed that much in the last twelve months.

Lee's calling me right now; he's looking for the spud peeler I think. He'll have to find it himself though. I want to finish this.

Of course the reason I've been writing so fast and furiously is that I want to get it up-to-date before we go out to meet the helicopter. After tonight, anything could happen. If there's something really urgent about to break we mightn't even get back here. We're taking light packs, and a rifle each, in case we have to move on somewhere else. We're leaving Fi and Kevin here with the kids, which isn't ideal, but it's all we can do.

So now that I've brought this up-to-date I can go back over Tailor's Stitch, knowing at least one part of my life is organised. I sure have written heaps since this war started. If the war ever ends maybe I could do something with it. In the meantime I've got piles of paper all over the place, most of it hidden in the tin box in the windowsill at the Hermit's hut, some of it back in New Zealand. Andrea's looking after that.

A feeling in my bones tells me that the climax is coming. It's not just the way Colonel Finley spoke on the radio; it's been growing on me for a while. I think we might be heading for the big showdown. If we are, I want to be part of it. I don't want to go back to New Zealand if there's a chance of helping at the critical time.

There's lots of things I'm hoping for though. I want to do whatever has to be done without letting anyone down. I wouldn't mind finding out what happened to the Kiwi guerillas. I want to see our country back in our control. And I want to find my parents.

When it's all said and done, the only things that matter in life are so damn simple. Family, friends, being safe and well. I think before the war a lot of people got sucked in by the crap on TV. They thought having the right shoes or the right jeans or the right car really mattered. Boy were we ever dumb.

Maybe people thought they could hide behind that stuff. Maybe they thought that if they wore Levis, ate Maccas and drank Pepsi no-one would look any further. No-one would see the real person.

War's stripped all that from us. I'm trying to think of any situation before the war when that happened. I can't think of many. Our Outward Bound course, yeah, after a couple of days with those guys we were more interested in what people were really like than what shop they bought their clothes from. When Jodie Lewis got hit by a car and was in a coma, that brought us together big-time, and we weren't too bothered by what shoes people wore. Suddenly people who normally never spoke to each other were hugging and crying together.

It seems like suffering's the only time we can see what's essential. If peace ever comes back I'm making a vow: I'll design myself special glasses. They'll block out whether people are fat or thin or beautiful or weird-looking, whether they have pimples or birthmarks or different coloured skin. They'll do everything suffering's done for us, but without the pain. I'm going to wear those glasses for the rest of my life.

In the meantime there's a war still raging, kids outside my tent whingeing, and less than an hour before I go up to Tailor's Stitch to take over sentry from Fi. If I hurry I can just get this down to the Hermit's hut, and put it in the tin box. I only hope it won't be the last time I get to write about me and my friends, and the things that have happened to us since the war began.